Praise for Sharon Sala

"Sharon Sala's Blessings, Georgia series is filled with unforgettable charm and delight!"

—Robyn Carr, #1 *New York Times* bestselling author

"Sharon Sala is a consummate storyteller. Her skills shine in her Blessings, Georgia series. If you can stop reading, then you're a better woman than me."

—Debbie Macomber, #1 *New York Times* bestselling author

"Ripe with amazing characters that bring Blessings to life... Blessings sure sounds like a great place to put down roots."

—*Fresh Fiction* for *Saving Jake*

"A strong and positive second-chance romance that fans of Robyn Carr and Susan Wiggs will enjoy."

—*Booklist* for *Come Back to Me*

"Will make anyone stand up and cheer. I look forward to reading more by this author and will be looking for more stories from Blessings, Georgia."

—*Harlequin Junkie* for *You and Only You*

"I loved this book and could not put it down...great backstories and a setting that is perfect."

—*USA Today Happy Ever After* for *I'll Stand by You*

"Sharon Sala works magic with words as she brings characters to life."

—*Long and Short Reviews* for *A Piece of My Heart*

Also by Sharon Sala

Blessings, Georgia

ONCE *in*
a BLUE MOON

SHARON
SALA

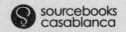
sourcebooks
casablanca

Copyright © 2020 by Sharon Sala
Cover and internal design © 2020 by Sourcebooks
Cover art by Chris Cocozza

Sourcebooks and the colophon are registered trademarks of Sourcebooks.

Published by Sourcebooks Casablanca, an imprint of Sourcebooks
P.O. Box 4410, Naperville, Illinois 60567-4410
(630) 961-3900
sourcebooks.com

Printed and bound in the United States of America.
OPM 10 9 8 7 6 5 4 3 2 1

CHAPTER 1

STREAKS OF MOONLIGHT SLIPPED BETWEEN THE BLINDS in Cathy Terry's bedroom, painting silver-white stripes across the dark hardwood floor. The lights of a passing patrol car swept across the wall where she lay sleeping, but all she saw was the man coming at her in her dream.

Blaine Wagner's face was twisted in rage—his fists doubled, ready to strike a blow.

"You're not going anywhere, dammit! Nobody walks out on me!"

Cathy was scared of him, but she'd had enough, and the luxury of their lifestyle was no longer the draw it had once been.

"I'm not nobody! I am your wife, not one of your whores, and I've had enough! You have cheated on me for the last time. I've already contacted a lawyer, and I'll be staying in the Luxor here in Vegas until I can find an apartment."

"Like hell!" Blaine roared, and swung at her.

Cathy ducked and ran, locking herself into their ensuite, and then called the police, crying and begging them to hurry as Blaine pounded on the door in continuing rage.

The sirens and the flashing lights pulling up to the house gave her the reprieve she needed. The moment she heard him leave the room to answer the door, she flew out of the bathroom, grabbed the bag she'd already packed from the closet, and followed him down the stairs.

He was already playing the part of the surprised spouse and telling the police it was all a misunderstanding when Cathy appeared. Her eyes were swollen from crying, and her fear was unmistakable.

"Help me! I've filed for divorce and he won't let me leave!" she said. She was trying to push past him when he grabbed her by the arm.

In the dream, she was struggling to get free, just like she had that night. The police had come into their house at that point, yelling at Blaine to let her go, and he was screaming in her ear, "I'll make you sorry. You'll never have another moment's peace as long as you live!"

Her heart was pounding when she heard a voice from her childhood.

Wake up! Wake up, Mary Cathleen! Wake up now!

She gasped, and then sat straight up in bed and turned on the lamp. The hundred-watt bulb put a whole new light on the moment, helping pull her out of the dream, but she couldn't deny what she'd heard. That was her mother's voice, and it had been two years since she'd heard it.

"Oh, Mama, you're still on my side, even from the grave." Cathy glanced at the clock.

It was twenty minutes to four, and going back to sleep after that dream wasn't happening, so she turned on the television, plumped up her pillows, and began scanning the available movies. She didn't much care what she watched. Anything to get her mind off her ex would suffice.

She was thinking about going to the kitchen for something to snack on when she saw actor Jeffrey Dean Morgan's face flash on the screen, and she stopped and upped the volume. He was one of her favorites, and being tall, dark, and handsome was the antithesis of Blaine Wagner's stocky build and blond hair.

That actor is one pretty man. I don't care what this movie is about. I can mute the whole thing and just sit and look at him. That should get my ex-husband's face out of my head.

But she didn't mute it after all and wound up watching almost two hours of the movie. It wasn't a happy-ever-after movie, but she didn't live in a happy-ever-after world and was fine with that.

Cathy ran to the kitchen during a commercial and made herself a peanut butter and jelly sandwich, then brought it and a glass of milk back to bed.

By the time the movie was over, the memory of the dream had mostly passed and morning was imminent. She turned off the television and took her dirty dishes back to the kitchen, started a pot of coffee, then headed back to her room to get dressed.

A short while later she was in the kitchen , contemplating her day of doing little to nothing here in Blessings, and remembering her old life in Vegas.

The divorce had taken six months to finalize, ending with a lump-sum payment of thirty million dollars to her bank account. It wasn't like Blaine couldn't afford it. He was a billionaire...a fourth-generation Wagner, a name famous in Nevada. In early days, it was silver mines, and during the past seventy-something years, casinos had become the family business.

After the divorce was final, she'd thought that would be the end of it. But she'd been wrong, and it was what he did on the courthouse steps as they were leaving that scared her.

When both lawyers walked off, Blaine stayed behind. Cathy thought it was for a final parting of the ways, until he grabbed her arm and whispered in her ear.

"You do understand I now view you as a threat. You know things about me and my life that aren't healthy for you anymore."

Cathy tried to pull away. "Don't be ridiculous."

"This isn't a joke, Cathy. I'm just giving you fair warning. I don't trust you anymore, and I have no intention of spending the rest of my life looking over my shoulder and waiting for the feds to come knocking. Your days are numbered."

Cathy's heart skipped a beat. *Oh my God. He's serious!*

"I don't have the faintest idea what you're talking about. Our world consisted of your country club, our personal friends, and hosting dinner parties for your business associates now and then."

His eyes narrowed. "Exactly."

"I still don't get it," Cathy said, pretending total oblivion, although she was beginning to remember that some of those associates had dubious reputations, even though she knew nothing incriminating about any of them. "Go away, Blaine. Just leave me alone."

She twisted out of his grasp and walked away, resisting the urge to run. This was a shock. She'd never seen this coming, but she needed to disappear, and she was going to have to be smart about doing it.

By the time she got home, she had a plan. The first thing she did was fill out papers online to change back to her maiden name. After two tense months of waiting, it was done, and that's when she amped up the plan. She was setting up a new life with a renewed driver's license, a new phone plan, and a new credit card.

She knew Blaine was having her followed. She didn't know if that was just intimidation, but leaving town with his knowledge of where she was going wouldn't assure her safety. He'd just have her tailed to other places, and if he was still in the mindset to get rid of her, it would be all too easy to make her death look like an accident.

But she already knew how to disappear. She'd spent the first twelve years of her life living off the grid in Alaska. The last thing Blaine Wagner would ever expect was for her to take to the back roads of America on foot.

Cathy ordered everything she needed online so her ex wouldn't know what she was buying, and thanks to him, every friend she'd ever had in Vegas had shut her out. No more lunch dates with girlfriends. No more girlfriends. So she holed up in her apartment and quit going anywhere, and when she got hungry, she ordered in.

The last thing she did was disperse the money from her divorce settlement into three different banks across the country.

And early one morning she walked out the back door of her apartment, caught the Uber she'd called to take her to the bus station, and took a bus to Colorado.

She got off in Colorado Springs and rented a motel room. She stayed long enough to buy a handgun and ammunition, and one morning just after sunrise, she shouldered her hiking gear and left the motel heading east.

She hiked along highways, sidestepping cities for the more rural areas, and the weeks went by until she finally reached Springer Mountain, Georgia—the beginning of the Appalachian Trail. It was a place she recognized true wilderness, and one in which she felt comfortable.

She knew how to forage, and how to fish from the rivers and streams teeming with fish. But the trail went north from there, and it was getting too close to winter to hike north, so she started hiking south. She made it all the way to a little out-of-the-way place called Blessings, Georgia, before something about it spoke to her, and there is where she stopped. And now here she was, in something of a holding pattern. Not really participating in life. Just hiding from it.

Cathy set aside the memories, finished her morning coffee, and got ready to go for her morning run.

It was mid-November, but it promised to be a nice day in the high fifties. She was wearing her running shoes, sweatpants, and a long-sleeved T-shirt as she pocketed her phone and left the house, pausing beneath the porch light to scan the area for signs of things that didn't belong.

The streetlights were already fading with the growing light of a new day. The morning was still, the sky cloudless. She walked to the edge of the porch and waited for the car coming up the street to pass, and then waved when she recognized the boy who delivered the morning papers. He saw her and waved back. She still didn't know his name, but this town was friendly like that.

She came off the porch, pausing in the driveway to stretch a few times, and then took off down the sidewalk at a jog, relishing the impact of foot to surface. The rhythm of her stride soon caught up with the thump of her heartbeat, and by the time she was making her second pass by the city park, she'd been running for an hour.

The fat raccoon scurrying through the green space was heading for the trees and the creek that ran through the park.

On the other side of the street, a young woman came running out of her house toward the old car parked in the drive. Cathy recognized her as one of the waitresses from Granny's Country Kitchen. From the way she was moving, she was likely late for work.

The thought of Granny's led Cathy to wanting some of the gravy and biscuits she'd had there before, but she couldn't go there all hot and sweaty and was wishing she'd pulled her hair up in a ponytail before leaving the house. Even though the morning was cool, the weight of the curls was hot against the back of her neck. She turned toward Main Street as she reached the end of the block, thinking to make one last sweep through Blessings and then head home.

Traffic was picking up on Main, and even though she'd been running every morning since her arrival, people still stared. No one jogged in Blessings, although she had seen some kids running at the high school track field, but she didn't care. She wasn't here to fit in. She wasn't planning to stay.

She ran past the florist, and then the quirky little hair salon called the Curl Up and Dye, and was moving past Phillips Pharmacy as a huge black pickup pulled up to the curb.

It had been months since she'd been behind the wheel

of any kind of vehicle, and she was toying with the idea of leasing one for the winter. She didn't know she'd caught the driver's notice, and it wouldn't have mattered anyway. She just kept running without noticing how far she'd gone until she saw the gas station at the far end of town and the city limits sign just down the road.

"Well, shoot," Cathy muttered. She made a quick turn on the sidewalk and was heading back into Blessings when she came down wrong on her foot, and before she knew it, her ankle rolled and she was falling.

The pain was instantaneous and excruciating, and as she was reaching out to break her fall, she jammed her hand against the concrete and then landed on her side with a thud.

"Oh my lord," she moaned, then slowly turned over onto her back, only vaguely aware of screeching brakes and then the sound of running feet.

It was just after 8:00 a.m. when Duke Talbot drove into Blessings and pulled up to the curb in front of Phillips Pharmacy. He was reaching for the list he'd put in the console when he caught movement from the corner of his eye and looked up just as a young woman in a long-sleeved T-shirt and sweatpants ran past the store. She was gone before he got a good look at her face, but all that curly red hair bouncing down her back was impossible to miss.

He couldn't remember seeing anyone jogging here before and was curious as to who might have taken it up. He didn't know any woman with hair that color, either, but considering the Curl Up and Dye was just down the street, Ruby or one of the girls could be responsible for that. He watched the jogger until she turned a corner and disappeared before he got out.

The bell over the door jingled as he entered the pharmacy.

LilyAnn Dalton looked up from behind the register and smiled.

"Good morning, Duke. You're out early," she said.

"Morning, LilyAnn. Just getting an early start on a long day." He picked up a basket from the end of the counter and started down the aisle where the shampoo and conditioners were shelved, then stopped and turned around. "Hey, LilyAnn, I just saw a redheaded woman with long, curly hair jogging past the store. I don't think I ever knew anyone to take up jogging here in Blessings. Who is she?"

"Oh, that's Cathy Terry. She's new here. She's living in one of Dan Amos's rental houses."

"What's she do?" he asked.

LilyAnn shrugged. "I don't know. She comes in here now and again. Really nice lady, but she sort of keeps to herself."

Having his curiosity satisfied, Duke began picking up the items he'd come for. It didn't take long for him to get everything on the list, and then he was back in his truck.

He stopped and used the ATM drive-through at the bank for cash, and then realized he was still a little early for his haircut appointment, so he headed to the gas station to get his oil checked.

He was thinking about the day ahead when he realized the redhead he'd seen earlier was on the sidewalk running toward him. He had a clear view of her face, and despite the pink flush on her cheeks, his first thought was how pretty she was.

Then all of a sudden she was falling, and he groaned aloud at how hard she hit. He stomped the brakes, slammed the truck into park, and got out on the run.

He was down on his knees beside her in seconds, and when he saw the blood on the palm of her hand, he knew that was going to burn later. Then he saw her ankle, and was shocked by how much it was already swelling.

"Your ankle! Don't move, it might be broken," he said.

And then she looked up at him, and Duke took a deep breath. He'd never seen eyes that blue, and they were swimming in tears. It took everything he had not to sweep her up in his arms, but he was afraid to move her.

"Did you hit your head?"

She wasn't sure. Maybe. She'd just watched a movie with Jeffrey Dean Morgan in it, and now either she was hallucinating, or his doppelgänger was leaning over her.

"Uh…I don't think so. Just the right side of my body. My ankle turned, and I think I need a little help getting up."

"My name is Duke Talbot. I saw you fall, and from the looks of your ankle, I think you need to go to the ER," Duke said. "Will you let me take you, or would you rather go in an ambulance?"

Cathy frowned. "I don't think I—"

"One or the other," Duke said.

She sighed. *Dictatorial male. Just what I don't need.* But both her hip and her ankle were throbbing now, and he did have a sweet, concerned expression on his face.

"If it's not too much trouble, maybe you could just drop me off at the ER, then."

"Yes, ma'am," Duke said, and then reached toward her hair, but when she flinched and then ducked, he frowned. Those were instinctive reactions someone might make from fear of being struck. "I'm sorry. You have a piece of grass in a curl. I didn't mean to startle you."

Cathy sighed. "Then, thank you," she said, and closed her eyes as Duke pulled it out.

When she opened them again, he was on his feet and she was in his arms, and he was carrying her toward his truck.

At that moment, a police car pulled up, and Chief Pittman got out on the run.

"Hey, Duke! We just had a call come in that someone fell. I see you beat me to her," Lon said, as he ran toward Duke's truck and opened the door.

"I saw it happen," Duke said, as he eased Cathy down inside and then quickly reclined the seat back. "I'm taking her to the ER."

"I'll lead the way," Lon said. He glanced in the truck as Duke was buckling her in and recognized who it was. "Miss Terry, I don't know if you remember me, but we were standing in line together at Crown Grocers last week. I'm Lon Pittman, the police chief here in Blessings. My wife, Mercy, and Duke's sister-in-law, Hope, are sisters, which in the South means we're all kin. You sit tight and we'll get you to the ER in style."

Cathy nodded, then closed her eyes. But even after he'd shut her in, she could still hear them talking. A couple of minutes later Duke got back in the truck, and as he made a U-turn in the street, she grabbed onto the console to steady herself.

"Lon's just ahead of us, leading the way with his lights

flashing. Just hang on for a few minutes more. Are you hurting very much?" he asked.

"Enough, and I really appreciate this," she added.

Duke glanced down at her briefly. Again, their gazes locked, but this time she was the first to look away. He could tell he made her uncomfortable, so he turned his attention to driving.

As soon as he pulled up at the ER, everything began happening at once. Two orderlies came running out so quickly that Duke guessed the chief must have radioed ahead that they were inbound. He jumped out as they were transferring Cathy from his truck to a gurney, and then walked beside her as they wheeled her inside.

"Is there anyone I can call?" Duke asked.

"No, but I'm fine, and thank you again for all your help," Cathy said.

Duke watched until they wheeled her out of sight and then shoved his hands in his pockets. He was still standing in the middle of the hall when Hope came around a corner. When she saw him, she came running.

"Duke? What are you doing here? Did something happen to Jack?"

"No, no, nothing like that," Duke said. "I came in to get a haircut this morning. I was going to have my oil checked when I saw a woman take a bad fall. I just brought her in."

"Oh no! Who was it?" Hope asked.

"Her name is Cathy Terry."

"Oh, Mercy mentioned her a time or two. She's renting from Dan Amos. Was she hurt bad?"

"I don't know. I felt bad leaving her here on her own, but when I offered to call someone for her, she shook me off. I think I make her nervous...not me personally, but me being a man."

Hope was a little surprised by Duke's insight and concern. Most of the time her brother-in-law was either critical or dismissive of just about everything and everybody.

"I'm working in the ER today. I'll check on her," Hope said.

"Okay. If she needs help, let me know," he said, then left the ER.

He got back in his truck and headed for the Curl Up and Dye for his appointment. The last barber had left Blessings some years back, so it was either a haircut at the ladies' hair salon, a drive all the way to Savannah, or do it yourself. Duke had only tried DIY once when he was twelve, and the results had been disastrous. But his thoughts were no longer on the day ahead of him. He was thinking of the little redhead he'd left all alone in the ER.

Cathy was disgusted with herself and, at the same time, a little anxious. Being self-reliant was fine when all your moving parts were working, but from the swelling on her ankle and the huge bruise already spreading on her hip, she wasn't going to be jogging for a while, and getting to the Crown for groceries wasn't going to be easy, either. She didn't have one person in town she knew well enough to ask for help, and she was wishing she'd already leased a car.

Cathy was watching Rhonda, the nurse who was cleaning the scrape on her hand, when another nurse walked in. She was tall, dark-haired, and looked vaguely familiar.

"Hi, Rhonda, how is she doing?" Hope asked.

"We're waiting for Doctor Quick," Rhonda said.

Hope moved to the other side of the bed.

"Hi, Cathy. I'm Hope Talbot. Mercy Pittman, the fabulous baker at Granny's, is my sister, and it was my brother-in-law, Duke, who brought you here. Has someone been in yet to get your personal information?"

"No, not yet," Cathy said, but now she knew why the woman looked familiar. She looked like the woman she'd seen at Granny's.

"Then they will do that shortly. Is there anyone I can call?" Hope asked.

"No, but I have a question. Does Blessings have a taxi service?" Cathy asked.

"We don't have an official taxi service, but we have a whole lot of good people who will gladly give you a ride home. Do you live alone?"

Cathy nodded.

Hope glanced down at Cathy's swollen ankle. "You won't be driving for a while."

"I don't have a car here," she said.

"Ah... Came in on the bus, did you?" Hope said.

"No, I had been backpacking for several months when I got to Blessings. I decided it was time to find a place to spend the winter."

Hope's eyes widened. "Wow! Go, you! As for getting home, that's no problem. We'll get you all sorted out. All it will take is one phone call. Have you met Ruby yet?" Hope asked.

"No, who's Ruby?" Cathy asked.

"Ruby Butterman. She owns the Curl Up and Dye. She's

the go-to person in Blessings when someone is in need. Her husband, Peanut, is the local lawyer."

"Her husband's name is Peanut Butterman? For real?" Cathy asked.

Hope giggled. "Yes. He always says his parents were smoking weed when they named him."

Cathy grinned, and then winced when Rhonda poured some antiseptic on the palm of her hand.

"I'll go make a couple of phone calls," Hope said. "I'll be back later to check on you. Don't worry. We'll get you home."

Once again, Cathy was struck by how friendly people were here, and as Hope had predicted, a couple of minutes later, a man came in and got her personal information, and as he was leaving, the ER doctor arrived.

Rhonda looked up. "Good morning, Doctor Quick. This is Cathy Terry."

He smiled. "Morning, Rhonda," he said, and then he shifted focus to his patient. "Hello, Cathy, I'm Dr. Quick. What have you done to yourself?" he asked, as he began eyeing the bruising and the swollen ankle.

"I turned my ankle and fell while I was jogging."

Dr. Quick was already feeling her ankle. "Can you move it?" he asked.

"Yes, it hurts, but I can move it," she said, and proceeded to show him. "Fell pretty hard on my right side. My shoulder and hip are beginning to hurt, too."

"Did you hit your head?" he asked, glancing at her thick, red curls.

"No."

Dr. Quick nodded. "Okay, I'm sending you down for X-rays. We'll know more after I see them. Just bear with us."

A couple of minutes later, an orderly arrived with a wheelchair, and all the way down the hall, Cathy kept thinking… *Nightmare or not, I wish I'd gone back to bed.*

CHAPTER 2

As soon as Hope was between patients, she made a call to Ruby at the Curl Up and Dye. The phone rang a couple of times before the call was picked up.

"Curl Up and Dye. This is Mabel Jean."

"Hi, Mabel Jean, this is Hope Talbot. I need to speak to Ruby, if she's free."

"Sure, hang on a sec while I put you on hold." Then she called out from the front of the shop. "Ruby, it's for you."

———

Ruby gave Duke a quick pat on the shoulder. "Give me a second," she said, and picked up the call from her workstation. "This is Ruby."

"Hi, Ruby, this is Hope. Sorry to bother you at work, but there's a patient here in the ER who's going to need a ride home in a while, and I wondered if you knew someone I could contact. She asked if there was a taxi service in town, and I told her no, but that I'd try to find her a ride."

"Oh my gosh! Of course. I'm certain I can find someone. Who's the patient?"

"Cathy Terry, the cute redhead who's renting from Dan Amos."

"Oh! I know who you're talking about. I see her jogging past the shop all the time. In fact, I just saw her running past this morning. What happened to her?"

"She took a bad fall while she was running. Turned her ankle and skinned herself up a bit. I don't think anything is broken, but we're waiting for Dr. Quick to make that determination."

"Well, bless her heart," Ruby said. "Don't worry. Just tell her someone will be there in the waiting room for her when she's ready to be released."

"I sure will," Hope said. "And thank you so much."

"Of course," Ruby said, and then hung up.

Vera and Vesta Conklin, the two other stylists, had eavesdropped on the call.

"What's wrong?" Vera asked.

Vesta frowned. "Sister, you don't have to know everything."

Ruby grinned. "That was Hope Talbot. I need to find someone a ride home from the ER."

Duke's heart skipped a beat. "Is it for Cathy Terry?" he asked.

Ruby's eyes widened. "Why, yes, it is. Do you know her?"

"Not really, but I'm the one who took her to the ER. I saw her fall. I offered to stay, but she said there was no need, and obviously, she now has a need. I'll do it. I didn't like leaving her like that anyway. Felt like I was leaving a job half-done."

"This is great!" Ruby said. "And I'm almost finished with your cut, so the timing is perfect."

———

Duke parked near the ER entrance and jumped out, then hurried inside. He didn't know when Cathy would be ready to leave, but he didn't want her to be somewhere waiting, so he went straight to the front desk.

"Hey, Carol Ann, I'm here to give Cathy Terry a ride home when she's ready to leave. Can you let somebody know?"

"Absolutely," she said.

Duke chose a seat that would give him a clear view of the hall. He didn't know how Cathy was going to take his reappearance, so being quiet and cordial might be his best bet. He was fine with cordial, but as Hope and Jack were fond of telling him, being quiet wasn't one of his better traits. He had a tendency to talk before he thought about what was coming out of his mouth, and he blamed it on having no one to answer to but himself.

While he was waiting, Dan Amos came in with a bloody rag wrapped around his left hand. Duke heard him say he might be needing stitches, and then they rushed him back into the exam area.

A few minutes later, Dan's wife, Alice, came running inside.

"What exam room is Dan in? He's here somewhere getting stitches."

"He's in 3A," Carol Ann said.

"Thank you," Alice said, and went through the double doors into the ER on the run.

Duke continued to wait, thinking to himself how fast someone's life could change, and remembering the day that drunk driver hit Hope head-on as she was coming in to work. If it hadn't been for her long-lost sister's appearance on that day to donate blood, Hope would have died.

He glanced up at the clock. It had been over two hours

since he'd dropped Cathy off here. He was beginning to worry that she might be seriously hurt when the doors suddenly swung open and an orderly appeared, pushing Cathy out in a wheelchair.

Duke stood up and smiled.

"We meet again. I happened to be getting a haircut when the call came in about you needing a ride home, and since I brought you here, I thought it would be okay with you if I took you home."

Cathy hated to admit it, but she was actually glad to see him. Even though their acquaintance had been brief, he was one less stranger to deal with.

"Of course it's okay, and much appreciated," she said.

"I'm parked nearby. Give me a couple of minutes, and I'll pull up to the entrance."

The orderly pushed Cathy to the door as Duke left at a lope.

"We'll wait inside until he arrives," he said.

Cathy heard but didn't comment. She was watching Duke Talbot run across the parking lot, wondering how old he was and guessing maybe late thirties, early forties, but then she decided it didn't matter. She wasn't looking. And if he wasn't already married, it was likely he had someone special in his life. Unless he was a complete jerk, anyone that good-looking would surely not be alone.

Within a couple of minutes he was at the entrance. He had the door open and waiting when the orderly wheeled her out. But when she tried to stand up, he just picked her back up as he'd done when she fell, and had her situated in the front seat of the truck and buckled in before she could brace herself for the impact of his touch.

Duke was rarely uncertain what to do, but today was an exception. He already knew she was leery of men. He didn't know why, or who had hurt her, but he didn't want his name on that list.

He got in, then glanced at her.

"Can I assume the fact that your ankle is wrapped instead of in a cast means it's a bad sprain and not a break?"

"You may," she said, and then grinned. "The rest of me is okay, too, minus a little skin. Kind of embarrassing, actually, since I hiked halfway across the country without so much as a stumble."

Duke blinked. "You hiked?" Then he stopped and took a breath. "By yourself?"

Cathy's smile tightened as her eyes narrowed. "Shocking, isn't it? A woman who can take care of herself without a man."

"I didn't mean it like that," Duke said, and started the truck. He left the hospital parking lot and then drove back to Main Street.

"Which way from here?" he asked.

Cathy was already regretting the challenge in her last comment. The man had been nothing but kind. A little bossy maybe, but it was only out of concern for her well-being.

"When you get back to Main, turn left. Then turn right at the stoplight, go down two blocks, and turn left on Cherry Street, and I'm sorry I was so defensive."

Duke sighed. "I'm sorry, too. I seem to have a propensity for saying the wrong thing to women."

Then he drove out onto Main and followed her directions all the way to the left turn onto Cherry Street.

"Which house?" he asked.

"The small blue one with the white front porch. I'm renting from Dan Amos."

"Nice," Duke said, and then added, "Dan was actually in the ER when you were. I saw him come in with a bloody hand, and then his wife came in a few minutes later. On-the-job injury, I suppose."

Cathy frowned. "Oh no. I hope it's not serious. He seems like a really nice man. Very helpful in finding me a place to stay for the winter."

Duke felt a moment of regret, and then disappointment. "So you're only passing through?"

She was silent for a few seconds before she answered. "I honestly don't know where I'm going. I just know where I don't want to be."

The lack of emotion in her voice was more telling than what she'd said. Duke wanted to know more, but he was already pulling up the drive. He parked beneath the empty carport, then got out and circled the truck to open her door.

Cathy had already unbuckled herself and dug the house key from her pocket when the door swung open.

"One more time?" he asked.

Cathy's lips twitched. "Now you're asking permission? Just do your thing, big man. I am so over this morning jog."

Duke grinned, then picked her up from where she was sitting, settled her more firmly into his grasp, and pushed the door shut with his elbow as they passed.

"I have the door key," she said as they started up the steps. "Now that we're on the porch, I can make it from here."

Duke put her down easy and held out his hand. "No, ma'am. I don't do anything halfway. My job isn't over here until I know you're safe inside and settled."

She sighed, then dropped the key in his outstretched hand.

Moments later, she was back in his arms and he was carrying her across the threshold.

"Where to? The recliner, or your bedroom?"

Cathy though about the shower she always took after a run, but right now, even if she unwrapped her ankle, standing up on it was too painful to think about.

"I think the recliner for now."

Duke settled her into the chair, looked around, trying to figure out how she was going to manage on her own.

"Do you have anything to make an ice pack?" he asked.

Cathy smiled at him. "Duke Talbot, you have been a godsend, and if I have offended you today, my sincere apologies. I have this chip on my shoulder I've been trying to dislodge for some time now, but you are officially relieved of further duty. I'll figure it out," Cathy said.

Duke didn't like the situation. There were too many chances for more problems here.

"I'm sorry, but this is the older brother in me not wanting to leave someone in need. Do me one favor and don't lock the door. I'm going to the pharmacy to pick up a couple of cold packs. The swelling on your ankle will go down a lot faster if you use them. It won't take me long, and then I promise I'll leave you alone."

He was gone before she could argue, and Cathy was hurting too much to care. She raised the footrest, then leaned back in the recliner and closed her eyes.

Duke was on a mission. It bothered him that Cathy was alone in this place. No friends, no vehicle, no job, just here with no plan or purpose. He drove straight to the pharmacy.

LilyAnn looked up when she saw him walking in and smiled.

"Forget something?"

"Not exactly," he said. "I need a couple of those gel packs that you freeze for ice packs, and a tube of that icy-hot stuff for sore muscles, and a bottle of painkillers. I also need to rent one of those rolling walkers…you know, the kind with a seat and a basket beneath it."

"That's all back in the pharmacy area. Let's go see what we have available."

Duke followed her. Mr. Phillips, the pharmacist, was behind the counter, and when he saw them looking at crutches and walkers, he came out to help.

"Exactly what are you needing, Duke? And do you want to buy or rent?"

"Rent," Duke said. "It's an injury that will heal. I want one of the walkers that has hand controls and wheels, with a seat and a basket beneath it."

"Yep, I have three of those for rent. They call them Rollators, and they're in the back. Follow me and take your pick."

"I'll get the rest of your stuff and have it at the register," LilyAnn said, and left the two men alone.

Duke followed Phillips into the back room, and after trying out all three walkers to make sure they rolled easily and that the hand brakes would set, he picked out the royal-blue one.

"How much do these rent for?" he asked.

"I don't have much call for these. I'll rent it for fifty dollars a month. Can you swing that?"

"Yes, and I'll be responsible for getting it back to you, too."

"You must have someone real stove-up at home."

"No, it's for a woman who took a fall this morning. She didn't break anything, but she has a badly swollen ankle, and I know her hip and shoulder have to be hurting, too."

"Well, that's real nice of you, Duke. Who got hurt?"

"Her name is Cathy Terry. She's new in town and renting one of Dan Amos's houses. I actually saw her fall."

"The lady with the curly red hair?" Phillips asked.

Duke nodded.

"I see her jogging past the store almost every morning. I'm sure sorry she's hurt. Here, let me send her a box of chocolates as a get-well from all of us here at Phillips Pharmacy."

"That's really kind of you," Duke said.

Phillips smiled. "Chocolate fixes a multitude of ills. Sometimes it's even better than the pills I peddle," he said, and picked a box of assorted chocolates and carried it up front to add with the other things. "LilyAnn, the chocolates are on the house. Don't bother ringing them up."

"Yes, sir," LilyAnn said. "That's a sweet thing for you to do."

The old man blushed a little and headed back to work while LilyAnn signed the walker out in their rental file, then checked Duke out.

"Need help carrying anything?" she asked.

"No thanks. I've got it," he said.

"I'll get the door," she said.

Duke loaded everything up and then backed away from

the curb and headed back up Main Street to Granny's Country Kitchen.

Lovey Cooper, the owner, greeted him as he entered.

"Morning, Duke! Good to see you."

"Hi, Lovey. I want to get some food to go. By any chance do you still have some biscuits and sausage gravy from breakfast?"

"Oh sure. That sells all day long. How much do you want? Enough for your family, or just you?"

"I want some for Cathy Terry. She had a fall this morning when she was jogging, and I was thinking she might not have eaten before her run."

"Oh no! She's been in here a few times since her arrival in Blessings. Is she hurt bad?"

"A bad sprain and some bumps and bruises. I don't think she'll be cooking for herself for a while."

"I'll get you fixed right up, and it won't take long. Just have a seat."

Duke sat down on the padded bench in the lobby and then took a deep breath. Yes, he was overdoing it, but that's how he did everything. When there was a need, he wanted to fill it. When something was wrong, he wanted to fix it. He'd spent his entire life taking care of people, and he didn't know any other way to be.

And...if he made Cathy feel like he was butting into her business without an invitation, maybe some of Mercy's biscuits would smooth the way.

He kept glancing at the clock, worrying about being gone so long, when in fact he'd left her house less than twenty minutes ago. Lovey came back within minutes carrying a large to-go sack.

"Here you go," she said. "Four biscuits and a pint of sausage gravy. And Elvis was just taking the first batch of fried chicken out of the fryer, so I wrapped up a couple of pieces of chicken and added a pint of mashed potatoes and gravy for her, too."

"That's awesome. What do I owe you?" Duke asked.

"Nothing. You're being such a Good Samaritan and I want to help. You tell her everyone at Granny's sends their love, and to get well soon."

Duke smiled. "Thank you, Lovey. You're the best."

He settled the sack of food on the front floorboard, then drove away. By the time he got back to Cathy's house, thirty minutes had come and gone.

He got the walker out of the truck bed and carried it to the porch, then went back for the two sacks. He knocked once, and then opened the door.

She had the recliner in full reclining position and her eyes were closed, but he could tell by the pained expression on her face that she wasn't asleep.

"Come in," she said, and raised the back of the chair into a sitting position.

Duke set the sacks down on the floor, then brought the Rollator inside.

"This is just a rental. You have it for a month." He rolled it over to her chair and began explaining how it worked. "If you push these handles down, it locks the wheels like brakes so it won't roll out from under you. And the seat lifts up so you can put things in the basket and move them from room to room."

Cathy was touched by his thoughtfulness and the endearing way in which he was instructing her in the walker's use.

"Thank you. I've never been so immobile before and wouldn't have thought of doing this."

Duke sighed with relief. She wasn't angry.

He went back for the two sacks. "I brought some icy-hot stuff for sore muscles. A bottle of painkillers just in case you didn't have any, and a couple of gel packs that need to freeze first. But once they're cold, you can alternate using one on your swollen ankle and then…well, you get the picture. Is it okay if I put these in the freezer for you?"

"Yes," Cathy said.

"Mr. Phillips, who owns the pharmacy, sent you a box of chocolates with his sympathies and said to get well soon."

Cathy was in shock. "Wow, there are some really nice people here in Blessings."

"There's more," Duke said. "Since you were out jogging so early in the morning, I was worried you might have missed your breakfast, so I went by Granny's and picked up some sausage gravy and some of Mercy's heavenly biscuits. That's what I call them, because they're so dang good, and when Lovey found out why I was getting them, she sent along a couple of pieces of fried chicken and some mashed potatoes and gravy for you to have on hand, and then wouldn't let me pay for it."

Cathy's eyes welled. It had been so long since anyone had been kind to her that the tears came without warning.

"No tears," Duke said, and laid a hand gently on her arm. "Are you hungry?"

"I thought of Granny's biscuits and gravy while I was running. I would love some."

"Will you let me make a plate for you?"

"Make a plate?"

Duke grinned. "That's Southern for putting food on a plate and serving you."

Cathy blushed. "Yes, you can make my plate, but just put it on the kitchen table and I'll roll myself in there to eat."

"Deal," Duke said. "Don't forget to set the hand brakes to brace yourself getting up."

"Okay," Cathy said.

Duke hesitated, then decided he'd done enough interfering.

"I'll just stand here to make sure you don't fall until you figure out the best way."

Cathy put the footrest down, then pulled the Rollator around in front of her, set the brakes, and then gingerly stood. Her hip hurt, her ankle was throbbing, but she was upright, and thanks to Duke Talbot, she would be mobile.

"Okay, now release the handbrakes before you go. Brace most of your weight on your arms. I know your hand is likely sore. I hope you can manage this, but it's the lesser of two evils."

"It's not that bad. Just missing a little hide, as my daddy used to say. I'll figure it out."

Duke didn't argue, and headed for the kitchen with the sacks. He put the gel packs in the freezer, then set the analgesic ointment and the bottle of painkillers on the kitchen table.

By that time, Cathy had made her way into the kitchen. She rolled herself up to the table, then turned the walker around and sat down on it like a chair.

"Plates are to the right of the sink. Flatware is in the top drawer to the left," she said.

Duke got out a plate and a fork, split two biscuits, poured

some sausage gravy over them, then carried the plate and the fork to the table and set it in front of her.

"Thank you so much. Did you get enough for yourself, too?" Cathy asked.

"No, I ate before I left home, but thank you. Maybe another time, okay?"

Cathy nodded, then took a bite and rolled her eyes as she chewed and swallowed.

"So good," she said, and went in for another bite.

"Want me to put the other stuff in your refrigerator?" he asked.

"Yes, thanks," she said.

Duke slid the containers onto an empty shelf, got a drinking glass from the cabinet, filled it with water, and then opened the bottle of painkillers.

"Hold out your hand," he said, and then shook a couple out into her palm.

Cathy took them gladly.

"I see you still have coffee on warm. Do you want some with your food?" Duke asked.

Cathy swallowed her bite of food and then looked up. He didn't look like Jeffrey Dean Morgan so much anymore. He just looked like the nicest man ever.

"Yes, and then you can stop waiting on me. You have done more than enough, and I owe you big time. Next time I see you, I can give you cash for the rental. How much do I owe?"

"It wasn't much, and it's on me. Do you have a phone?"

"Yes."

"Then I'm going to write down my cell number. I want you to promise that if you need anything...anything at all...that you'll call me. Since I'm my own boss, I come and go as I please, and it would please me to help."

He picked up the notepad and pen at the end of the kitchen counter and wrote down his number, then poured her a cup of coffee anyway and set it beside her plate.

"I guess I'll be going now," Duke said.

Cathy looked up. "I went running to get rid of a nightmare and was rescued by a knight in shining armor. Thank you for everything."

Duke grinned. "And I came into town to get a haircut. I always wanted to be a knight in shining armor for someone. I hope to see you again soon. Those gel packs should be ready to use in a couple of hours. I'll turn the lock on the door and let myself out. Rest well. Keep your feet up."

And then he was gone.

Cathy heard his truck start up and drive away, and stayed at the table long enough to finish eating. As soon as she got back into the recliner, she leaned back with a groan and closed her eyes.

Her tummy was full of biscuits and sausage gravy, and her heart was full to bursting from the kindness of strangers. The thought of seeing Duke Talbot again did not bother her, and it should have. She wasn't here for a relationship. Her plans had nothing to do with that.

She was almost asleep when it dawned on her that she didn't have any plans, so that claim held no water...no water at all.

CHAPTER 3

Moses and J.B. Gatlin hadn't been to Blessings since right after the hurricane, when they went there to tell their sister-in-law, Alice Conroy, about their mother, Beulah, being dead.

Their reception at that fancy house Alice was sheltering in had been nothing short of brutal, and they both admitted it was nothing more than they'd deserved. They'd had every intention of leaving Georgia, but it didn't happen.

After their mama blew up the house, they didn't have a change of clothes between them. With no job skills beyond being the hill people that they were, they'd pooled what money they had left, along with what Beulah had put by in the bank, and bought themselves a used trailer house and put it up where their house once stood, while Alice went on to marry Dan Amos, the man who'd given them shelter during the storm.

They did odd jobs for people in the area—and made enough money to keep their utilities on and food in their bellies—but they were barely getting by.

Then one morning when they went outside to feed their laying hens, there was a cow grazing near the barn.

"Looky there!" Moses said. "Someone's cow got out. Who do you reckon it belongs to?"

J.B. stood and looked at it for a minute, and then shrugged.

"Well, it's down at our barn, eating our grass. I reckon it belongs to us," he said.

Moses frowned. "No sir. We aren't thieves. Go put it in the pen. Someone will surely come looking for it."

J.B. went down to the barn and did as his brother told him, but the thought was still in his mind that they could sell the cow at an auction somewhere and pocket a little extra cash.

And after three days without a single soul coming to look for the cow, J.B. loaded it up and took it to a cattle auction in another county and came home with over eight hundred dollars.

Moses was at the house when J.B. came back, and the look on his face made J.B. a little nervous. He drove the pickup to the back of the barn, unhooked the stock trailer, and then drove back to the house, took the money out of his wallet, and got out.

"What the hell did you do with that cow?" Moses yelled.

J.B. just handed his brother the money and went into the house.

Moses stared at the wad of money, then counted it in disbelief. Eight hundred and twenty-three dollars.

"Lord, lord," Moses muttered.

He looked down at his old work shoes, then up at where they lived. It was falling down around them. He looked back down at the money again, and then followed J.B. into the trailer.

"Well?" J.B. asked.

Moses opened a cabinet and pulled out the round oatmeal box that they used for a bank, and put the money inside, then put it back in the cabinet without saying a word.

"I already fed the chickens, and I got a call from a man

up near Savannah who wants some windows hung tomorrow. We need to be there by 8:00 a.m."

"All right," J.B. said. "What's he paying?"

"I told him we'd do it for three hundred," Moses said.

"How many are we hanging?" J.B. asked.

"I reckon he said five of them. They're regular-size windows and all on the ground floor."

J.B. nodded.

"All right, then."

They stood for a minute looking at each other, and knew they'd both crossed a line that would have shamed their mama. But then they weren't too happy with her, either. If it wasn't for her, they wouldn't be in this shape, so they let the guilt slide.

They went to bed after the sun went down, Moses in his room, J.B. in his across the hall. But neither one of them could sleep. J.B. had sold something that didn't belong to him, and Moses had abetted the crime by taking the money from the sale.

It was a fitful night for both of them, and when the alarm went off at 5:00 a.m., they were up without complaint.

They came home that evening with two hundred and fifty-one dollars to add to their stash. They'd had to buy their own lunches and put gas in the truck coming and going, but it was money honestly earned.

It was another month before the brothers crossed the line again, but this time it was easier. They saw three steers out grazing in a bar ditch, and when they drove up on them, the steers turned and ran ahead of the pickup.

"You need to stop, or they'll run all the way to our place," Moses said.

"Yeah, they probably will," J.B. said, and kept driving,

and the steers kept running up that gravel road all the way to their homeplace. But when J.B. parked at the trailer, the steers finally stopped running.

Neither brother commented, but they both walked down to the barn. One opened the gate to the corral, and the other herded the steers inside. They began grazing on the overgrowth in the corral.

"You feed the chickens. I'll start supper," Moses said, and that's how the evening went.

They ate sausage patties and fried potatoes until they were gone, then cleaned up the kitchen together.

"How long do you reckon we oughta keep them steers?" J.B. asked.

Moses shrugged. "Someone might show up looking for them tomorrow."

J.B. nodded. "Yeah, we'll wait and see."

"Right. We'll wait and see," Moses said.

They kept them four days, then hauled them to a different auction house in a different county and came home with more money than they'd ever had at once.

After that, their consciences no longer bothered them like they had before, and they began looking for easy marks.

It was Moses who remembered that the Talbot property butted up to Old Man Bailey's place, and it was Moses who also knew the old man was in a nursing home.

They scouted the place out one day, just to see if they could see any cattle in the Talbot pasture, and saw nice ones that would bring a good price.

Before, they'd just been availing themselves of wandering cattle, so this was their first venture into outright rustling. They were going onto other people's property, cutting fences, and stealing livestock.

"If we get ourselves a good load, then we won't have to do this anymore," Moses said.

"What do you mean?" J.B. asked.

"Well, with what we already have, and what we'll get from a big haul, we'll be sittin' pretty come winter when the work dries up," Moses explained.

"Yeah, I guess you're right," J.B. said. "When do you want to do it?"

"I say let's come back here just before sunup. The cattle will come up for feed, and we'll get what we want and be gone before either one of the Talbots even gets out of bed."

J.B. grinned. "Good thinking, Moses."

They made a quick run to a nearby town to get a couple of sacks of cattle cubes, and then went home for the day. Before sunrise the next morning they were ready.

It wasn't all that far to the old Bailey place from where they lived, and they were there within fifteen minutes. They followed their own tracks back through the overgrown pastures to the backside of the Talbot farm, then cut the fence and drove right out into the pasture, looking for the herd.

They found them just over the hill from where they'd come in, still bedded down. But when the cows heard the pickup and the trailer rattling over the rough ground, they got up.

Moses turned in a half circle so that they were now facing the cut fence for a quick exit, then got out and opened the back gate to the trailer.

"Let's get the feed," Moses said, so they got a sack apiece, emptied them in a circle, and waited.

The cattle came running, pushing and shoving a little to get to the cubes. The Gatlin brothers let them eat a little, and then J.B. got a cattle prod, and Moses had a pole. They got on either side of a couple of steers and just turned them around from where they were standing with the pole. Then with one poke of that prod, the first steer jumped forward right into the trailer and the other one followed. They got three head in the front half of the trailer, then shut that gate, and then took some of the feed and led two more inside. They didn't know one of the cows they loaded up had a calf until it followed her inside and began to suck.

"Score," J.B. said, when he saw it.

They shut the back gate and locked it, then took off for the truck and drove away, back through the fence they'd cut, and then through the Bailey property and back out on the road. They went straight to their place long enough to remove the ear tags from the cattle, then headed to the auction house J.B. had used when he sold that first cow.

They left the auction house with over four thousand dollars and went straight to the bank in Savannah to deposit the money into the account they'd opened after their second sale. The people there didn't know them as anything other than cattle jockeys—men who bought and sold cattle for a living—and thought nothing of it, and after the account had been opened, the brothers made a point of depositing all of their money from odd jobs there as well.

It made them feel like regular people to have a bank account, and adding in the little dabs of legal earnings to go with the rustling business made them feel better. They'd almost convinced themselves that making a deposit with legal money canceled out the money they'd made from selling stolen property.

"This was our last run," Moses said.

"Yeah, I remember," J.B. said.

"And we're not doing this again," Moses added.

J.B. shrugged. "Whatever you say."

Once they got home, they washed the fresh cow poop out of the trailer, then took it to the barn. Just for good measure, they sprinkled some dry dirt into the trailer bed, then filled it up with junk and old wire from inside the barn to make it look like it hadn't been used in ages, and dragged it out into the weeds behind the barn and left it there. The next morning they drove into Savannah to pick up some much-needed supplies.

They didn't know Jack Talbot had already found the broken fence, but they wouldn't have cared. As far as they were concerned, they'd gotten away unseen, the cattle were sold, and that was the end of that.

Duke was on his way home when his phone rang, and when he saw Jack's name pop up in caller ID, he knew his brother was checking on him. He answered, then put it on speaker and kept driving.

"Hello."

"Are you okay?" Jack asked.

"I'm fine. I'm almost home," Duke said.

"Well, okay then. I was getting worried. Didn't think you'd be gone this long and—"

"Yeah. Kinda got caught up in a little incident in Blessings and wound up taking a lady to the ER."

"Oh hell, did you have a wreck?"

"No, nothing like that. I just happened to witness her take a bad fall, and then Lon showed up and escorted us to the ER. I went to get a haircut after that, and then Hope called Ruby looking for someone to take the lady home. I was getting ready to leave, and I'd already taken her to the ER, so I thought I might as well offer to take her home. And that's where I've been."

"Oh wow! That sounds serious. Who was it who fell?"

"Her name is Cathy Terry. She's new to Blessings."

There was a long moment of silence—enough that Duke thought they'd been disconnected.

"Jack? Are you still there?"

"Uh, yeah…I was just…I was just surprised you went to all that trouble for a woman you didn't know."

Duke was floored. He didn't even know how to respond. Jack waited. "Duke?"

"I'm here."

"What's wrong?" Jack asked.

Duke sighed. "Is that what you guys really think about me? That I'm too self-absorbed to help a woman in need? Any woman? Even a stranger?"

"No, brother, no…I'm sorry. I didn't mean it to sound that way. Look, I'm sorry. I didn't meant to hurt your feelings."

Duke was still in shock, but he laughed it off.

"You didn't hurt my feelings. So did you get the cattle fed this morning?"

"Yes, but there was fence down in the back pasture. I came home to get wire stretchers and some stuff to go fix it, but the wire looked cut, not broken."

Duke frowned. "Do we have any cattle missing?"

"Well damn, I didn't think to check," Jack said. "I'll go—"

"Just wait for me to get home and change, and I'll go with you," Duke said.

The brothers disconnected, and by the time Duke got home, the topic of conversation had become the fence. Duke changed into work clothes, put on his old denim jacket, and started out the door, then stopped and went back inside. When he came out carrying a rifle, Jack was shocked.

"What's that for?" he asked.

"If the fence was cut, someone was up to no good. If we're missing cattle, then we're dealing with thieves. I'm just being cautious."

Jack eyed his older brother with renewed respect.

"That's something I should have thought of, too. It's a good thing we're in this together. I don't know how Mom and Dad did this on their own when we were kids. It takes the both of us…two grown men, to keep this place running."

"You forget that five years ago we added two hundred acres and thirty more head of cattle to go with the fifty-three we already had," Duke said. "Get in. I'm driving."

Jack laughed as they both got in the old farm truck. He'd already loaded up the wire cutters, fence stretchers, and a roll of wire to repair the break.

"You always do this so I have to get out to open gates."

"There has to be some kind of perk for being the oldest," Duke said.

He started up the truck and drove down to the barn to load up a few sacks of cattle cubes, then drove across a cattle guard, heading toward the fenced-off pastures beyond.

"Where to first?" Jack asked.

"I think the west field where the big herd is, just to make sure we don't have any other fence down there. We can get a head count there before we go to the north side," Duke said.

"I don't know for certain it was cut. It just looked like it," Jack said.

"If we're missing any cattle there, then we'll know for sure," Duke said, as he pulled up and stopped. "First gate, little brother."

Jack jumped out and opened it, and as soon as Duke drove through, Jack fastened it shut and got back in the truck.

A few minutes later they were driving the boundaries of the west pasture, and as they expected, the sound of the old truck brought the herd running.

"I'll spread the cubes. You drive," Jack said. He got out again, but this time got up in the truck bed and opened the first sack. "Ready!" he yelled, and then braced himself as Duke started moving, pouring cattle cubes over the side of the truck, leaving a trail of them in the grass. Jack opened two more sacks and emptied them before he stopped, and by that time all the cattle were lined up and head down, eating.

At that point, Duke got up in the back of the truck with Jack and they both began a head count.

"I got fifty-three," Duke said.

"So did I," Jack said. "That means they're all here. Now on to the north pasture."

They got back in the truck, going through one more gate, then followed Jack's tire tracks from before through the field.

"What are you doing?" Jack asked. "It's shorter if you cut across to—"

"Just making sure I don't mess up some kind of trail that thieves might have left," Duke said.

"Why would you think to do that?" Jack asked.

"All those *North Woods Law* shows I watch, I guess," Duke said.

Jack grinned. "You do have a thing for them," he said. "You know…when we were kids, nobody ever asked us what we wanted to be when we grew up. It was just understood that we would take over the family farm."

"I know," Duke said. "Did you ever want to do anything else?"

"No. After Mom and Dad died in that accident, you stepped up big-time and got me through my last year of college. You knew I wanted to come home to work with Dad, and the family farm was still here when I graduated because of you. You used to talk about taking your degree and going to work for the National Park Service."

Duke was silent for a moment, and then he shook his head. "It was just talk. I didn't want to lose the farm any more than you did, and we're doing just fine."

Jack sighed. "You gave up a lot for me."

"I didn't give up a thing. You and Hope are my family."

"And you put the farm and us ahead of every personal dream you might have had," Jack said.

Duke grinned. "Well, there were those few weeks when I thought Hope's sister, Mercy, should just marry me and move into the house with us, and that would solve my single status."

Jack laughed. "Yeah, you had everything figured out except for the fact that you two could barely get along, never mind falling in love."

"It was a moment of madness," Duke said. "I don't know what the hell I was thinking, other than it was kind of like buying more cattle to add to the herd."

Jack burst out laughing. "Oh, my God, Duke. No wonder you're still a bachelor. You've got to do something about that mindset. You're still plenty young enough to get married and raise a family."

"I'll leave the babies up to you and Hope," Duke said. "And enough about orchestrating my future. Butting in is my forte, not yours."

Jack pointed to a section of fence up ahead. "That's where the fence is down."

"Yes…I see it. Start watching for truck and trailer tracks. We should be coming up on the herd soon, and then we'll get a head count here. I might have jumped the gun on thinking theft was involved, but better safe than sorry," Duke said, and slowed down even more so they could watch for fresh tracks.

A couple of minutes later, Duke noticed something up ahead and hit the brakes.

"What do you see?" Jack asked.

"Looks like someone put feed out here, but we don't dump feed all in one spot like that. I want a closer look," Duke said.

He took the rifle with him as they got out, and even as he was walking up on the spot, he knew his fears were likely true. What remained to be seen was how many head of cattle the rustlers took.

"Look! They even left two empty feed sacks behind," Jack said.

"Wait. I'm taking pictures," Duke said, and snapped pictures of the trampled grass and the feed sacks before moving forward.

"Duke! Look here. Footprints!"

Duke ran over to where Jack was standing. "Boot prints, and there's a weird line running through the heel on the left foot. I think it's a big cut in the leather." He squatted down and took a couple of pictures, and then suddenly stopped, took off one of his boots, and put it beside the footprint for size reference.

"You are a size 13, so I'm saying that's about a size 11 boot," Jack said.

"With a serious slash in the heel," Duke added. "Wait here. I'm going back to get the truck, and then we'll go find the herd. We need to know how many are gone before we call Sheriff Ryman."

"Dammit," Jack said. "This makes me sick. Who would do such a thing?"

"The Baileys own the land that butts up to our back fence, but nobody's been living there since Mr. Bailey went into the nursing home, and that's more than a year ago," Duke said, and then ran back to get the truck.

He drove way out around the site to pick Jack up.

"I would have thought we'd already be seeing cattle," Jack said as he got back in. "They usually hear us coming."

"Not if they're all down at the south end," Duke said, and headed that way.

It wasn't until they topped a small hill and started down to the grove of trees below that they saw the cattle grazing.

"Stop and let me get in the back," Jack said. "They're going to come running when they see us."

Duke stopped again, and as soon as his brother Jack was back in the truck bed with another sack of cattle cubes, he started driving down the hill.

When they got closer, Jack started pouring feed out over the side, leaving a trail behind them as they went, then emptied another feed sack before they stopped.

Again, Duke got up in the back with him to count.

"Well, hell. I only count twenty-four, and there should be thirty," Duke said.

Jack nodded. "I had the same count."

"So we're short six head," Duke said, and took out his phone. "I'm calling Sheriff Ryman. It'll take us a bit to get back to the house, and if we're lucky, we won't have to wait all afternoon for someone to come out. I want to fix that break, but he needs to see it as is. Maybe we need to just move the herd into the east pasture and take away the convenience."

"The grass is short there," Jack said.

"So we'll start feeding round bales a little sooner than planned. It's better than losing more cattle," Duke said.

"Agreed. Get in," Jack said. "I'll drive back so you can talk."

"And get you out of gate duty?" Duke said.

"Fair's fair, brother," Jack said, and jumped out of the truck bed and got in the driver's seat.

Duke was already reporting the theft as they drove away.

While Duke was dealing with cattle rustlers, Cathy had finally managed to get herself into the shower. She'd done exactly what they told her not to do and unwrapped her ankle, but she felt dirty and gritty, and a spit bath wasn't going to suffice.

She was exhausted and hurting by the time she was finished, but she was clean, and she had rewrapped her ankle.

She rolled herself back into the kitchen, took a couple more painkillers, then went back to the living room and collapsed into the recliner. She got her foot up and was almost getting comfortable when someone knocked at her door.

She groaned. Just when she was beginning to get easy. But before she could move, she heard a familiar voice.

"Cathy, it's me, Dan Amos. Are you there?"

"I'm here. Give me a second," she said.

"I know you fell. I can let myself in if you're okay with that," he said.

She was taken aback for a moment, and then realized that as the landlord, he had access to all of his rentals, and relaxed.

"Yes, yes, come in."

She heard a key in the door, and then as the door swung inward, Dan and his wife came in.

"We heard through the grapevine that you got hurt, and came to see if you needed any help," Dan said. "And I don't think you've met my wife, Alice."

"It's a pleasure, Alice. Please, both of you have a seat," Cathy said, pointing to the sofa nearest her chair, then eyeing the bandage on Dan's hand. "Duke Talbot told me you came into the ER while he was waiting to bring me home. What happened to your hand?"

"Oh, carelessness mostly. I was replacing windowpanes in an empty house, and one of them broke in my hand. It's not a bad cut, and because it's in the palm, they just glued the cut rather than using stitches or staples."

"It sure scared me," Alice said. "Dan is my everything."

"Ditto, honey," Dan said. He gave Alice a quick smile and then shifted focus back to Cathy. "I know without a car you're still afoot. What can we help you do? Do you need groceries or prescriptions filled?"

"I think I'm okay with all that," Cathy said. "I had been toying with the idea of leasing a car. I should have acted on the thought sooner."

"Can I bring you some supper tonight?" Alice asked.

"Thank you for the offer, but I already have food. Duke got some for me before he left, and Lovey sent fried chicken and potatoes and gravy for later."

Alice smiled. "Lovey is the best, but I don't like to think about you here all hurt and alone. I want to leave my phone number for you. If I do, will you promise to call if you need anything?"

"That's really sweet of you," Cathy said. "There's a pad and pen in the kitchen. Duke already wrote his number on it. You can leave yours, too, if you want."

"Yes, I want to. A while back, my two kids and I showed up here in Blessings without anything but the clothes on our back. I don't know what would have happened to us if it hadn't been for the people of Blessings. And then, of course, Dan came to town and saved us."

Dan chuckled. "Well, I fell in love with them first. Then I did the hero thing."

Alice poked him on the arm and then went to the kitchen to write down her name and number.

Cathy was just beginning to realize what a jewel of a place she'd stumbled into. It was beginning to feel like a place to heal in more ways than one.

"Okay, you have my number," Alice said, as she came back into the room. "Do you have to go back to the doctor for any kind of follow-up?"

"Not unless I have problems," Cathy said. "As soon as I feel like it, I can walk on my ankle, but as you can see, Duke rented this Rollator to make sure I had a way to get around until it heals."

"The Talbot family is well thought of in the area," Dan said. "He's a good friend to have. Now, if you're sure we can't do anything for you, we'll get out of here and maybe you can get some rest. I'll lock the door on my way out."

"Thank you for coming to check on me," Cathy said. "I never expected anything like this. I mean...I'm a stranger here."

Alice just laughed. "Oh, honey, in Blessings, no one is a stranger for long. Get some rest. Your personal phone number is on the rental application. I'll call you sometime tomorrow and check in on you, just to make sure you don't need me to run an errand, okay?"

"Yes, okay, and thank you for coming," Cathy said.

Dan locked the door behind them as they left.

The house was quiet now, but Cathy didn't feel so alone anymore. There were people here who knew her name, and who cared about her welfare. It was more than she'd had in almost a year, and the feelings washing through her were overwhelming. She reclined the chair again and closed her eyes, suddenly grateful she'd followed her knee-jerk reaction to winter here.

———————————————

Blaine Wagner had been AWOL from Vegas for almost a month, cruising on a friend's yacht along the California coast and then down the Mexican Riviera. They'd spent a week docked in Cabo San Lucas, then Puerto Vallarta, then gone as far as Acapulco before heading back.

He didn't realize his ex-wife was no longer showing up anywhere in Vegas until he got home and checked in with Rand Lawrence, the private investigator he'd hired to watch her apartment. The whole time he'd been gone, he'd been trying to decide whether to just let her be or remove the threat of her altogether.

He woke early, more than anxious to get back to the office and into his normal routine, but in the back of his mind, he wanted an update on his ex.

He ordered his driver for a nine o'clock pickup, and then showered and dressed before going down to breakfast. After weeks of rich food and more liquor than he'd like to think about, he asked his chef for bacon and eggs and a couple of toasted English muffins, then downed them with multiple cups of black coffee and headed for the office.

As soon as he arrived, he issued orders to his secretary, checked to make sure the board meeting was still on for the afternoon, and then went into his office.

The scent of fresh brewing coffee met him at the door,

and he poured himself a cup from the coffee bar before sitting down at his desk.

His computer was on and waiting for him to go through his personal emails, so he spent a couple of minutes scanning what was there before he reached for his phone to call Rand Lawrence, then counted four rings before the PI answered.

"Hello, Rand speaking."

"Good morning, Rand. This is Blaine Wagner. I'm checking in for an update on my ex-wife."

"I don't have much to tell, Mr. Wagner. I haven't seen her come in or out since you left. I finally put up a security camera in the hall that's aimed straight at her door, and it hasn't opened once since I installed the camera."

Blaine's heart skipped a beat. Could he be so lucky as to hope she'd become despondent and offed herself?

"Do you think she's still there?" Blaine asked.

"I have no way of knowing that," Rand said. "All I know is that I saw her go in weeks ago, and her car is still in the parking garage."

Blaine frowned. This was not what he wanted to hear.

"Do a follow-up and see if she booked any trips. Check airlines for overseas flights. Check cruise ships. She might have gone on vacation somewhere—and get back to me on this ASAP."

"Yes, sir," Rand said.

Frustrated, Blaine disconnected. He was too impatient to wait for Rand to run all those traces, and thought about checking in with the apartment manager and having them do a welfare check. Then he tried to think of who he knew at her bank that might break FDIC rules for him and see if she'd withdrawn a large amount of money.

He had a meeting later in the afternoon, but it would freaking make his day if someone found her dead in her apartment. He knew the manager of her complex and made a call to the office. He was put on hold just long enough to tick him off, and then the call was picked up.

"Good morning, Mr. Wagner. This is Eric. How can I help you?"

"Morning, Eric. I have a favor to ask. I know it's a little unorthodox, but I'm a bit concerned about my ex-wife, Cathy. I've been out of town for a while, and I come back to all kinds of messages from her old friends that are concerning to me." It didn't faze him one bit that he'd just lied, as long as he got the answers he wanted. "She's in one of your apartments and hasn't been seen anywhere for some time. Her friends have called without getting answers. Her car hasn't been moved in weeks, and now they have me concerned. She could easily be vacationing, I suppose. But we'd all rest easier knowing she hadn't suffered a fall or taken ill and is unable to call for help. Is there any way you could do a kind of welfare check? You surely have spare keys to the apartments, right?"

Eric Mitchell was immediately on alert. The last thing he needed was for someone's dead body to be rotting in one of the apartments. It would cost a fortune to strip the place down and fix it after something like that.

"Yes, yes, I can do that for you. I'll check my records to get the building and apartment number and get back to you soon."

"As soon as possible, please," Blaine said. "I have meetings this afternoon and can't be disturbed then."

"Yes, just give me about thirty minutes and I'll call you back."

"Thank you so much," Blaine said, and then disconnected. He glanced up at the clock. It was a quarter to ten. He wasn't in the habit of drinking before noon, but he set aside his coffee and headed for the wet bar, while on the other side of Vegas, Eric Mitchell was scrambling for pass keys.

Eric wasn't looking forward to this. He could have sent someone else to do it, but Blaine Wagner had asked him personally, and he was stuck.

He jumped in his car and drove down to the building, then headed inside, rode the elevator up to the eighth floor, and walked down to 802. He paused outside the door and inhaled, but didn't smell anything resembling a rotting body, so he rang the doorbell and waited. And then waited. Then he rang it again and waited. And waited some more.

Satisfied there wasn't going to be an answer, he put the key in the lock and turned it. Only afterward did it occur to him that it could have set off a security alarm, and he breathed a sigh of relief when he was met with silence.

The air-conditioning was on, so there was no musty smell as he called out.

"Cathy! Cathy Wagner! Anybody here?"

Silence.

At that point, he began walking through the rooms, choosing the kitchen first and going straight to the refrigerator. There were a couple of leftover cartons of moldy food and a partially full bottle of milk that was almost two months out of date. He closed the door and went through the living room and into the office. There was a laptop on the desk, but when he checked, it was off, and the battery had gone dead.

He moved into the bedroom, and the first thing he saw was her purse sitting on the bench at the foot of her bed. He looked inside, and when he realized everything she would have carried was still in it—her wallet, her ID, credit cards, car keys, sunglasses, even makeup—his heart skipped a beat. No woman willingly left all of this behind. Now he was getting concerned.

He went straight to the big walk-in closet. It didn't take but a few moments to notice there were no empty hangers to indicate she'd packed clothes. There was no sign of a struggle or any kind of abduction. She was just gone.

Eric was still in her bedroom when he called Blaine. He must have been waiting for the call because he answered on the first ring.

"This is Blaine."

"It's me, Eric. I'm in her apartment, and I don't really know what to tell you except that she's not here. There's food in her refrigerator that has molded. The milk is out of date almost two months. The laptop in her office is off, and when I tried to turn it on, the battery was dead. I'm standing in her bedroom right now, and her purse is here with her wallet, money, credit cards, and ID still in it. Her car keys are in it. I checked her closet. There's no sign of her packing any clothes because there are no empty hangers. It's as if she just vanished. Do you want me to call the police?"

Blaine's heart skipped a beat. He knew exactly what she'd done. The bitch! She'd walked away from it all to get away from him, and he'd never seen it coming.

"No. Let me do some more checking first, and for now, let's keep this between us."

"Yes, sir," Eric said. "So, I'll just lock it back up as if I was never here. Her lease is paid up until May of next year anyway."

"Thank you again," Blaine said, but he was cursing a blue streak by the time he disconnected.

The last confirmation he needed would be to check the damn bank account. They wouldn't tell him where they'd moved money, but he could find out if the account was still active. He just needed to find the right person. Someone with access to viewing those accounts surely needed a little extra something. He banked there as well, and had seen a couple of bank employees regularly in the casinos in which he was invested. If they liked to gamble, he had a feeling they wouldn't turn down the money to snoop.

It cost Blaine five thousand dollars to get the info he wanted about Cathy's checking account. There was less than two hundred thousand dollars left, which was more than enough for the automatic withdrawals for her utility bills until her lease ran out. But since she'd left all her credit cards behind, they were useless in trying to trace her.

Now he had to decide if he wanted to just kiss her absent ass goodbye and consider he'd won by running her out of town, or if she was too much of a threat. But that was for another time. Right now, he was doing lunch with an associate, then going from there to the board meeting being held at the Luxor, so he slid into the back seat of his limo, closed the window between him and his driver, and made a call to a brunette named Angel.

He smiled when she answered. "Hello, big boy. You're back. I have missed you and your hot body so much," she said, and then made a little purring sound that raised the hair on the back of his neck.

"Missed me enough to go to dinner with me tonight?" he asked.

"Ooh, yes, baby. And do I get to spend the night? You know how I love waking up next to you."

"Absolutely," Blaine said. "I'll pick you up at seven. I have dinner reservations at Joel Robuchon's at the Grand for seven thirty."

"Oh yum. You spoil me," Angel said.

Blaine laughed. "See you then," he said, and disconnected.

Duke and Jack were back at the scene of the crime, with Deputies Treat and Butler from the County Sheriff's office. Butler was taking pictures of the tire tracks and had made a plaster cast of the boot print with the cut in the left heel. They had already taken pictures of where the wire had been cut and of the feed sacks left behind while Jack and Duke were repairing the downed fence.

"So, you say you're missing six head?" Butler asked.

Jack nodded. "Three big steers and two cows, one with a calf."

Treat was making notes as Butler asked questions, but he soon popped up with one of his own.

"Who owns the place that backs up here to yours?" he asked.

"Mylo Bailey, but his daughter, Rhonda Bailey, who's a nurse at the hospital in Blessings, had to put him in a nursing home over a year ago. As far as we know, the house and the place have stood empty ever since," Duke said.

"Property with no one in residence is a good way to get in and out without being noticed. It's obvious they came across it because the tracks are visible on the other side," Treat said. "We'll be heading over that way as soon as we leave your place. Oh, one other thing. Are your cattle branded?"

"No, but they all have numbered ear tags and the initials DJT below the numbers…for Duke and Jack Talbot," he added.

"Okay. We'll be checking in with local auction houses, too," Treat said. "I think that's all for now. If you own game cameras, it might be a good idea to put some up. If the rustlers make a return trip, you might get lucky."

"Good idea," Duke said, and then he and Jack led the way out of the fields back to their house. The deputies left as Duke and Jack went inside.

"I'm making coffee," Jack said, as he went to the kitchen sink to wash up.

"And I'm going to the office to work. Let me know when the coffee is done, and I'll come get some."

"Oh, I'll bring you a cup," Jack said. "Go do your thing. I'm getting meat out to thaw for supper. I don't know about you, but I'm starved. We missed dinner. Want me to bring you a sandwich to go with your coffee?" he asked.

"Sure. Whatever we have," Duke said, then hung his

work jacket on the peg by the back door, washed up, and then went down the hall to the office.

But as soon as he sat down, his thoughts flashed on the little redhead he'd taken home this morning, and he wished he'd had the nerve to ask for her phone number. He wanted to call her just to hear her voice again, but he couldn't. And then it dawned on him that the hospital might have it in their records, so he turned on the computer. While it was booting up, he sent Hope a text, then pulled up the farm account and began posting the bills and payments. When Jack brought the sandwich and coffee a few minutes later, Duke stopped long enough to take a bite, then kept working.

He had finished half of the sandwich and was working on the last half when his phone signaled a text. He wiped his hands, then grabbed the phone to read what she'd sent.

> Dear Brother-in-law, we're not supposed
> to give out patient information. Go see
> her tomorrow and ask her yourself. If she
> wants you to have it, she will give it to you.
> P.S. I love you, but not enough to get
> fired. LOL

Duke sighed. He hadn't thought that through, and he returned the text.

> *My bad. I didn't think about that. Sorry, Hope.*

Then he added a smiley-face emoji and hit Send, finished off his sandwich, and went to refill his coffee.

Deputies Treat and Butler drove straight to the Bailey property. The empty two-story house looked a bit forlorn. The yard hadn't been mowed in ages, and there was a layer of dust all over the windows. It was a shame. The house itself had once been a showstopper in the area.

The central part of the house was two-story redbrick, with white clapboard, single-story wings on either side. It had white shutters in need of paint, and there were a few missing shingles.

The old barn behind the house was a big two-story with a gambrel roof and a loft opening above the doorway below. It had once been painted white, but was mostly gray now, and the pen built behind the barn appeared to be made of welded pipe that was red with rust.

It didn't take them long to find obvious tracks coming and going in the dirt driveway, and after taking more pictures, they matched up the tire treads at the Bailey place to the ones they'd seen at the Talbots'. The kicker was finding the same boot print with the slash in the heel. They photographed it and then walked back to their car.

"They definitely used the empty property as their access," Treat said. "I think now we need to question the daughter, Rhonda Bailey, to see if she's rented out this property to anyone."

"The Talbots said she worked at the ER in the Blessings hospital. Why don't you call and see if she's still on duty, and if she's not, get her personal phone number."

"Will do," Butler said. He was already on the phone as Treat backed up and then left the property.

Rhonda Bailey was just coming out of an exam room in the ER when one of the nurses at the desk waved her down.

"Phone call for you on line three."

Rhonda slipped behind the nurses' station to take the call, pressed Line Three, and then answered.

"This is Rhonda."

"Miss Bailey, this is Deputy Butler with the County Sheriff's office. We need to ask you a couple of questions about your father's property."

Rhonda was immediately apprehensive. With her father no longer capable of making his own decisions, she and her brothers were responsible for it.

"Oh no! Has something happened?"

"No, nothing like that. Have you rented it to anyone, or given anyone permission to be on the property?"

"No. Absolutely not. What's wrong? Has property been damaged?"

"No, ma'am, but it appears some cattle rustlers used it as access to get to the back side of the Talbot property and made off with a half-dozen head of their cattle."

Rhonda gasped. "I am so sorry! That's terrible! I didn't know people were still doing things like that."

"Yes, ma'am, unfortunately, thievery is a healthy business, and for people who raise cattle, rustling is a real threat."

"There aren't any other neighbors close by Daddy's house, so that made it easy for them to come and go without being seen," she said.

"Yes, ma'am. That's what we noticed. Okay, sorry to have

bothered you at work, but you've cleared up some questions we had. Thank you for your time."

"Yes, of course," Rhonda said, and then hung up.

The other two nurses couldn't help but overhear Rhonda's side of the conversation, but before they could question her, Hope Talbot walked up. One look at their faces, and she knew something had happened.

"What's going on?" she asked.

Rhonda sighed. "Have you talked to Jack this afternoon?"

"No, but I saw Duke earlier in the day when he dropped Cathy Terry off for treatment."

"Sorry to be the one to break the bad news, but that was a deputy from the County Sheriff's department on the phone. Someone used Dad's old place as access to get to the back side of the Talbot property. They stole some of your cattle. The sheriff's deputy wanted to know if we'd rented it out to anyone, and of course we had not, so there's no way of telling who did it."

Hope groaned.

"Oh my God! I need to call home," she said, and headed for the break room.

She already knew Duke and Jack were going to be upset, and she was just sick about the loss. As soon as she found a quiet place, she called her husband.

"Hello, honey. I was just about to call you," Jack said. "We've had some trouble out here today."

"I just heard," Hope said. "Some deputies from the county called Rhonda Bailey to ask her about her dad's property. She said the people who stole the cattle gained access through her dad's place."

"So, they've already confirmed what we thought. Duke thought that might be the case," Jack said.

"I'm so sorry," Hope said. "Do you think we have any chance of getting them back?"

"I'd say slim to none. If they took them straight to an auction, they're probably already gone."

"But we had them all ear-tagged," Hope said.

"Yes, but those tags can be removed. What's done is done. We can't change it. But we did move all of the cattle that were in that pasture up closer to the house. Rustlers would have to go through gates and be really gutsy to come this close to the house now and try for more. What I am surprised about is how they even knew cattle were in that back pasture, and how they knew they could get to it through the Bailey property."

"Sounds like someone local, doesn't it?" Hope said.

"Yes, it does, but I can't imagine who it might be. Hopefully, the sheriff's deputies will figure it out, and that will be that," Jack said.

"Are there any clues at all?" Hope asked.

"Not really... Oh, we did find an interesting boot print they left behind. The heel on a left boot has a long slash on it. It was deep enough that it showed up in the dirt that way."

"Did you get pictures?" Hope asked.

"Yes, and so did the deputies. What time do you get off this evening?"

"Not until six. I won't be home until sometime after six thirty, maybe closer to seven, and if something happens in the ER and they need the extra help, you know I'll have to stay. If I'm going to be delayed, I'll let you know," she said.

"We'll keep supper warm for you. Love you, honey."

"Love you, too," Hope said, and disconnected, then put her phone back in her pocket and went back out onto the floor.

The distant rumble of thunder and the sound of rain on the roof woke Cathy up, and then for a second she looked around in sudden confusion before she figured out where she was.

The ice pack on her ankle was warm, the house was dark, and the streetlights were shining in through her front windows. She turned on the lamp beside her chair, then turned on the TV and got up to pull the drapes, grateful for the walker.

Once she felt safe behind the curtains, she turned on the lights and made her way to the bathroom. When she came out, she headed for the kitchen. It was almost 8:00 p.m., and she was grateful for the cold fried chicken and potatoes and gravy Lovey sent. She got the containers out of the refrigerator and took them to the counter, put some food on a plate, and popped it in the microwave, then used her walker to get it into the living room to eat.

The television was on Mute, so the rain hammering the roof was easily audible, and the rising wind was evident from the rain being blown against the windows.

She turned up the volume as she took a bite of the chicken, and as she ate, she thought about how grateful she was for the food and shelter. She'd spent several stormy nights out on the road with nothing but her waterproof tent for shelter and was glad to put that behind her.

Cathy looked around at the little house, at the simple furnishings and the less-than-elegant ambiance, remembering the opulent lifestyle she'd had, all of the jewelry and designer clothing, a mansion full of servants. But when she took another bite of chicken, she knew in her heart that she fit the simplicity of this place better.

Later, after she'd cleaned up in the kitchen and gone to bed, she kept thinking of how quickly she'd gone from solitude to a houseful of new friends today, and all because of a fall.

She'd taken a hard fall from grace in Vegas and been ostracized for it. But here in Blessings, one stumble and people she didn't even know had come to her rescue.

Blessings had possibilities. It might just become her forever home, instead of a stopping-off point.

She sighed, then shifted her foot to a more comfortable position and fell asleep to the sound of rain on the roof.

CHAPTER 4

CATHY WOKE UP STIFF AND SORE. THE EFFECTS OF HER fall were setting in, and she ached all over. She got to the kitchen and started coffee, then went back to her bedroom to shower and wash her hair before she put the ankle wrap back on. She was letting her hair air-dry as she put on pants and a T-shirt, then rewrapped her ankle before going to the kitchen.

After a few sips of coffee, she heated up the last of the biscuits and sausage gravy, and thought of Duke Talbot with every bite. She couldn't imagine why someone that good-looking was single, but her spidey senses hadn't set off any warnings that he was bad news. Still, she reminded herself she'd just met him. There could be any number of reasons he was unattached, none of which were her business.

She took a couple of pain pills after she ate, then grabbed an ice pack and went into the living room, covered herself over with a blanket, and settled into the recliner with the cold pack on her ankle, waiting for the pain pills to kick in.

Duke woke just after daybreak, but when he heard rain on the roof, he knew morning chores were going to be messy. He rolled over on his back and began mentally going over the tasks for the day.

He'd still been up when Hope came home last night, and

he knew today was her day off, so she was likely sleeping in a bit.

Jack tried to be protective of Hope, but she was just as strong-willed and independent as her sister, Mercy, and somehow that became what was most special about her. Lord knows, Jack was forever smitten.

Duke sighed. He really didn't want to grow old alone. He wanted to be smitten, too, but for whatever reason, he'd never found that certain someone. And the very next thought that went through his mind was of Cathy Terry.

He wondered if she'd been able to sleep much last night and if she needed help with anything. He'd left his number with her, but he knew she wouldn't call. That left the next move up to him, so he got up, showered, shaved, and dressed, then made his bed before going downstairs to start breakfast. Because of Hope's work schedule, he and Jack did most of the cooking and cleaning, while Hope kept up with most of the grocery shopping because she was in Blessings almost every day.

Duke began by starting coffee brewing, then stirred up a batch of drop biscuits and put them in to bake before browning some sausage patties. When they were done, he took the meat out of the skillet and made gravy in the drippings.

By then, the biscuits and coffee were done, and he could hear Jack moving around upstairs. Likely, the aromas of frying sausage and fresh coffee were hard to ignore. Duke cracked a half-dozen eggs into a bowl to scramble, and then poured them in a skillet to cook. He was putting them into a bowl when Jack and Hope came into the kitchen.

"Morning, you two," Duke said, and then winked at Hope. "I thought you might sleep in a little this morning."

"I planned to until I smelled breakfast," she said, and poked him on the arm as she went to pour herself a cup of coffee.

They filled their plates from the bowls and pans on the stove, then sat down to eat in companionable silence. After a couple of minutes, Hope got up to get some jelly from the refrigerator.

"Has anyone heard anything from the sheriff's office about the stolen cattle?" she asked.

Jack shook his head. "I think they'll call if they have news. Otherwise, we go on about our business."

"I am going to put up game cameras today. We have three that I know of, but I'll need to replace batteries. I can't remember the last time we used them," Duke said.

Jack reached for another biscuit to finish off the gravy on his plate. "I do," he said. "About three years ago, when there was that cougar sighting up by Gray Goose Lake. Remember?"

"Oh, I remember that," Hope said. "I was leery of going into outbuildings for a long time…afraid I'd walk up on one waiting to pounce."

"That's not exactly their natural behavior," Jack said. "They don't like to be around people any more than people like being around them."

She shrugged. "I know, but we have chickens, and at the time, we had three small calves that we were bottle-feeding in the barn, remember?"

Duke nodded. "You're right. If a cougar is hurt or injured in some way and unable to hunt, they will come to the easy prey. Only this time I'll be on the lookout for rustlers, not cougars, and I'm pretty sure we don't have near enough batteries to replenish three game cameras. I'll feed the chickens before I go check on the cows, then I'll head into Blessings for batteries. If anyone needs anything else, make a list."

"You cooked. I'll clean up," Jack said. "And call if you need help. Don't do something stupid on your own."

Duke gave Jack a look. "I don't do stupid things."

Hope laughed out loud as Duke grabbed a rain poncho from a peg in the utility room and pulled up the hood before going out the back door.

The rain was really coming down and already forming puddles as he headed for the chicken house first. He ducked into the feed room just off the henhouse for a bucket of feed, then walked across the covered breezeway and into the henhouse.

The chickens that weren't in the nests were either perched on the roosts or milling around down on the ground. But when he came in and began pouring chicken feed into the feeders, they greeted him with gentle little clucks.

"And a good morning to you," he said, then grabbed an egg basket from a peg on the wall and gathered over two dozen eggs from the nests. He set the basket out in the breezeway and went to fill up the chickens' water. He scattered some grit and crushed oyster shells as supplements, then picked up the eggs and headed back to the house, where he left all his rain gear on the porch and headed inside with the eggs.

"Wow, we're getting quite a few eggs now every day, aren't we?" Hope said as he set the basket on the counter.

"A little over two dozen this morning. I'm going to change clothes and get my raincoat," Duke said.

"Are you going to see Cathy Terry?" Hope asked.

"I might, why?" Duke asked.

"I thought I'd send a dozen fresh eggs if you were," Hope said.

"Okay, sure. Get them ready. I'll take them by," Duke said, and left the kitchen.

A short while later, he was clean and dry, wearing his good raincoat and the waterproof cover over his Stetson when he picked up the eggs and the grocery list.

Jack and Hope were nowhere to be seen, and Duke guessed they were going to take advantage of having the house all to themselves while he was gone. Hope was really good-natured about the Talbot brothers' living arrangements, but Duke knew the day might come that she and Jack wanted a house of their own.

He settled the eggs onto the floorboard of the pickup and headed out of the drive, glad for the heavy layer of gravel all the way to the blacktop that would take him to the highway into Blessings.

———————————————

Mercy Pittman was up to her elbows in flour at Granny's Country Kitchen, turning out her famous biscuits as fast as the oven could bake them. On a normal day, Granny's was the place for locals to congregate at breakfast time, even if they'd already eaten at home first. They could always drink another cup or two of coffee and have some biscuits and jelly. But when rain interfered with all the people who normally worked outdoors, they came to Granny's.

Mercy was just putting two more huge sheet pans of biscuits in the oven when the power flickered.

Everyone in the kitchen gasped. The ovens and the flat-top grill were gas, but the diner needed power for everything else. But before they could panic, Lovey's son, Sully Raines, who had begun helping her run the café, came flying into the kitchen.

"It's all good! I had that generator wired into the power here last week, remember? If the power goes out, the generator will kick in."

Mercy sighed with relief. "Oh, that's right! Thank goodness."

He gave her a thumbs-up and then headed back to tend to business.

While Granny's was safe from power outages, the same could not be said down at the Curl Up and Dye.

Ruby Butterman, who owned the hair salon, was a little nervous. Vesta was already in the middle of coloring her first client's hair, and her twin sister, Vera, was rolling perm rods into her client's hair. Ruby's first customer was due in at any moment, and there would be a hair disaster of tragic proportions if the power went out.

When the power flickered, Vesta gasped. "Oh Lord, Lord! Please don't let us lose power!"

Mabel Jean, the manicurist, was doing a mani-pedi on Clara Jordan, the Baptist preacher's wife, and when Vesta called on the Lord, the preacher's wife took it upon herself to beseech Him some more.

"Let us pray!" Clara said.

Mabel Jean froze, right in the middle of a down stroke on one of Clara's fingernails.

Vera's client immediately jerked and lowered her head, causing Vera to lose hold of the paper and the curl she was rolling up. The little white perm rod went flying one way, and the paper the other.

Vera sighed. She had no option but to follow along.

Ruby sat down in the chair at her station and bowed her head, too. She'd been to luncheons when the preacher's wife said the blessing, and knew this was going to take some time. Clara had a tendency toward sermon-length prayers.

Fortunately for everyone, Clara hadn't been praying more than a couple of minutes when the bell jingled over the front door. Ruby's customer had arrived, and as fate would have it, Clara was right in the middle of taking a breath when Ruby jumped out of her chair and said, "Amen, and thank you for that, Clara. Ladies, proceed."

Vera rolled her eyes at Ruby and reached for another perm paper and a fresh perm rod, and Vesta returned to dabbing color on her client's roots.

Rachel Goodhope, who ran the Blessings Bed and Breakfast, was standing by the front counter, looking a bit confused.

"Did I interrupt something?" she whispered, as Ruby came up to greet her.

"Clara felt called to pray to the Lord not to let the power go off here," Ruby said.

Rachel grinned.

Ruby didn't have the luxury of agreeing, so she changed the subject.

"Come on back and let's get started. We should be good to go now, since both Vesta and Clara have prayed to the Lord for the electricity to stay on here."

Melissa Raines, Sully's wife, owned the only dry cleaners in town, and losing power there would shut everything down. She'd gone there this morning to hand out paychecks and just happened to still be there when the power flickered.

When it did, the employees paused, waiting to see if it stayed on. Melissa was in the back checking inventory to see what supplies needed reordering when it flickered, and like everyone else in the shop, she paused, holding her breath. But when the lights stayed on, she hurried to finish.

"Okay everybody, I'm going back to my office to get this order in. If you have troubles, you know how to get in touch with me," she said, then stepped outside beneath the awning to open her umbrella and made a run for her car.

It wasn't power flickering that woke Cathy. It was the loud crack of lightning, followed by a distinct grumble of thunder that made her jump. The sudden movement not only hurt her ankle, but also made the cold gel pack she had on it slide onto the floor, taking part of her blanket with it.

"Oh crap, that hurt!" she moaned, and slowly lowered the footrest on her recliner.

It felt like she'd been asleep for hours, but it was only ten thirty. She managed to stand up, picked up the gel pack, and then put it on the seat of her walker before making her way to the kitchen to put it back in the freezer.

The coffee maker had shut itself off, and she was debating with herself about reheating some in the microwave when she heard a knock at the door.

"Who in the world would be out in this weather?" she

muttered, as she turned the walker around and went to answer it.

The fact that Duke Talbot was standing beneath her porch roof and already shedding clothes did something for her heartbeat, but as it turned out, the only things he took off and left on her porch swing were a raincoat, his boots, and a cowboy hat with its own rain cover.

He gave her a tentative smile and then held up the carton of eggs.

"It is not my habit to go to anyone's home unannounced, but I didn't have your number, and I come bearing a gift. Hope sent you a dozen fresh eggs. Is that enough to get me in the door?"

Cathy grinned. "It's more than enough."

Duke was enchanted as he went inside and closed the door behind him. She had a dimple. Just one, and only visible when she smiled.

"Is it okay if I put these in the refrigerator for you?" he asked.

"Of course. I'm sorry I don't have hot coffee, but I fell asleep and the coffee maker shut itself off."

Duke frowned. "I hope I didn't wake you."

"No. It was that lightning and thunder a few minutes ago. I was in the kitchen when you knocked."

"Okay, then," Duke said, and headed for the kitchen in his sock feet. Cathy went to the hall and turned on the central heat to take the chill off the house, then followed him and sat down at the table.

"If you don't mind reheated coffee, pour yourself a cup and microwave it," she said.

Duke glanced at her. "Do you want some?"

"Sure," she said.

He filled two cups, popped them in the microwave, then brought them to the table and sat down with her.

"How is your ankle?" he asked.

"Still swollen and painful, but I'm managing just fine, thanks to you."

Duke eyed the flash in her eyes and wondered what she was thinking. But instead of asking, he made a painfully boring comment.

"You make good coffee."

The praise was so simple, but for Cathy, who'd rarely gotten a compliment from her ex other than how she looked, it pleased her.

"Thank you."

Duke was trying to think of some witty comment that might prompt a conversation when his cell phone rang. When he saw it was from the County Sheriff's office, he sighed.

"I'm sorry. I know this is rude, but I really need to take this call."

"Do you need privacy? I can go—"

"No, nothing like that," he said, and then answered. "Hello, this is Duke."

"Good morning, Duke. Deputy Treat here. We just wanted to catch you up on the investigation. We did confirm the rustlers came directly through the Bailey property. We tried to locate a place where they might have purchased the feed sacks they left behind, but that brand is sold all over the state, and anyone with cattle might have purchased it."

Duke sighed. "Have you been around to any of the cattle auctions yet?"

"Not yet. That's on the agenda, but as you know, they're only open on sale days, so the ones that were open yesterday aren't open today. We're going to take a quick run through the ones holding auctions today, and maybe we'll get lucky and find someone with a slash on his boot heel who's trying to sell six head of cattle."

"We appreciate anything you can do," Duke said.

"Sure thing, and we'll be in touch," Treat said, then disconnected.

Duke slipped the phone back in his pocket. "Sorry. That was one of the deputies who's investigating our case. After I got home from Blessings yesterday, we discovered we were missing six head of cattle. The fence wires had been cut, and we found where the rustlers had loaded the cattle up and left through a neighbor's property. The man who owns it is in a nursing home now, so it was way too convenient for them to come into the back of our property without ever being seen."

Cathy gasped. "Rustlers? I didn't realize that was still an ongoing thing for farmers and ranchers!"

Duke shrugged. "Yes, it's a pretty big problem for people with cattle herds. Over the years, I've become something of a cynic. No matter what you own, someone will try to steal it."

"I'm so sorry. Is there any chance of getting them back?"

"Slim to none," Duke said. "I came into town to get some batteries to put up some game cameras, in case the rustlers try to make a return visit."

Cathy reached across the table before she thought and put her hand on his arm.

"Are you in danger?"

"I don't think so. But I always carry a rifle when I check cattle. Never know when I might run across a predator. But enough about our troubles. Were you able to get any sleep last night?"

Cathy frowned. She didn't like knowing this was happening…and that he might be in danger. She hadn't expected this kind of thing to be happening in a small town. This felt like big-city trouble. Then she remembered he was waiting for her to answer.

"Uh…oh…not a lot. But I've already had almost a two-hour nap this morning."

"Is there anything I can do for you? Or any errands you need me to run? I'm totally competent to help with pretty much anything. Our parents died when Jack was still in college, and I kept the farm going and him in college on my own."

Cathy was not only instantly empathetic, but wondering if family responsibilities like that had anything to do with his single status.

"I lost my dad when I was twelve. Mom died a couple of years ago. I got a divorce soon afterward." She was silent a moment, and then added, "Something I should have done a long time ago."

Duke hesitated. He wanted to know everything about her, but wasn't going to pry.

"I remember you said you were backpacking when you got here. How did you learn that? Was it something you and your husband used to do together?"

"No. He's a native of Las Vegas. His life is all money, women, and casinos."

"He gambled?"

"No. He owns casinos and has interest in others. He played the women, not the odds."

The bitterness in her voice was obvious, and Duke was sorry he'd asked.

"I didn't mean to pry, and as I told you before, I always say the wrong thing around women. I'm sorry. So tell me about your backpacking. Have you been lots of places? What's your favorite place?"

Cathy's eyes were suddenly alight. She leaned forward, her elbows on the table, her chin resting in her hands.

"Alaska! I grew up there! Mother and I didn't leave until after Dad died. But it's so beautiful there if you don't mind the snow. You were talking about growing up on your farm. We raised a garden, dried food, dried and salted meat for winter...that kind of thing. The land there is so fertile, but the growing season is short. We lived off the grid the first twelve years of my life. I learned a whole lot about surviving in the wild. It was only after we moved to what people call civilization that my troubles began."

Duke's eyes widened, trying to picture a little redhead in snow gear tromping around the Alaskan wilderness.

"That's the most amazing thing anyone has ever told me about where and how they grew up," he said.

Cathy smiled. It was getting easier and easier to be around this man.

Then Duke glanced at the time. "When I was putting away the eggs, I noticed there's nothing in your refrigerator to make for your dinner...except the eggs. If you were able, I'd take you out to eat, but I think your comfort matters most. How about I go get some takeout and bring it here? My treat."

"That would be much appreciated," Cathy said. "But you've treated me enough. I have money to—"

"Nope. Just tell me what you're hungry for. Granny's has takeout for anything on the menu. We also have Broyles Dairy Freeze, with awesome chili dogs and fries, and a barbecue joint as well. Jack and Hope will tell you that I like everything, so what sounds good to you?"

"Chili dogs? I can't remember the last time I had a chili dog. That sounds so good. I think maybe that, and fries."

"They have really good malts and shakes, too," Duke added.

"You're tempting me now. Throw in that chocolate malt, and I'll be toast for the rest of the day."

Duke got up from the table like he'd been ejected from the chair.

"Awesome. One chili dog, or two?"

She laughed. "Only one, for sure."

He sighed as the laugh washed through him. "I'm not locking the front door, and I won't be long."

He was gone before Cathy had time to say goodbye. It was still raining, and she could hear him out on the front porch putting his boots and rain gear back on as she began clearing away their coffee cups.

She was getting a frozen gel pack from the freezer when she heard him leave, but it didn't deter her. She went back to the living room to ice her ankle. The sooner she got back on her feet, the happier she would be.

CHAPTER 5

DEPUTY RALPH HERMAN WAS HUNKERED DOWN beside a car at the south end of Main Street, helping Peanut Butterman change a flat tire. Despite their raincoats, they were both soaked by the time the tire was changed. Peanut tossed the flat in the trunk and turned and shook Ralph's hand.

"I sure do thank you for stopping to help."

The deputy turned slightly against the rain blowing in his face.

"No problem. It's just an all-around nasty day to have a tire go flat. I was happy to help. You take care," he said, and got back in the cruiser, made a U-turn in the street, and drove back uptown.

Peanut drove straight to the service station at the other end of town to drop off the tire to get fixed, and called Ruby on the way, smiling to himself when she answered. Just the sound of her voice made everything right in his world—even a flat in a downpour.

"Hello, honey. Have you started home from the courthouse in Savannah yet?" Ruby asked.

"I'm already back in Blessings, but I had a flat just inside the city limits. Deputy Ralph stopped to help me, or I'd still be messing with it. I'm about to drop it off to get fixed, and then I'm going home to change into some dry clothes before I head back to the office. Do you want me to pick up lunch for you and the girls?"

"Oh, that would be awesome. We've already had power flickering here at the shop, so nobody is willing to take the time to go get lunch. We're trying to finish up on our clients without leaving them with wet heads. I'll find out what the girls want and call you back, okay?"

"Everything you do is okay with me," Peanut said. "Love you."

"I love you, too," Ruby said, and then sighed as she hung up.

Vesta looked at Vera and giggled. "I wonder who Ruby was talking to just now."

Ruby looked over at her and grinned. "You just hush. Peanut offered to get lunch and drop it off here for us, so figure out what you want. I told him I'd call him right back."

When the twins' focus shifted to food of any kind, all joking was set aside.

Vesta thought for a moment before offering a suggestion.

"What if we all order something from Broyles Dairy Freeze? That way he won't have to get in and out of the car a bunch of times. He can just go through the drive-through, and if he'll bring it to the back door and honk, we can go out to get it."

"That is so sweet of you," Ruby said. "He just had a flat coming into town and said he was going home to change into dry clothes first. He'll appreciate your thoughtfulness."

Vera shook her head. "Bless his heart. A flat in this kind of weather."

"I think I want a burger, fries, and a vanilla malt," Vesta said.

"I want the same, except make my malt chocolate," Vera added, and then tapped her client on the shoulder. "Time's up, sugar. Let's go rinse out that perm solution so I can get the neutralizer on you."

Mabel Jean had already finished the mani-pedi on Clara and walked her to her car, holding an umbrella over both of them. But now she was chilled and nursing a cup of coffee.

"I'll take one of their chili dogs and a package of potato chips. Thanks to the weather, I'm too cold for a malt, so I'll stick to coffee."

"Duly noted," Ruby said. She'd just finished the shampoo and style on Rachel Goodhope, so she reached for the hair spray and gave Rachel's hair a quick once-over, then removed the cape and handed her a mirror. "What do you think?"

Rachel took a few moments to check out the back of her hair and then nodded.

"Love it, but then I always do. Thank you, Ruby. I'd better get home. We have someone due to check in at the bed-and-breakfast around 1:00 p.m., so I need to make sure Bud remembered to put cookies in the guest room."

As soon as Rachel was gone, Ruby texted their lunch orders to Peanut and then went to clean up her station.

Peanut got the text with their orders and was grateful they'd chosen the Dairy Freeze. As he drove into line at the drive-through, he saw several cars coming in behind him. It appeared everyone had the same idea in this miserable weather.

He'd already called in the order on the way down Main, and when he pulled up to the window, the woman working saw him and smiled.

"Hey, Peanut! We got your to-go ready. Do you need to add anything to it?"

"No thanks," Peanut said, and handed over his credit card.

He got the card back and his order, and waved as he drove away.

He was just about to drive back out onto Main Street when a small rain-soaked dog ran across the street in front of him.

"Oh crap!" he muttered, wincing when the dog barely missed getting hit by a passing car. Then it dawned on him that he knew that little dog. Everyone in Blessings knew that little red King Charles spaniel. He rolled down his window and whistled.

"Mister! Hey, Mister! Come here, boy!" he called.

The little dog stopped, then turned around and looked back.

Peanut whistled again, and then got out in the downpour and opened the back door to his car.

"Come here, Mister. Come here, boy. Wanna go home? Let's go home."

The little dog took off running toward Peanut, and once again, Peanut was soaked, but this time for a good reason. Despite very short legs, Mister cleared the leap in one try, hunkering down on the floorboard, shaking.

"Good boy!" Peanut said. "Good boy, Mister. Sit down, boy. We're gonna go home."

The little spaniel was shivering, but his huge black eyes were fixed on Peanut in a grateful and trusting way.

Peanut jumped back in the car, and instead of turning left to go to the salon, he turned right and drove straight to Miss Earline Woody's house. He pulled up beneath the portico where her 1980 Chrysler was parked and got out. Then he opened the back door and picked Mister up from the floor of the car and carried him up the steps.

Like Miss Earline, the grand old house had seen better days, but it had good bones and Miss Earline came from good stock, which was why they were both still standing.

He heard footsteps, and then the door swung inward. He could see the old woman had been crying, and when she saw Peanut standing on the threshold with her missing puppy in his arms, she threw her hands up in the air.

"Hallelujah! Thank you, Jesus! My prayers have been answered." Then she held out her arms. "Mister. My poor little Mister. Come to Mama."

The little dog whined as Peanut handed him over.

"Oh, Peanut, thank you, thank you. He was out beneath the umbrella doing his business when a big old clap of thunder sounded, and before I knew it, he was running. I tried to catch him, but the gate was ajar, and I'm not so spry anymore, and he was gone. I didn't think I'd see him again."

"You almost didn't," Peanut said. "I saw him running on the street in front of Broyles Dairy Freeze. Traffic just missed him, but when I stopped and called him, he came back to me and jumped right in the car. I think he was ready to come home."

"Well, God love you, son. You don't know how much this little mess means to me. Now I need to get us both cleaned up and dried off. Thank you again."

Peanut grinned. "You're welcome. You might want to have that latch on your gate looked at."

"Yes, yes, I surely will," Miss Earline said. "You be careful, and I'm sorry you got your nice suit all wet."

Peanut laughed. "It's my second one today. All the more business for the cleaners. You take care now," he said, then closed the door behind him and ran back to his car.

He drove up to the back of the salon, got the sacks of food, and went inside.

Ruby looked up, saw him all wet, muddy, and bedraggled, and shrieked.

"What happened to you? I thought you were going to change into dry clothes before you went to get the food."

He handed her the sacks and kissed her cheek.

"I did. This is the second set of wet clothes for the day."

"What happened?" Ruby asked.

"Miss Earline's little dog, Mister, escaped. I saw him running down the street in front of the Dairy Freeze, and by the time I got him in the car and then back home to her, this is the result."

Ruby laughed. "Oh, honey. You are a good, good man. That little dog means the world to her."

"I know. Everybody in town knows Mister. But he was so wet, I almost didn't recognize him. So, rest assured your food is fine. It was in the front seat. Mister was on the floor in the back seat. Dog and chili dogs did not comingle."

Ruby laughed. "Good to know. Now get yourself home and into more dry clothes. Just leave all the wet stuff in the utility room. I'll get it to the cleaners."

"Thanks, babe," Peanut said, then winked at all the girls. "Enjoy your dinner," he told them, and then ran out the back door into the rain.

While everyone else in Blessings was bemoaning the inclement weather, Cathy had pulled back the curtains in the living room so she could watch it. After all the years she'd lived in Las Vegas, a state with a startling lack of rainfall, a good downpour was an enjoyable experience.

It also gave her a good view of the street and her driveway so she could watch for Duke to return. Twenty-four hours ago, she hadn't even known he existed, and now he had been to her house twice.

And so she sat within the quiet of the little house, lulled by the rain on the roof and watching it turning into a curtain between her and the world as it ran off the porch.

All of a sudden, a small, bedraggled figure walked into her line of vision, dragging what looked like a black garbage bag. She was leaning forward, trying to focus through the rain, when it finally dawned on her that it was a child.

Ignoring the pain in her ankle, she got up and quickly hobbled out onto the porch, staring in disbelief. She looked up and down the street, unable to believe a little guy like that would be out in this weather on his own.

She called out: "Hey!"

He looked at her without breaking stride and kept walking.

Cathy knew immediately something was wrong. And he was way too little to be in this storm on his own. She didn't think twice as she hobbled down the steps and then out into the rain, moving as quickly as the pain would allow until she caught up with him halfway down the block. Once she got in front of him, she stopped and got down on one knee.

She was pretty sure he was crying, because his eyes were red, but it was hard to tell because of the rain. His brown hair was plastered to his head and down the back of his neck, and his clothes were sodden and clinging to his little body.

"Hey, my name is Cathy. What's your name?"

"Melvin Lee."

"So, Melvin Lee, are you lost?" Cathy asked.

"No, ma'am. I'm a'goin to my granny's."

Cathy frowned. "Does your mother know where you are?"

And just like that, he set his jaw and glowered.

"I ain't a'goin' home, and you can't make me."

By now, Cathy was soaked and freezing, and could only imagine how cold he must feel.

"Are you running away from home?"

"Yes, ma'am."

Cathy stood. "I'm pretty cold. How about we go sit up on my porch out of the rain and talk some more, okay?"

"I ain't supposed to talk to strangers," Melvin Lee said.

"I understand, but you're probably not supposed to be running away, either, right? Look at my ankle. See how it's all wrapped up?"

He nodded.

"So, I hurt it yesterday, and I can't stand up on it for long, and I sure can't run, so you could outrun me in a second if I was mean, right?"

He saw the wrapping on her ankle, and then looked straight into her eyes.

"I reckon I could sit on your porch for a bit."

"Good. I need to sit down, too," Cathy said, then held out her hand.

He took it without hesitation, while she picked up the garbage bag. They walked back to the house together, then up onto the porch. The moment they were out of the rain, Cathy saw the tension in his little body let go. She helped him up into her porch swing and put the bag he was carrying up against the wall.

"I'm gonna go inside and get us a blanket, okay?"

He was starting to shake and just nodded in agreement.

Afraid he would run, Cathy hobbled quickly into the house to call the police.

Avery, the day dispatcher, took the call.

"Blessings PD. This is Avery."

"This is Cathy Terry at 311 West Cherry Street. There's a little boy at my house who says his name is Melvin Lee. I don't know what's going on, but I saw him walking past my house in this downpour dragging a garbage bag. I thought he was lost, but he says he's running away from home, and he's soaked to the skin."

"Oh my word! Yes, ma'am. We'll get someone right there," Avery said and disconnected, but before he could dispatch a cruiser, the 911 line rang.

"Blessings 911. What is your emergency?" he asked, then heard a lot of kids crying and a woman who sounded on the verge of hysterics.

"This is Junie Wilson. My son, Melvin Lee, is missing. I called him to come eat lunch, and he didn't answer. He's not in the house. I've looked all over, and oh my God, I don't know what happened to him," she wailed. "I can't go look for him on my own because I've got all these babies and it's pouring."

"Someone just found him and called it in. I'm about to dispatch a car to go pick him up," Avery said.

Junie wailed again. "Oh thank God…thank God. Is he okay? Where was he? Who found him?"

"Ma'am, all your questions will be answered in time. Just calm down. He's safe, and someone will be bringing him home."

"Yes, yes, okay. Thank you, again," Junie said, and disconnected.

Avery sighed, and was about to send out the call when Chief Pittman came up to the front desk.

"Chief! A lady named Cathy Terry just called reporting she'd found a runaway kid. He's at her house and needs to be picked up. And…I just took a call from the frantic mother who just discovered he was missing."

Lon frowned. "Same kid, I presume?"

"Yes, sir. Melvin Lee Wilson. The oldest of Danny and Junie's kids."

"You said Cathy Terry found him?" Lon asked.

"Yes, sir. Do you know her?"

Lon nodded. "Yes, and I know where she lives. I'll take the call."

"Okay," Avery said. "I'll log it in."

Lon had just taken off his raincoat, but he turned back around to put it on again.

Now that Cathy had notified the police department, she grabbed the blanket from her recliner and hurried back outside.

"I'll bet you're freezing," she said, and wrapped Melvin Lee up in the soft, thick covers. "We can keep each other warm a bit, okay?" she said, as she pulled him up in her lap, and then cuddled him close.

Melvin Lee nodded.

"How old are you, honey?" Cathy asked.

"Almost eight."

"Then you must be a second grader. Did you run away from school?"

He started crying. "I'm supposed to be a second grader, but they held me back in first grade 'cause I couldn't read so good. My mama keeps me out of school a lot to help her with the babies."

Cathy hugged him a little closer, patting his shoulder as she began to rock them both.

"Are you the oldest?" she asked.

"Yes. Then Willy, then Arnie, then Lucy."

Cathy was trying to imagine having four children under the age of eight and couldn't. She'd never even had one.

"Why are you running away?" she asked.

"Mama told us today she's havin' another baby, and I don't want no more brothers or sisters to take care of," he said, and started to wail. "I don't wanna be the dumb kid in the class. I need to learn myself how to read, and how to count money and stuff."

"Oh, honey," Cathy said, and then held him closer.

She was still holding him when she saw Duke's truck, and then she saw the look of concern on his face as he pulled up in the drive and got out with the sack of food.

"Cathy! What happened? You two are soaked to the skin."

"This is Melvin Lee," she said. "Melvin Lee, this is my friend, Duke Talbot."

Duke frowned. "Are you one of Danny Wilson's kids?"

"Yes, sir," Melvin said.

"I went to school with your daddy. Are you hungry?"

The little boy wiped the tears off his face.

"Yes, sir."

"Do you like chili dogs and french fries?" Duke asked.

Melvin Lee's eyes widened. "Yes, sir."

"I've got plenty. Come inside where it's warmer. Both of you," he said.

Melvin Lee let go of the blanket and slid out of Cathy's lap, but Duke was looking at Cathy. She was soaked to the skin, and her ankle was bound to be throbbing. Her curls were even tighter and clinging to her head and down the back of her neck. But it was obvious her concern was solely focused on the little boy.

Duke handed the sack to Melvin Lee and picked her up and carried her into the house, then into the kitchen.

"You are something else," he said softly. He put her down in a chair, then proceeded to get out plates and glasses and start dividing up the food.

He poured half of his chocolate malt in a glass for the little boy, then put one of the chili dogs and some fries on a plate and scooted it toward him.

"Dig in," Duke said.

Melvin Lee didn't have to be told twice. He was chin deep in his chili dog, and talking a blue streak.

As soon as he paused to take a breath and another bite, Cathy asked, "Want ketchup on your fries?"

"No, ma'am," Melvin Lee said, talking around the bite he was chewing.

"So where's your daddy working these days?" Duke asked, and dunked his fry into a well of ketchup on his plate.

"Somewhere up in the Pennavanna."

"In Pennsylvania?" Duke asked.

Melvin Lee nodded. "Yeah. That. He ain't never home long. He says he has to keep a-workin' to feed us all. I wished he could find work closer to home so when Mama is having one of her bad days, he could stay home and take care of the young'uns, and I could stay in school."

Cathy glanced at Duke. "His mama made an announcement this morning that kind of rocked his world," she said softly.

Melvin Lee nodded. "Yep. I heard her talkin' to Daddy on the phone. She told him she was preggers again, and I decided it was time to move out. I ain't takin' care of no more babies. I gotta learn to read good and do my numbers. I don't wanna be the dumb kid in the class no more." Then he took another bite of the chili dog. "This here chili dog sure is good."

Duke smiled. "I agree," he said, and then poured a little more of his chocolate malt into Melvin Lee's glass.

Cathy was smitten with both of them. The little guy's view of the world was old far beyond his years, and Duke's calm acceptance of what made little boys tick was endearing.

And then she heard a knock at the door.

"I'll get it," she said, and jumped up and rolled out of the room before Duke could do it for her.

————————

Chief Pittman was standing on the threshold when she opened the door.

"Hello, Chief. Melvin Lee doesn't know I called you, so…"

"I understand. That's Duke's truck in the drive, right?"

She nodded.

"Good. Just lead the way and let me do the talking," Lon said, leaving his raincoat on the porch swing.

Cathy went back into the kitchen with Lon right behind her.

"Something smells good," Lon said as he walked in. "Hey, Duke. Did you get one for me?"

Duke grinned. "I ate it," he said.

"I'll remember that next time Mercy invites all of you to dinner," Lon said, and sat down in the chair beside Melvin Lee. "Hello, son. You're sure wet. I'll bet you're cold, too, huh?"

"A little," Melvin Lee said, and stuffed a french fry in his mouth.

"I'm Chief Pittman. You're Melvin Lee Wilson, aren't you? I know your mama and daddy."

Melvin nodded, and kept chewing.

"Your mama just called the police station in a panic. She was crying. She doesn't know where you are, and she's scared for your safety," Lon said.

"She just wants me to watch the babies," Melvin Lee said.

Lon looked a little startled, and then glanced up at Duke and Cathy.

"Melvin Lee is a little overwhelmed with life," Duke said.

"His mama's having another baby," Cathy added.

"She makes me stay home from school and babysit. I done been held back one year already. The kids call me stupid. I'm not stupid. I'm just a little behind," Melvin Lee said, and then stared down at his plate.

Cathy's heart hurt just looking at him. He was so little to have such a big burden.

Lon laid a hand on the little boy's shoulder. "If you'll let me take you home, I'll have a talk with your mama about school."

Melvin Lee looked up. "You will? You'll tell her she can't keep me home to babysit no more?"

"Yes, I will," Lon said.

"I reckon I'll go on home, then," he said.

"Not before I get a hug," Cathy said.

The little boy sighed as he got up and went to where Cathy was sitting.

"Thank you for being my friend," he said.

Cathy took her napkin and wiped the chili off of Melvin Lee's chin, and then off the corners of his mouth.

"It was my pleasure," she said, but when she hugged him, she was not prepared for the surge of emotion she felt when his arms slid around her neck, or when he buried his face against her shoulder.

"You tell your daddy I said hello, okay?" Duke said.

"Yes, sir. I will next time I see him," Melvin Lee said. "Is my bag still out on the porch?"

"Yes, it is," Cathy said.

"I'll be needing to take it with me," he said, and then walked out with the police chief as if he was going to jail and not back home.

After they were gone, Cathy got up to start clearing the table, and burst into tears instead.

"He's too little to feel that defeated."

Duke groaned. "Now you've gone and done it. I can't stand to see a woman cry," he said, and put his arms around her.

"I'll get your clothes all wet," she sobbed.

"It's okay. Just don't cry, honey. Lon will get him all

sorted out. You'll see. Now will you do something for me?" Duke asked.

"What?" Cathy asked as she pulled away and began fumbling for a tissue.

"Take a hot shower, put on some dry clothes, and lie down for a while. Rest yourself and your ankle, too."

Cathy wiped her eyes and then turned around and just looked at him.

"Yes, I will, and thank you for caring, for helping me with Melvin Lee, and for being the thoughtful man you are."

It was all Duke could do not to take her in his arms and kiss her senseless, but that's not what she needed. Yes, Cathy Terry had a sore ankle, but she was already one of the walking wounded when she showed up in Blessings, and she needed to heal from the damage one man had done to her life before Duke dared broach the subject of wanting more.

"I have a request," he said. "If I had your phone number, I wouldn't be intruding into your life without prior warning."

"Does this mean your visits aren't going to come to an end, even after my ankle is well?"

He grinned. "That's the plan, unless you change it for me."

"Then you can absolutely have my number," Cathy said.

"Wait a sec," Duke said, and pulled up his contact list to add her name. "Okay, I'm ready," he said.

Cathy gave him the number, and felt a sense of something imminent as he hit Save. They were connected now. She had his number in her phone, but had only felt the freedom to use it should she need help, because that was the offer when he left it.

"Got it," Duke said, and then dropped the phone back in his pocket. "I guess I'd better get those batteries for the game cameras and get back to the farm. Today is Hope's day off, and I usually find something to do so that they have some time at home together."

"So you've all always lived together," Cathy said.

"Yes, but I've always thought that if they ever decided to start a family, I would move out. I should probably do that now, but the convenience of Jack and me being in the same place tending the farm is too easy to give up. Maybe I'll just build a house of my own somewhere on the property…or they might want the new house, in which case I'd happily stay with the family home. Even if it's too big for one person, it's still home."

"I'll bet it's lovely out there," Cathy said.

Duke looked at her, trying not to drown in those deep-blue eyes.

"I'd love to show you sometime…when you're up to a trip and a little walking, of course."

"Oh, I would love that," Cathy said.

"Awesome," Duke said. "Thanksgiving will be here before we know it. If you don't already have other plans, I am officially inviting you to dinner with the family, and just know that will also include Mercy and Lon, and whoever else Hope and Jack might invite."

"I can't think of anything better," Cathy said. "I happily accept."

Duke beamed, and before he thought, took her by the shoulders and was about to kiss her on the cheek when he caught himself and stopped. Instead, he just gave her shoulders a quick squeeze. "I'll talk to you soon. Call if you need me," he said and then let himself out.

Cathy sighed. There for a moment she'd thought he'd

been going to kiss her. She wasn't sure whether to be disappointed it hadn't happened, or relieved things weren't moving too fast.

Duke put all of his rain gear back on and made a run for his truck. Once inside, he glanced up at the house and saw her standing at the window.

He waved.

She smiled and waved back.

He didn't remember one single minute of the drive home.

CHAPTER 6

LON WAS WELL AWARE OF THE DEJECTED LOOK ON THE little boy's face. He'd never had a runaway like this one before.

"Uh…you said your mother kept you out of school a lot?"

Melvin Lee nodded. "Yes, sir. They held me back in first grade 'cause I can't read so good. I missed too much school, I reckon."

"So, is it rough being held back?" Lon asked, as he braked at the stoplight, then saw the little boy's eyes well.

"The guys laughed. They said I must be dumb."

"Didn't your school tell your mother you can't miss a lot of school?"

"I don't know," Melvin Lee said. "All I know is I don't get to go every day. You sure you're gonna talk to her?"

Lon nodded. "I'm absolutely positive. Don't worry. Your life is about to change in a good way. That I can promise."

Melvin Lee beamed.

"Thanks, Chief!"

"No problem," Lon said.

The light turned green and he accelerated through the intersection, then took a right at the next street and pulled up in the driveway of a pretty yellow house with brown trim.

"Here we are," Lon said.

Melvin Lee looked up just as his mother came running out onto the porch. He sighed, then unbuckled his seat belt and grabbed the bag with his clothes.

"Hang on, Melvin Lee. I'll get the door for you," Lon said. He got out in the rain and circled the car to get his passenger, then kept his hand on Melvin Lee's shoulder as he walked him up the steps to the house, carrying the bag with the little boy's clothes.

Junie fell to her knees and wrapped her arms around his shoulders.

"Melvin Lee...you scared me to death. What happened? Why did you run away?"

Lon's hand was still on the boy's shoulder. "Tell your mama, then go on in the house."

"I'm not taking care of no more babies," Melvin Lee said, and then shrugged out of her arms and dragged his bag into the house.

Junie stood abruptly, and she was frowning. "What's going on here?"

Lon stared straight into her eyes. "Keep in mind I can check this for myself, but I'm expecting you to answer me truthfully. Has the school been sending you letters about Melvin Lee's absences?"

Junie's chin jutted out. "You don't understand. I need help at home while my husband is away."

"No, ma'am. What you don't understand is that you aren't allowed to use your child as unpaid help when he's supposed to be in school. It's against the law. You do not want to get social services in your business, and that's what's about to happen. You hire help. You call on your adult family members if you need help, but you figure it out now, because your little boy is so overwhelmed by the responsibilities you've dumped on him, and by being called stupid at school because he was held back, that when he found out you were pregnant again, he took off in a thunderstorm and had no intention of coming back."

The defiance on Junie Wilson's face faded as the shock washed through her.

"I didn't know kids were making fun of him," she said. "I need to talk to him."

"Yes, you do. And you will assure him that you will never keep him out of school to watch your babies again. Those are his siblings, not his responsibility. Do we understand each other?"

Junie's shoulders slumped. "Yes, sir."

"Now...go inside and get him dried off and dressed for school. I'll wait. I'm taking him to school this afternoon, and I will be checking at school every day to make sure he's not absent again."

Junie bolted inside. Lon heard kids screaming and a toddler crying, and winced. Poor Melvin Lee.

Within minutes, the little boy came flying out of the house in dry clothes, wearing a little green raincoat.

"Mama says you're taking me to school!"

"Yes, I am. Pull up your hood," Lon said, and a few minutes later, they were pulling up at Blessings Elementary. "I'm going to walk you inside," Lon said.

"Yes, sir," Melvin Lee said, eyeing the steady downpour. "Reckon we oughta run?"

Lon grinned. "I reckon we should."

And so they did.

Duke was still smiling to himself when he pulled up at the back of the house and got out. Having Cathy as a guest at their house for Thanksgiving had changed the whole vibe of the holiday for him. He got out on the run and dashed through the rain to the back porch, then shed all of his rain gear at the door before going inside.

He could hear laughter in the front of the house, and he could smell lemon oil. Cleaning house was in progress.

"I'm home!" he called out.

"We're in the living room," Jack shouted. "Grab a dust rag. Hope is on a tear."

Duke sighed. He'd been on the receiving end of Hope's penchant for cleaning house before. He paused in the kitchen long enough to get some cleaning cloths, and headed toward the front of the house in his sock feet.

The vacuum cleaner was in the middle of the floor, and Jack was standing on a ladder with a long-handled feather duster, wiping down the blades of a ceiling fan. Hope was near the fireplace, polishing the ancient wood on the mantel, which explained the scent of lemon oil.

"What's all this about?" Duke asked.

"Since this is my day off, I'm using it for holiday cleaning," Hope said. "You can dust the books and the bookshelves first, and then we'll do the dining room table and chairs next. I'm not running the vacuum until all of the wood has been dusted and cleaned."

"Speaking of holidays, I invited Cathy Terry to Thanksgiving and she accepted," Duke said.

Jack stopped and looked down from the ladder.

Hope paused and turned around.

"Way to go, Duke. That's a first," Jack said.

Duke ignored the insinuation and headed for the bookshelves.

"That's great," Hope said. "You know how I feel about holiday dinners. The more, the merrier. How is she feeling?"

"I guess okay," Duke said. "She's managing enough that she took off out of the house barefoot and limping to go rescue a little boy she saw out in the storm."

Sensing a story, Hope paused and sat down on the huge stone hearth.

"Oh my gosh! Was it a toddler? Was he lost?"

"No. Nothing like that. It was Danny and Junie Wilson's oldest son. He's seven, almost eight, he said, and he was running away from home."

Jack climbed down from the ladder. "I remember running away once. But that was because I broke a window."

Duke grinned. "I remember, and Dad sent me to find you."

"So Cathy went after him?" Hope asked.

"Yes. I went to get lunch, and when I got back, they were both soaked to the skin and she had him in her lap out on her porch swing, wrapped up in a blanket."

"Bless his heart," Hope said. "Why did he run away?"

Duke turned around and leaned against the bookshelves to finish the story.

"It appears his mama has been keeping him out of school so much to help her with the three younger children that the little guy is having to repeat first grade. The kids are making fun of him and calling him stupid, and I guess his breaking point came this morning when he overheard his mama telling his daddy over the phone that she was pregnant again. He told Cathy he wasn't gonna take care of no more babies. He packed some clothes in a plastic garbage bag and took off."

Hope grimaced. "That's terrible that she did that to him. I thought there were laws about parents getting in trouble for not sending their kids to school."

"There are. Of course, Cathy had already called the police department to report she'd found him, and they'd just received a frantic call from Junie that he was missing, so Lon came and picked him up. Last thing I heard, Lon was promising the little guy that he'd make sure his mama didn't make him miss any more school just to babysit, and then he took the boy home."

Jack grinned. "Your life has certainly become more exciting since rescuing Cathy Terry."

"I guess, but I'd put our cattle getting stolen as a bigger issue," Duke said. He turned his back on both of them and resumed dusting.

The reminder that had happened shifted their focus enough that they stopped teasing him. By midafternoon, the house was shining, they all smelled like lemon oil, and the rain was beginning to let up.

Over two thousand miles to the west of rain-soaked Georgia, Blaine Wagner was in his limo on the way to a business lunch at the Venetian in Las Vegas when his cell phone rang. He set aside his glass of wine, and when he saw caller ID, he closed the window between him and his driver, then answered.

"Hello, Rand. I'm expecting updates."

Rand Lawrence had his notes pulled up on his iPad to make sure he didn't forget anything.

"Yes, sir, I have some, and interesting ones, for sure. Cathy Wagner filed paperwork to reclaim her maiden name as her legal name."

"So, she's Cathy Terry again?" Blaine said.

"Yes, sir, which does explain why she left all of the credit cards and her identification behind. She had canceled all of the accounts anyway, so the cards and ID info are worthless."

"Do you know where she is?" Blaine asked.

"No, sir. But she left Vegas by bus with a one-way ticket to Denver, Colorado. She did arrive there, but has since disappeared. I received your text about her moving her money out of her bank, but there is no credit card trail anywhere, and while I have some hacking skills, I'm not comfortable trying to find out where she's moved her money. That's messing with the FDIC and federal banking laws."

"Understood," Blaine said, but his thoughts were in freefall. "Listen, here's what I want you to do. Just keep the case open, and if anything pops up on any of your searches, let me know. Okay?"

"Yes, sir. Will do. Should I invoice your office, or you privately?"

"Privately, and thank you for asking."

"Yes, sir," Rand said, and disconnected.

Blaine dropped his phone back in his pocket and then reached for his wine as the limo pulled up to a red light. The black tint to the windows in the rear of the limo gave him complete anonymity, which also gave him a sense of security. A man with his standing in this city always had to be careful.

He eyed a gaggle of tourists crossing in the walk lane, viewing them all as money in his pocket. He could tell which ones were just sightseers, and which ones came to play.

Even though the people who played the slots and the tables were part of the bloodstream of Vegas, the whales who came to the private games were the ones Blaine catered to. Those were the high rollers who received lavish comps because they wagered large amounts of money during their frequent stays.

Everything in Vegas was a game and a gamble, including the people who came and went, and today Blaine was having to come to terms with the fact that his ex-wife was gone. But what was she doing? Where did she go? He was beginning to realize he should have kept his mouth shut and not threatened her. That was all the warning she'd needed.

And then his gut knotted.

What if she went to the feds out of spite? What if the feds put her in witness protection? I need to put out some feelers and see if there's anything stirring that might come back on me.

He took another drink and then set the wineglass aside and opened the window between him and the driver.

"Paddy, replace this wine. I don't like it. I'd prefer something from the German pinot noirs, I think."

"Yes, sir," the driver said, and accelerated through the green light.

A few minutes later, they arrived at the Venetian Resort hotel and casino. Paddy jumped out and circled the limo to open the door for his boss.

Blaine exited the car and was immediately greeted by an employee who escorted him to where the private lunch was being held. As soon as Blaine walked into the room, his blood pressure settled and his wayward thoughts about

his ex disappeared. He was in his element and on familiar
ground.

—————————————

Dan Amos came by Cathy's house after the rain finally
stopped, bringing a Mexican casserole and a tres leches cake.

"Alice sent food, and I'll confess it took an extreme
amount of my willpower not to sample it on the way over.
Her saving grace is that she made the same thing for us for
supper tonight, so your food is intact."

Cathy inhaled as he carried it into the kitchen for her.

"Wow, that smells good," she said.

"I put the cake in the refrigerator. She said to tell you
it needs to stay cold. The casserole will be fine sitting out
until after you've finished supper."

"Thank you so much…both of you, and please tell Alice
how much I appreciate it."

"Will do," Dan said. "Before I leave, do you mind if I get
up in the attic to make sure the roof doesn't have any leaks?
You're the first renter who's lived here since the hurricane,
and I want to make sure the roof repair held."

"Oh sure, do you what you need to do," Cathy said.

"Thanks," Dan said.

He stepped back out onto the porch, then brought in
a ladder, carried it down the hall to the attic access, then
climbed up and crawled in.

She could hear him walking around above, and felt
grateful for having a competent and honest landlord. A few
minutes later he climbed down.

"It's all good and dry as a bone up there," Dan said. "I'll

get out of your way now. I have a couple more houses I need to check before I quit for the day."

"Here's hoping they're all nice and dry," Cathy said.

Dan gave her a thumbs-up and left with his ladder.

Cathy watched him loading up and then driving away and wondered what had happened in his life that made him give up the high-powered lifestyle of a prominent criminal lawyer and settle in this little town doing his own repairs on his rental properties. Then she shrugged. Everybody had a story to tell, even her, although nobody here in Blessings knew a thing about hers—except Dan.

A short while later, there was another knock on her door, and the woman standing on the porch holding a sack of groceries immediately introduced herself.

"Hi, sugar! I'm Ruby Butterman. I run the Curl Up and Dye salon, and I heard through the Blessings grapevine—otherwise known as the gossip circle—that you're a bit incapacitated right now. So, these goodies are from me and the girls at my shop. When you get to feeling like it, stop by for a free shampoo and style."

Cathy was enchanted. "Thank you so much. I run by your shop almost every morning…or at least I did before I messed up my ankle. I appreciate the offer and the goodies so much. Please pass on my thanks to the girls as well."

Ruby set the groceries on the seat of Cathy's walker and then handed her a card from her shop.

"This has all my contact info on it. Call if you ever need anything, okay? I've got to get back to the shop. I have a client coming soon."

She waved, then turned and dashed off the porch and drove away.

Cathy rolled the sack of groceries into her kitchen and put up a quart of milk, a loaf of fresh bread, some meat and cheese for sandwiches, and a couple of frozen dinners.

"I swear, these are the nicest people ever," she muttered, and then found a Snickers candy bar in the bottom of the sack, and grinned. "Score. That's a woman after my own heart."

She took the candy bar into the living room with a glass of iced tea and enjoyed the unexpected treat.

———————————

Melvin Lee had the best day ever at school—even if it had only been for the afternoon—because the chief of police made Mama promise never to keep him home to babysit again. He didn't even pay any attention when one of the guys from his old class laughed at him in the hall and called him *dummy*. He wasn't gonna be dumb forever.

Rain was letting up when he boarded the school bus for in-town kids and rode it to the corner of his block. Raindrops splattered on the hood of his little green raincoat, making it sound like rain on a roof. He and two other kids got off at the same stop, but he was on the only one who lived down the street, so he headed for home.

At first Melvin Lee was happy, but the closer he got to the house, the slower his steps became. He was dreading helping feed the kids and getting them ready for bed when it dawned on him that Granny's little blue car was in the drive. He loved his granny and started running, splattering through the puddles.

He was running up the steps when the front door opened and his mama appeared.

"Stop right there," she said. "Take off your wet shoes and raincoat out here."

Mama's voice sounded squeaky, which meant she was all stressed.

He sighed, said, "Yes, ma'am," and did as she asked.

She picked everything up and went back inside. Melvin Lee followed her, taking care to close the door behind him.

Within moments, he heard his granny's voice and then the sound of her footsteps hurrying up the hall. Granny was an older version of Mama, but happier and way more fun.

"There's my sweet boy!" Minna said. She swept him up into her arms and gave him a big kiss.

Melvin Lee was grinning so big it made his lips stretch.

"Hi, Granny! Are you gonna stay for supper? Will you sit by me?"

Minna Atkins leaned over until she was face-to-face with him and cupped his face.

"I'm staying for supper, and for a long, long time, Melvin Lee. I moved into Sissy's room, and she's gonna sleep in your mama's room with her."

Melvin Lee gasped. "You are?"

Minna nodded, then lowered her voice. "I'm so sorry about what happened, honey. I didn't know, or I would have been here a long time ago. I'm going to be your mama's helper from now on. You just get to be Melvin Lee Wilson, whoever he turns out to be."

Melvin Lee's eyes welled, and he threw his arms around her neck.

Minna picked him up in her arms again, but this time she carried him to the sofa and sat down with him clutched against her chest, his face buried against her neck. He wasn't crying out loud, but he was shaking, and after the call she'd gotten from her daughter, she knew the decision she'd made to leave her retirement community was the right one.

Junie had been listening. She was still horrified and humiliated that the police chief not only gave her a stern talking-to, but a veiled threat as well. The worst thing she could have imagined was losing her children, and the last thing she wanted was to get Social Services involved in her life.

It had been hard to call her mama to ask for help, but it was even harder to call her husband, Danny, and tell him Melvin Lee had run away and why.

Danny's stunned silence soon went from shock to anger. He was already upset that Junie was pregnant again, when she was supposed to be on reliable birth control. But to find out it was Melvin Lee's absences and not his intellect that caused him to have to repeat first grade broke his heart.

Junie knew Danny was mad at her, and disappointed in her as well. But she'd made this mess, and it was up to her to fix it.

She sighed. Sissy was playing in her playpen, but Junie needed to check on the boys. Anytime they got quiet was a time for concern, so she went down the hall to see what they were doing, leaving Minna and Melvin Lee on their own.

Supper was over, and Melvin Lee had already had a bath and was in his pajamas getting ready for bed. He had school tomorrow and didn't want to be late.

Granny promised she'd come and tuck him in and read

him a story, so he was going through the books on his shelf, trying to decide what he wanted her to read, when he heard the phone ring. A few moments later, his mother came into his room carrying her phone.

"Daddy's on the phone. He wants to talk to you."

Melvin Lee beamed and reached for the phone.

"Hi, Daddy! Granny's here. She's gonna read me a story before I go to bed."

"That's great. Are you okay now?" Danny asked. "Mama told me you ran away."

Melvin Lee sighed. "Yes, but I won't have to do that no more. Chief Pittman said so."

Danny Wilson was horrified that the chief of police had to be the one to take care of his son's troubles. It should have been him. He should have been home.

"Mama told me. I just want you to know I'm so sorry. I didn't know, son. I didn't know, but it won't ever happen again, okay?"

"Okay, Daddy. Are you coming home soon?"

"Yes, and when I get home this time, it will be to stay."

Melvin Lee gasped. "Forever and ever?"

"Yes, forever and ever. Now you tell Granny I said hi, and sleep tight tonight. I'll be home by the weekend. I love you, Melvin Lee. You are such a good boy. I am so proud of you."

"I love you, too, Daddy. See you soon," he said, and then handed the phone back to his mother.

Junie was crying as she turned around and passed her mother who was on the way to read Melvin Lee's story.

Minna didn't have much sympathy for her daughter, so the tears didn't move her. Instead, her focus was on her grandson.

"Hey, honey, did you pick out a story?" she asked.

"*Curious George*! George is funny, Granny."

Minna took the book.

"A great choice! You lay yourself down now, and I'll tuck you in. Then you can listen to the story, okay?"

Melvin Lee scooted beneath the covers, sighing as his granny covered him up and brushed the hair away from his forehead. He shivered from the sheer joy of feeling safe and knowing someone was finally going to take care of Mama and the kids besides him.

He watched his granny open the book, then waited for her wink. She always winked before she started a story. As she began to read, he got lost in the story.

Minna read all the way to the end, even though Melvin Lee had already fallen asleep. He'd had such a big day. Such a hard day. She laid the book aside and leaned over and brushed a soft kiss on his forehead.

"Night, night, my little man. Granny loves you forever," she whispered, and then turned out the light, leaving a small Thomas the Tank Engine night-light burning beside his bed.

Cathy had her nightgown on and was getting ready for bed when her cell phone rang. She glanced at caller ID and smiled as she answered.

"Hello."

"Hey, it's me," Duke said. "I hope I'm not calling too late."

"No, not at all," she said.

"So, I'm making sure you're okay. You got soaked today. You didn't reinjure your ankle, did you?"

"I'm fine. The only thing that's a mess is my hair. Naturally curly hair sort of explodes in damp weather."

He chuckled. "Your hair is kind of amazing…like you."

Cathy's heart skipped a beat. "Why, thank you, Duke Talbot. That's one of the nicest things anyone has ever said to me."

"I have my moments," Duke said. "I just wanted you to know that we'll be really busy out here tomorrow. We have to work cattle, and it will likely be a long, muddy day, but if it's okay, I'll call you again tomorrow evening."

"It will be something to look forward to," she said.

"Crown Grocers has a delivery service. I checked. It's something new that was added after the Piggly Wiggly went out. All you have to do is call in your order, and they'll deliver it right to your door."

"I didn't know that!" Cathy said. "I will definitely call in an order tomorrow, but as soon as my ankle gets a little better, I've decided to lease a car. That will end my lack of mobility, too."

"I'm not sure they have cars to lease in Blessings," he said.

"No, they don't. I'll do that in Savannah. Don't worry about me. I know my way around all that."

"Okay, but if you need a ride to Savannah, or anything like that, just call."

"I've got it covered," Cathy said. "Hope all goes well for you guys tomorrow, and be careful working cattle."

"Thanks," Duke said. "Talk to you soon."

Cathy heard him disconnect and then put her phone back on the charger and turned out the lights. But instead of going off to sleep, she lay there in the dark thinking about her life.

When she'd first left Las Vegas on that bus, she'd had no goal in mind except escaping her ex-husband's reach. And she'd been wandering aimlessly until she'd found Blessings. She'd chosen it because it was so far away from where she'd come, and because nobody knew her here, she'd felt no threats.

But now that she was making friends here, she'd discovered another facet of Blessings she hadn't expected. It was beginning to feel like it could be home, and Duke Talbot's abrupt arrival in her life was another plus. Even though they'd just met and he was intriguing, she was guarding her heart as closely as she was guarding her location.

CHAPTER 7

THE PASSING DAYS IN BLESSINGS WERE CHANGING FOR a lot of people.

Melvin Lee's enforced life of babysitting was over, and he'd made peace with repeating first grade after his daddy came home. Danny Wilson still hadn't settled on what kind of job he was going to look for, but it would be a local one and that's all that mattered.

Minna Atkins settled into her room and the routine of the Wilson family's life better than she had imagined, and Junie was elated to have her husband home for good, but considered her morning sickness as due punishment from the universe for all of her misdeeds.

Duke and Jack's cattle loss was entered into the farm account as a very expensive loss, and Hope found out she was pregnant. It wasn't exactly planned, but she wasn't unhappy about it, and Jack was over the moon.

After Duke congratulated them properly, he had to face the fact that the day had finally come when a separate residence was becoming a reality for either them or him. That evening as they were all cleaning up the supper dishes, Duke made an announcement.

"In light of the upcoming blessed event, I'm calling a family meeting."

Jack hung up the dish towel he'd been using, and Hope put the last of the leftovers into the refrigerator, and then they all gathered back around the kitchen table they'd just cleared off.

"So what's up?" Jack asked, and reached for Hope's hand.

Hope saw a look on Duke's face that she'd never seen before, and it scared her.

"Is something wrong, honey?"

Duke smiled. "No, no, nothing like that. In fact, everything is right, even perfect, and I have a proposition to make that has to do with our growing family. I've been thinking about this for a couple of years now and just let time get away from me without talking to you two about it. I think it's time that I found a place of my own."

Hope gasped, and Jack was so stunned he couldn't speak.

"Oh, don't take it like that," Duke said. "For God's sake, it should have happened years ago when you two first got married. Hope, bless her heart, didn't just move in with one man. She moved in with two, and frankly, honey, I don't know how you stood me."

Hope's eyes welled. "I always knew that the farm and you were part of the deal and considered myself fortunate. I don't want to be the reason it's breaking up."

Duke clapped Jack on the back to punctuate his sincerity.

"You guys are missing the point. We're not breaking up. We're growing! I'm thinking that big library we hardly ever use and the old room Mom called the sewing room would make an awesome master bedroom and nursery."

"But that leaves the whole upstairs for you," Jack said.

"No. You're missing the point," Duke said. "This is a special time for the both of you, and you deserve the freedom to be yourselves and share this time together, without wondering if I'm going to come walking in the house. Those bedrooms will fill up in the years to come."

"What are you planning for yourself?" Jack said. "There

are a lot of great places on the farm to build. We don't want to lose you, Duke."

"You're not losing me. I'll be here every day just like I am now, and we'll still work the farm together, and life will go on. I'm not sure about building a house, though. I've been thinking about Mr. Bailey's place. I don't know if it's for sale, but I'm going to check it out. It already has a house on it, and the land backs up to ours. It would be a good addition to our farm, and all that extra land would be an opportunity to build up the herd."

"That house is old," Jack said.

Duke grinned. "No, it has character, and that's what I like about it."

"You *have* been thinking about it, haven't you?" Jack said.

Duke nodded. "Yes, and long before baby Talbot was on the way."

Hope sighed. "Okay. I can accept that reasoning, but only if you promise you still call this place home. If you don't feel free to come and go as you've always done, you're going to hurt my feelings."

"And mine," Jack said.

"It's all good, guys. I just wanted you to know now, so you can start renovations to the downstairs and be done long before the baby arrives."

"Fine, but we're not messing with anything inside the house until after the holidays," Hope said. "I have plans, and they include all of us and our guests, including Cathy Terry, remember?"

"I'm not forgetting anything," Duke said. "Look at it this way. After I'm gone, you two have the run of the house. Hell, you can run naked anytime you want to."

Hope rolled her eyes. "I'm about to lose the running-naked body and turn myself into a big fat baby incubator."

Duke grinned. "I know I'm notorious for always saying the wrong thing, but right now I got nothin'."

It made both Jack and Hope laugh, and when bedtime finally rolled around, the shock of the news had worn off, and Duke was thinking about calling Rhonda Bailey the next morning to see if her dad's place was for sale.

Phone calls between Duke and Cathy continued through the next few days along with a couple of quick trips to her house. Once to bring her fresh eggs again, and once to bring her flowers, because Duke liked to watch the dimple come and go when she smiled.

Finally, the swelling in Cathy's ankle was gone. It was still a little tender if she was on it too much, but it felt good to have her feet back under her again, and she rolled the walker back to Phillips Pharmacy on her own.

LilyAnn saw her coming and held the door open for her as she entered.

"Out shopping?" she asked.

"Yes, but I'm also returning this," Cathy said.

"You know it's paid up for the month, right?" LilyAnn asked.

"Yes, but I really don't need it anymore and someone else might."

"Okay, I'll register it as having been returned. You should have seen Duke Talbot when he first came to rent it for you. He was such a sweetheart. So concerned for your welfare and that you were so hurt and lived alone."

"Really?" Cathy said.

"Oh yes! He went back into the storage room with Mr. Phillips to try them all out, and then I thought it was so sweet when he also thought of the ice packs and the pain-killers for you. You can tell he's used to taking care of people, can't you? I mean...he stayed on the farm and made sure Jack got to finish college after their parents died. He had to step up and take charge, and I think that is what kept him from ever marrying. He just wouldn't take the time away from responsibilities to devote to building a relationship."

Cathy nodded to indicate she was still listening as she picked up a basket and began going down an aisle to get some shampoo. And all the while, LilyAnn followed her, still talking.

It wasn't lost on her that the day of her accident, a total stranger had been more considerate of her than her own husband had ever been, and it was already a given that he was good-looking. And he was calling her every morning, and then again every evening before she went to bed. It was an amazing feeling to know that someone alive on this earth actually cared what happened to her.

Hearing LilyAnn bragging on him, too, was reassuring in a whole other way. Cathy had to keep reminding herself that everybody in Blessings knew everybody, and they knew all about the residents' character and honesty. She was the outsider. But instead of distrusting her, like she'd been inclined to distrust all of them, they'd made her feel welcome—inviting her into the inner circle of Blessings. To be accepted in this way was a gift, and she wasn't taking it lightly.

Finally, she finished her shopping and went up front to

pay. LilyAnn was still chatting when Cathy finally had to cut her off.

"I guess I'd better get back home. I have a roast in the oven," she said.

"Umm, sounds so good," LilyAnn said. "My husband, Mike, loves pot roast and veggies. Oh…by the way, have you made plans for Thanksgiving?"

Cathy nodded. "Duke invited me out to the farm to spend it with his family."

"Oh really?" LilyAnn said, and then grinned. "So, any chance that fall you took might turn into another kind of fall…as in falling for one of our eligible bachelors?"

"You are so jumping the gun," Cathy said, and laughed. "He's just a friend who's been super-nice to me. I think he felt sorry for me because I don't have any family."

LilyAnn shook her head. "Nope. Duke has never been much of a social person. I think he's a little fascinated by you, and that's a first."

Cathy didn't comment because she didn't know what to say, but she liked the validity of knowing her invitation wasn't just an afterthought.

"Like I said, I need to get home and check on the roast. Have a nice day," Cathy said.

"You too," LilyAnn said, and then waved as Cathy left.

Cathy took a shortcut home through an alley and could smell the roast as she walked up the steps onto her porch. She hurried inside to check it.

"Another five minutes and you're coming out," she said as she put the lid back on it and took her purchases from the pharmacy to her room, then went back into the kitchen to finish up the meal.

The roast was out and resting when her timer for the potatoes went off. She took them off the burner and was draining the water so she could mash them when her cell phone rang. She set the pan aside and went to answer, happy when she saw it was Duke.

"Hi, you," she said, unaware of the big smile she'd put on Duke's face.

"Hello to you, too. You sound like you're in a good mood."

"I'm always in a good mood," she said.

"Are you in a good enough mood for a drop-in visitor?" Duke asked. "I had to pick up some chicken feed and didn't want to leave Blessings without getting a chance to see your pretty face."

"That flattery will certainly get you in the door. Are you on the way?" she asked.

"I'm already in town at the feed store loading up."

"Well then, if you don't have other plans, come eat dinner with me. It's roast and vegetables, and it's almost done."

"I have no plans beyond you, and I would love to eat with you. Can I bring anything?" Duke asked.

"Just yourself," Cathy said.

"Then I'll see you soon," Duke said, and disconnected.

She was still savoring *I have no plans beyond you*, when it dawned on her she needed to hurry. All of a sudden, her solitary meal had taken on a whole new vibe.

She threw some butter in the potatoes and started mashing them, adding seasonings and cream, then turned the fire off from under the pan of green beans and made a dash to the refrigerator to get the makings for a salad.

Cathy hadn't planned on all of this, but she wanted everything to be nice. This was the first thing she'd been able to do for him as thanks for all he'd done for her.

She had everything ready except dressing on the salad when she heard his footsteps on the front porch. Her heart skipped with anticipation, and she paused in front of the little mirror in the hall to eye her appearance.

A few curls had taken flight, and the sprinkling of freckles across her nose could have used a little powder, but the long-sleeved blue T-shirt she was wearing matched the color of her eyes, and her cheeks were flushed with excitement.

Then she reached toward the mirror and touched her reflection.

"Calm down, girl," she whispered. "Don't let your heart outrun your good sense here."

And then he knocked, and she stuck her tongue out at herself and hurried to the door.

"As always, your timing is perfect," she said. "Come in, come in."

Duke took one look at her and wanted nothing more than to take her in his arms and kiss her senseless. Instead, he crossed the threshold, letting her shut the door behind him. But when she turned around to take his jacket, he put his hands on her shoulders.

"I'm not sure if it's the curls or the freckles or the smile on your face, but fair warning here, lady. I'm about to kiss you hello."

His mouth was on her lips, and the newness of it made her heart skip a beat. He didn't let himself linger, but the kiss was delivered with unapologetic fervor before he stepped away and took off his jacket and laid it across the back of the sofa.

Cathy's cheeks felt hot, but the smile on her face was total reflex.

"Am I still invited to dinner?" he asked.

"I think it's safe to say you're definitely welcome here... anytime," Cathy said. "Come with me while everything is still hot."

Duke grinned.

"Are we referring to food here?"

That's when she realized what she'd just said, and laughed out loud.

"Just shut up and follow me," she said, and led the way into the kitchen.

"Hey, you're not limping," Duke said as he paused to wash his hands at the kitchen sink.

"I know. I returned the walker to the pharmacy this morning, too."

He frowned. "You didn't have to do that. I would have taken it for you."

She eyed the frown on his face and shook her head.

"You do everything for everybody, don't you, Duke Talbot? Dinner is ready, so sit yourself down, and let someone do something for you."

Duke was so touched by what she'd said that he sat without another word, watching as she dished up the food and began carrying it to the table.

"Do you want coffee or sweet tea?" Cathy asked. "I have both, so take your pick."

"It's Georgia. Unless it's breakfast, I'll always pick tea, and my afternoon drink is ice-cold Coke," he said.

Cathy took note of that information as she removed the pitcher from the refrigerator and set it on the table, then iced two glasses and set them at their places before joining him.

"This is exciting," she said. "You are the first guest I've entertained since I came here. Welcome to my kitchen, and please help yourself."

He eyed the juicy slices of beef roast on the platter and took two, then added mashed potatoes and ladled gravy she'd made from the pan drippings over both. He scooted the platter and bowls closer to her, then added green beans to his plate and salad to the small bowl.

"I only have two kinds of salad dressing," Cathy said. "Italian and the traditional ranch dressing I have come to appreciate here in the South."

"And I like both of them," Duke said, and reached for the Italian dressing as she chose the other.

He didn't hesitate as he cut off a bite of roast, swiped it through the brown gravy, and popped it in his mouth, then chewed. Seconds later, he was rolling his eyes in delight.

"Mmmm, Lord deliver me. The lady is adorable and she can cook, too."

Cathy sighed. Success. Now she could enjoy her own meal, so she started eating.

The first couple of minutes were fairly silent, and then Duke finally paused to take a drink of tea.

"We had a bit of exciting news out at the farm a couple of days ago. I'm gonna be an uncle," he said.

Cathy gasped. "Hope's pregnant? Oh, that's wonderful!"

"Yes, she and Jack are so excited. I'm just an onlooker, but it's still cool to know our family is going to grow." Then he took another bite, chewing thoughtfully as he watched her.

"Is she feeling okay, or has morning sickness hit?" Cathy asked.

"So far, she's doing great and still working like nothing has changed. And, she has informed us that she has big plans for the holidays, so be prepared for a big Talbot-style Thanksgiving dinner."

"I can help," Cathy offered.

"I'll let her know," Duke said. "But she has Mercy for backup, and between those two sisters, I'm not worried about a thing."

Cathy thought about her solitary life up in Alaska. She had always wanted a sibling, but it didn't happen. And now that she was divorced, she had no actual family left anywhere on earth. She'd been so focused on escaping Blaine's anger that it hadn't dawned on her how alone she really was in the world.

"What are you thinking about?" Duke asked.

She blinked. "Uh...just what you said, I guess. Why?"

"You looked...not sad, but kind of wistful."

"Oh. Well, I guess you read my thoughts pretty clearly, then. Mother always said everything I thought could be read on my face, so I guess my emotions are an open book. I was thinking about when I was growing up, and that I'd always wanted a sister or a brother to play with, but it never happened."

Duke nodded. "I get that. I have a younger brother, but he was enough younger than me that we didn't have all that much in common until we both grew up. I was his babysitter, and the instructor of all big-brother duties when we were young."

Cathy smiled. "That was Daddy for me. Growing up in Alaska was a whole other way of life."

Duke's eyes widened. "That was your childhood?"

She nodded. "I was homeschooled at first, so my whole world was Mother and Daddy, and his sled dogs. I learned a lot of things early on, not the least of which was how to shoot a gun. It was the difference between life and death there. We were always hunting for food, or protecting ourselves from becoming food for some furry four-foot."

"I am in awe," Duke said. "No wonder backpacking across the country did not faze you."

She shrugged, thinking of the elaborate lifestyle she'd abandoned so willingly.

"It all came back to me when I needed it to," she said, and then paused. "I need to tell you something that only Dan Amos knows. I had to tell him so he would rent me the house without running a credit check."

Duke's stomach suddenly knotted. He'd guessed from the start she had secrets.

"I'm listening."

"I was twelve when Daddy died, and Mother and I left Alaska. She moved us to Las Vegas. She moved us to a desert, with no forests or rivers, and the shock of desert life was hard on me, but it saved her. I look back now and know she had to leave, because she couldn't be in Alaska without him. Everything there was a reminder of him. So I began public school, which was a whole other thing I had to conquer after being homeschooled, and she went to work as a hostess in a casino. I finished growing up there."

"That must have felt like another world," he said.

She nodded. "In so many ways. But when I got old enough, I went to work in the same casino, and that's where I met the man I married."

"Was he an employee there, or a customer?" Duke asked.

Cathy hesitated, but if they had any kind of chance of making this friendship into a relationship, she wasn't keeping secrets to make it happen.

"No. He owned it…and had interests in two others. His family goes four generations back into the history of Nevada. From silver mines to the gambling world of Las Vegas. I lived in a mansion. I had servants. And we traveled the world…when he wanted to. At first, I was seduced by the money and the lifestyle, and it took Mother away from hustling drinks for gamblers and into her own house on the estate, but it didn't take long for the shine to wear off. He was often verbally abusive when something displeased him, so I didn't displease him."

She didn't know there were tears in her eyes until Duke reached across the table and took her hand. She took a breath and kept talking.

"I lived that life for many years…too many. And then Mother died. And I no longer had to pretend his anger was okay. And I no longer had to pretend I didn't know about all his other women. It took a couple of years for me to get the courage, but I finally filed for divorce, and when I told him, he went nuts. He wasn't a man who lost at anything. He didn't want me anymore. He didn't love me. But I belonged to him, and if anyone was going to make life-changing decisions, it would be him."

"Did he hurt you?" Duke asked.

"He tried. I locked myself in the bathroom and called the police. They escorted me and the bag I already had packed out of the house, and I got my own apartment. He fought the divorce every step of the way because he didn't want to give me alimony. He kept saying I had abandoned him. But I knew stuff about his lifestyle he didn't want made public, and Nevada divorce laws were in my favor. We hadn't signed a prenuptial agreement, and the judge ruled a huge settlement in my favor. It was a pittance compared to what he has, but it was millions—literally millions—way more than I would have ever expected.

"And then the day it was final, he threatened my life—said I knew too much about the people he did business with—and hinted that I needed to watch my back and that my days were numbered. The divorce turned him into something of a stalker. I knew he had someone watching everything I did, so I legally returned to my maiden name, waited until I knew he was out of the country, moved all the money from my divorce settlement into three different banks across the country, then disguised myself, and took a bus to Denver, Colorado. I left every credit card, my driver's license, everything of mine that had his name on it in the apartment I had leased, plus all the clothes, all the jewelry, and disappeared. I'm sure he knows by now I skipped out, and that all the money is no longer in that account, and I don't know if he's going to just let me go…or if he might try to find me.

"I was running for my life when I stumbled into Blessings. I didn't expect to do anything more than winter here, but it has begun to feel like the home I once had with my parents. A place where I felt like myself. A place where I felt like I might belong. I'm living under the radar now, so if all this is horrifying to you, and you want nothing more to do with me, I understand. I might never have told you this, but then you kissed me, and I won't deceive you in any way."

Duke had heard enough. He got up, circled the table, and

took her in his arms and just held her. He was so angry on her behalf he couldn't speak, but she'd just broken his heart.

Cathy felt the first tears finally rolling down her face as she leaned into his strength. He was so big and so strong, and he was holding her tight—so tight.

God help me. I'm already too attached to this man to let go.

"Is this hello or goodbye?" she finally asked.

Duke kissed her again, and this time, he held nothing back. There was no mistaking the passion, and no way to tell where the moment would have taken them until he made himself stop. His voice was rough with emotion as he wiped the tears from her cheeks and then cupped her face.

"I'm never going to tell you goodbye again. I don't quite know what to do with a rich woman, but there's also the fact that I didn't know what to do with a poor one, either. I had a serious relationship that ended when my parents died. She had planned on me following her to Oregon. Her job was with the National Park Service.

"But I couldn't leave Jack in limbo. He was still in college. And I wasn't going to sell the farm, because that's all Jack ever wanted...to come home and take over when our parents retired. I guess if I had loved her enough, I wouldn't have let her go, but I chose my family and the farm and let my life slide." He brushed his thumb across her cheek, and his mouth across her lips. "I don't want to be on the sidelines anymore. I'm in your life for as long as you'll have me, and we'll go from there. If it's all right with you?"

Cathy's breath caught on a sob.

"It's beyond all right and more than I could have hoped for," she said, and then threw her arms around his neck and kissed him, but it wasn't until she heard him groan and then wrap his arms around her that she knew there was no longer a need to keep running.

———————————

Cathy was still walking on air long after Duke had gone home. The kitchen was clean and the leftover food had been put away, but she was restless. She needed something to do. She was still thinking about leasing a car when it occurred to her that while that service wasn't available here, maybe renting cars was. She grabbed her phone and made a quick call to her landlord.

"Hello, this is Dan."

"Dan, this is Cathy Terry. Nothing is wrong at the house. I just have a question."

"What's up?" he asked.

"I already know there's no place here to lease cars, and I'll have to go to Savannah to do that, but by any chance is there a place here that rents them?"

"Yes, there is. It's downtown in the same office as the insurance agency. I'll give you the name and number, and you see what they have on hand. Give me a second to look that up for you."

"Oh, thank you," Cathy said, and then wrote down the information.

"You're welcome. If you need a ride down there, give me a call back. I'm heading to Bloomer's Hardware in about thirty minutes. I can swing by and pick you up on the way."

Cathy sighed. "You must be the best landlord in the world," she said. "If they have anything, I'll give you that call." Then she heard him chuckle.

"I don't know about best landlord, but it is truthfully the best job I've had. Way better than arguing court cases."

He disconnected, and she quickly made the call. After a brief conversation, she realized she had her choice of three different cars, but since she didn't have insurance of her own anymore, she'd have to get insurance to go with it. Whatever it took to be mobile again was fine with her, and she called Dan right back.

"I'll be needing that ride," she said.

"Pick you up in about ten minutes."

"I'll be watching for you, so don't get out. Just honk."

"What about your ankle?" he asked.

"Oh, it's all better. No problems there."

"Okay, then I'll see you soon."

Cathy disconnected, then went to get her purse and make a quick change of clothes. The first thing she was going to do after she got wheels was go shopping in Savannah. All the clothes she owned now were what she'd had in that backpack.

She was sitting out in the porch swing in a clean pair of jeans, a white tee, and her jean jacket when Dan pulled up into her drive. She picked up her purse and headed down the steps to his work truck and got in.

"I've ridden in this truck before," Cathy said.

Dan grinned. "Yes, I remember. I picked you up in front of Crown Grocers and took you to look at houses."

She grinned. "House. I picked the first one you showed me, remember?"

"That you did. Are you settling in okay here in Blessings?" he asked.

She thought of Duke and smiled.

"Yes, I'm settling in just fine."

CHAPTER 8

"THANKS FOR THE LIFT," CATHY SAID, AS DAN DROPPED her off in front of the insurance agency.

Dan grinned and gave her a thumbs-up, then drove away as she went inside.

She smiled at the woman sitting at the front desk.

"Hello. I'm Cathy Terry. I just called about renting a car."

"Oh. Yes. We have three cars. A white Ford Focus, a black Jeep Cherokee, and a tan Hyundai...our economy model."

"I think the Jeep Cherokee," Cathy said. "And as I mentioned, I haven't had a car of my own in a while, so I don't have insurance. We'll need to take care of that through the rental agreement."

"Yes, ma'am," the clerk said. "I'll need your driver's license and a credit card."

Cathy had a couple of credit cards, but she had yet to use them. "I'll use a bank debit card for that," she said.

"That's fine," the clerk said. "Just have a seat while I get the paperwork together."

Cathy sat down beside the desk. It did cross her mind that doing this might somehow reveal her location, but she was counting on the fact that Blaine had given up. Kind of an out-of-sight, out-of-mind reaction. It was time to trust the universe on this one, because she was tired of running.

A few minutes later, the clerk finished the paperwork, and Cathy signed the rental agreement.

"You've rented it for two weeks, so if you think you're going to need it longer, let us know," the clerk said.

Cathy nodded. "Yes, I will, but I'm certain I won't. As soon as I can, I'm going to Savannah to lease or buy one."

"If you have any problems with this one, you have our number. They're bringing the Jeep around to the curb, and they'll explain all of the features to you."

"Thank you," Cathy said, then took her paperwork and went out the front door.

A couple of minutes later, she saw the car coming and smiled. It was a far cry from the white Lexus she'd driven in Vegas, but it suited her.

The driver pulled up to the curb and got out. After they checked out the Jeep's condition together, Cathy got inside and started it up. The driver explained a few more details, and then Cathy backed away and drove straight to the Crown for groceries. It was wonderful not to be dependent on others anymore.

She went inside without a grocery list. It was the first time since her arrival that she hadn't had to choose her purchases based on what she was able to carry home, and today she was stocking up.

She pulled a shopping cart from the stack and was moving toward the baking aisle when Alice Amos waved at her from the checkout stand.

"Hi, Cathy! Good to see you out and about."

Cathy smiled. "Thanks. It feels good to be mobile again."

The greeting was nothing more than a simple hello between acquaintances, but it made Cathy feel like she belonged. Someone knew her. And the longer she was here, the more people she would meet. It felt good just to be in the world where someone else knew her name.

After that, she got down to serious shopping, and by the time she checked out and loaded up to go home, there were seven sacks of groceries in the back of her car. Canned goods. Baking goods. Extra cuts of meat for her freezer. Fresh vegetables and eggs. Extra dairy. And since Duke had mentioned it was his favorite soft drink, she had a six-pack of Coke. Now all she had to do was get home, unload it, and put it away.

But having a car made her curious about parts of Blessings she'd never seen, and for the first time since she'd come, she turned left at the end of town instead of right and drove down across old railroad tracks into a neighborhood far less welcoming than she would have imagined.

The poverty level here was a slap-in-the-face reality, which didn't go along with the image she had of this little town. People had been so good to help her. Why weren't they helping down here as well?

She only drove through a couple of blocks before she realized people were aware of her presence. She was a stranger in their neighborhood, and they were wary. She didn't want them to feel anxious in any way, so she turned at the end of the block and left.

But the memory of that place, and the hopelessness she'd felt, stayed with her.

Moses Gatlin went to town to pick up some new skirting to winterize their old trailer house. Georgia wasn't known for hard winters, but weather was so strange these days that they didn't want to take a chance on their pipes freezing.

J.B. stayed behind to finish removing the old skirting and clean up around the trailer. They didn't have a lawn mower, but they'd set their trailer where the old house used to be, and the grass didn't grow much where it had exploded and burned. Still, there were enough grass and weeds around the steps and at the ends of the trailer to make the place look shabby. And now that they were in the money from the cattle-rustling venture, J.B. was trying to elevate their lifestyle.

So he went to the toolshed to poke around for some kind of clippers and found his granddaddy's old scythe instead. He had vague memories of the old man using it to cut the grass down back in the day and decided if Granddaddy could do it, so could he.

But the scythe was rusty as hell and hadn't had an edge sharpened on it in at least two generations, so he took it back to the trailer, got the whetstone they used to sharpen their hunting and kitchen knives, and set to work.

It took a while to get that rust off before J. B. could even begin to start whetting the cutting edge, but he knew how to do it. He'd been at it for almost an hour when he finally paused, then ran his thumb lightly against the edge to see if he had it sharp enough to take down the grass. After a couple more strokes of the whetstone, he set that aside and got up to try it. When it took the tops off the grass without effort, he grinned.

"Now that's what I'm talking about," he said, and began swinging it back and forth across the grass, just like he remembered Granddaddy doing it.

A few minutes later, he heard the sound of their old truck coming up the road. That meant Moses was back, and

J. B. wasn't quite through. In his haste to finish up, he moved closer to the concrete steps than he meant to, and on the downswing, the tip of the scythe hit the hard surface and bounced right back against his leg. He screamed out in pain, then grabbed at his leg as the blood began to gush.

Moses drove up into the yard just in time to witness the accident and got out on the run, then dropped down on both knees beside his brother.

"Let me look. Let me look," Moses said, and when he saw how deep the gash had gone, he yanked off his belt, wrapped it around J.B.'s leg just above the cut to form a tourniquet, and all but dragged his brother to the truck.

"What are you doing?" J.B. cried.

"I got to get you to the hospital in Blessings, or you're gonna bleed to death. That cut went all the way to the bone. Now hold onto that belt and keep it tight. This is gonna be a wild ride."

And it was.

The old truck bounced around through the dried ruts, and then spun out when they hit gravel before they finally reached blacktop. After that, Moses stomped the accelerator all the way to the floor.

"How fast are we going?" J.B. asked.

"I ain't got time to look," Moses muttered, as he passed the city limit sign going into Blessings and then was forced to slow down drastically once he started through town. By the time he pulled up to the ER entrance, he was shaking.

"Stay here," he said, "I'm getting help," and he jumped out running.

Seconds later, an orderly and a nurse came running out pushing a gurney. They transferred J.B. onto it and pushed him into the entry, leaving a blood trail as they went.

Hope Talbot was on duty in the ER when they pushed him past the nurse's station, and she followed them and Dr. Quick into a trauma bay. Within seconds they had his work boots off and the leg of his jeans cut all the way to his thigh.

"Aw, man…you ruined my pants," J.B. groaned.

"Just shut it, brother. You need your leg worse than you need your pants," Moses said.

So J.B. shut it, talking only to answer questions from the doctor or the nurses.

It wasn't until Dr. Quick was beginning to suture the wound that Hope noticed the bloody boot prints around the bed where Moses Gatlin had been standing.

For a moment, she forgot to breathe as she stared down at a gash in the heel of the left boot. That looked just like the one in the pictures Duke had taken from the site of the rustling. She knew orderlies would start mopping this all up the moment they were finished, so she grabbed her phone and snapped a couple of pictures.

"I'm sorry, Dr. Quick. Excuse me a moment," she said, and ducked out of the room.

Dr. Quick looked at the other nurse and grinned.

"Bless her heart. I told her being pregnant and working the ER was going to be tough."

But he couldn't have been more mistaken. Hope wasn't sick at her stomach. She was on the trail of rustlers.

She sent the photos to Jack, then called the police department.

"Blessings PD. This is Avery."

"This is Hope Talbot. Is Chief Pittman on duty?"

"Yes, ma'am."

"Ask him to come to the ER stat, but with no sirens. I think I might have found our cattle rustlers."

"Yes, ma'am. On the way," Avery said.

Hope disconnected as Avery dispatched the chief.

Lon was on patrol and had just driven past the park when he got the call. He headed to the ER running hot, then cut the siren before he turned off Main Street and headed to the hospital.

Hope was standing outside the entrance. He pulled up behind an old pickup already parked at the doorway and got out on the run.

"What's happening, honey?" Lon asked.

"I didn't know who else to call but you. I know you didn't work the incident, but I didn't want them to get away or have the opportunity to dispose of the evidence. I might have found our rustlers."

She showed him the photos Jack had just sent her of the boot prints from the site, and then she showed him the bloody prints from the ER.

"Wow," Lon said. "Who do those belong to?"

"Moses Gatlin," Hope said. "As you know, their place isn't all that far from ours. And it's even closer to Mr. Bailey's place where the rustlers gained entrance to our place. I know it could be a coincidence, but—"

"You did the right thing," Lon said. "If you'll send those photos to my phone, I'll take it from here, and you won't have to be further involved."

He waited for them to show up on his phone. As soon as they did, he gave her arm a quick pat.

"You're off the hook now, sister. We don't need you or baby getting any deeper into this mess."

Hope hugged him. "Thank you. You're the best brother-in-law ever," she said, and ducked back inside.

Lon made a quick call back to dispatch.

"I'm gonna need some backup at the Emergency Room, and tell them to hurry."

Moses was focused on Dr. Quick's instructions for how to take care of the wound and when to change the dressings when there was a commotion at the door, and then Chief Pittman and two officers walked in.

"Dr. Quick, I'm going to ask you and Rhonda to step out of the room now," he said.

Quick blinked. "I'm just finishing up. If "

"Is his life in danger?" Lon asked.

"No, sir. He's good to go. I was just giving instructions."

"Then I'm going to ask you both to step out."

Quick glanced at the men, wondering what they'd done, but he didn't hesitate. He took his nurse's arm and escorted her out.

Both brothers were in shock.

"Get some pictures of those," Lon said, pointing to the telltale prints in the blood. He wanted his own photo proof of the scene, too.

Deputy Ralph quickly obeyed.

"What's going on?" Moses asked. "If you think this injury had to do with a fight or something, then, no sir, it did not. He cut his leg with a scythe while he was cleaning up the yard."

"It's not about his leg," Lon said. "Whose footprints are those?" he asked, pointing.

Moses turned. "Why, I guess those are mine."

Lon pulled up the photos from the site of the rustling that Hope had just sent.

"Do you recognize these prints?" he asked.

Moses stared down at the mud and the grass and the clear boot print in the mud that matched the one in the blood, and all of a sudden his heart skipped a beat.

"How about this picture?" Lon asked, and flipped to a broader scene showing the empty cattle cube sacks and the cut fence wires.

Moses looked. His mind was spinning. There were a thousand things he could think to say, but he couldn't get them said. He'd known. In the back of his mind, he'd known the risks the day he took the money from the sale of the first steer.

"What the hell are y'all carryin' on about? Let me see!" J.B. cried.

Lon held out the photo of the bloody boot print, and then showed him the same print in the mud and then the scene at the fence.

All the color in J.B. Gatlin's face went south. His eyes rolled back in his head and he fainted.

Moses shrieked, "Doctor! Doctor! Come quick!"

Dr. Quick dashed back into the room, saw his patient, and glared at the chief.

"What did you do to him?" he cried.

"Showed him a couple of pictures that linked them to some cattle rustling. I'd guess he fainted."

Quick checked J.B.'s vitals, then sighed. "Yes, he's fine. Sorry for shouting. Proceed as you will," he muttered.

Lon looked at Moses.

"Anything you want to say to me now?"

Moses shuddered. "We did it. We weren't raised this way and I knew it was wrong, and we did it anyway. I'm sorry. If I could take it back, I would, but it's done."

"Turn around, and put your hands behind your back," Lon said. "Moses Gatlin, I'm arresting you for—"

At that point, all sound faded as Moses turned. He felt the cold steel of the handcuffs around his wrists, and then dropped his head. The possibility of frozen pipes in the trailer had just become the least of their worries.

By the time J.B. came to, Moses was already at the jail being processed. Lon and the other officer transported J. B., booked him, and put him in the cell next to his brother.

"What's gonna happen to us?" J.B. asked as Deputy Ralph closed the cell door behind him.

"County has the case. Sheriff Ryman will transport you both to the county jail, and you'll go from there. Sorry you boys took this route in life. I have to say, it sure did surprise me," Ralph said.

Moses ducked his head.

J.B. just looked away.

As their mama used to say…what's done is done.

———————————

Jack was a slightly shorter, stockier version of his big brother, Duke, but when it came to taking care of family, they were just alike.

He tried to call Duke after Hope called him, but it went to voicemail, so he just sent her the pictures she'd requested, left Duke a message, and took off into Blessings to make sure Hope was okay and the rustlers were behind bars.

Finding out the rustlers' identities had been shocking. Jack had gone to school with J.B. Gatlin. He and his brother had never been anything but law-abiding people, but Jack had heard they'd fallen on hard times after their mother, Beulah, died. It appeared they'd taken the easy way out to recoup their losses.

The ER was busy by the time he arrived, so Jack didn't do much more than check Hope out, give her a hug, and praise her for being so observant.

"You get off work at 4:00 p.m., right?" he asked.

"Yes. Shift will change at three, but it'll take every bit of an hour before I can get away from here," Hope said.

"So how about I pick up something for dinner and take it home. We have all kinds of stuff to make side dishes. I just thought it would save a lot of fuss and mess if we weren't cooking some kind of meat. Does anything sound good to you?"

Hope laughed. "Everything sounds good. I'm going to have to be careful and not eat my way through the next seven months. I know...get some ribs from Granny's, and if there's any of Mercy's chocolate pie left, bring me a piece."

"Will do," Jack said, then gave her a quick kiss and left.

Hope sighed as she watched him go. "Best husband ever," she muttered, and then went back to work.

———————————————

By nightfall, Hope Talbot was the talk of the town, and as it always was with gossip in Blessings, the story had morphed from Hope seeing the bloody boot prints and putting two and two together to being the one who'd put the cuffs on Moses Gatlin herself.

When Duke finally realized Jack had left him a voicemail, he listened to it on his way back home and was shocked by what he heard, but even more so at learning the identity of the men who'd stolen their cattle. Like Jack, it sickened him to think it had been their own neighbors who'd done it.

When he finally reached the house, he parked at the back entrance as he always did, then sat for a few moments, contemplating the facts of what he was about to do.

He had never lived anywhere else in his life but on this property, in this house, and he felt a twinge of sadness that things were going to change.

But he wouldn't deny for a moment that this change was all for the better. On a phone call to Rhonda Bailey earlier, she had confirmed that they were already thinking of putting their old place up for sale, and they would certainly give him the first option. They were having the property appraised, and once they did, they would let Duke know what the family wanted to ask for the property.

He'd asked permission to go through it, and she told him where they'd hidden the key. That's where he'd been when Jack was trying to call him—walking through the rooms and checking out the structure and the floors and the roof.

The bones of the old house were sound, and most everything inside was in good to decent condition, but it was all out of date and needed remodeling. If everything went as planned, he was going to make Rhonda Bailey a fair offer on behalf of her father, and he was guessing they would gladly accept it. Her father's nursing-home care was costly.

Finally, Duke got out of the truck and went inside. He was thinking about what kind of meat to take out of the freezer to make for their supper when Jack got home. When he saw Jack carrying in a sack from Granny's Country Kitchen, and then he smelled the aroma, he smiled.

"I see you cooked supper tonight, via Granny's," Duke said.

"Hope wanted ribs from Granny's and a piece of Mercy's chocolate pie," Jack said.

"So do I. I hope you brought enough for all of us," Duke said.

Jack laughed. "You know I did, so stop worrying. Hope should be here around four thirty or so. I'm going to put the ribs in the warming oven and the pie in the fridge."

"Sorry I didn't get your call earlier," Duke said, as Jack began putting away the food.

"Yeah, where were you?" Jack asked.

"Over at the old Bailey place. I'd already walked the land, and I wanted to go through the house, too. Rhonda said the family is going to put the house up for sale, and I think I'm going to make an offer. The house is amazing, but it needs some TLC for sure," Duke said.

Jack frowned. "It needs more than tender loving care. It needs an overhaul. Are you sure you want to redo an old one instead of building something new?"

Duke nodded. "Yeah. You know me. I like vintage way better than modern."

"You like a little redhead, too, don't you?" Jack asked.

"Maybe, but I'm not discussing her," Duke said.

Jack grinned. "Dammit. I never thought I'd see the day, but I do believe you are finally falling for a girl."

"She's no girl. She's a woman…a beautiful woman," Duke said.

Jack grinned again. "I stand corrected."

Rand Lawrence was working from home today, running searches on Cathy Terry. His soon-to-be wife, Kellie Steele, was making cookies. He could smell them from his office. Kellie was used to his lifestyle and the times he was on stakeout. It was part of his job. But she didn't like that he was working for Blaine Wagner. She hadn't said so, but he could tell how she shut down every time Blaine called him.

She used to work as a hostess at The Still, a restaurant in the Mirage, and she'd told him how Wagner, who was still married, always hit on the pretty young women who worked there.

When Kellie came into his office carrying a plate of warm oatmeal cookies, he groaned.

"Honey, those smell amazing. You're so good to me," he said, and hugged her around the waist as he grabbed a cookie and took a big bite. "And they're delicious. Thank you."

She smiled as she ran her fingers through his hair, then began massaging the back of his neck.

"Oooh, that feels as good as these cookies taste," Rand said.

"You've been in here for hours. I figured the muscles were tight. What are you doing?" she asked.

"Running a couple of searches for a client."

"Who's the client?" she asked.

He sighed. "Blaine Wagner. He's trying to locate his ex-wife."

Kellie frowned. "But you said she left Vegas. Why does he care where she went? They're divorced."

Rand shrugged. "I have no idea," he said, and put the last half of the cookie in his mouth and went back to work.

"Do you want something to drink?" Kellie asked.

"Maybe a refill on my coffee?"

She gave his shoulders one last squeeze and then picked up his empty cup. "I'll be right back."

Rand glanced back at the screen, then rolled his eyes. There were so damn many females with the name Cathy Terry that there was no way he was ever going to find her.

He knew she had a new driver's license. He'd verified that with the Nevada DMV, but she'd left her Lexus in the parking garage at her Las Vegas apartment. There was no record of her registering a car title for a new car. No record of her leasing a car, and there were a million places to rent that would never run background checks on anyone. She could be anywhere—even out of the country with a fake passport and a fake name, for all he knew—and he wasn't into hacking into government databases. He did have her social security number, which would not change, despite whatever name change went with it.

The fact that she'd gotten thirty million dollars in the divorce settlement was probably a factor in her not trying to find a job, which would have ultimately revealed her location when her paychecks were issued. He had to give it to her. Cathy Terry sure knew how to disappear.

CHAPTER 9

CATHY WAS AT PEACE WITH HERSELF FOR THE FIRST time in years. She didn't have to pretend she knew nothing about Blaine's other women. She didn't have to pretend to their social circle that everything was wonderful about being married to one of the wealthiest men in Nevada. And hopefully, she'd gotten far enough away to be safe from his threats.

Renting the car shifted her perception of being powerless, too. Even as she was making herself some supper, she was planning a shopping trip to Savannah tomorrow. She needed clothes and shoes. The little boutique in Blessings was great for a special-occasion outfit, but she needed to replace a wardrobe, and that meant hitting a mall somewhere.

She also needed a good basic cookbook. She knew how to cook, but she didn't remember the ingredients that went into all of the recipes from when she and her mother were together. And after she married, the chef and the servants had done everything for them. She'd lost herself in that world and forgotten who Mary Cathleen Terry had been and everything her daddy had taught her. But it was all coming back. She was reclaiming her sovereignty, and it felt good. What she wasn't ready to do was reconnect herself to the World Wide Web and negate everything she'd done to disappear.

So, without the cookbook, she'd settled for a molasses

cookie mix—one of the add-egg-and-milk-and-stir mixes. But the scent of cookies baking was amazing, and if they tasted half as good as they smelled, she was in for a treat.

She was taking the pan of cookies out of the oven when her phone rang. She set them aside, turned off the oven, and then ran to answer.

"Hello!"

"Hi, honey. Just wanted to touch base with you before the day was over."

"Duke! Your timing is great, but you're in the wrong place. I just took molasses cookies out of the oven."

Duke could hear the smile in her voice and wished he was there. "You are such a tease. Have you had a good day?"

"Yes, it was great! I rented a car, and for the first time since I came here, I stocked up on more than just basic groceries."

"Now you're mobile. That's great! Oh…I don't know if you heard the news or not, but Hope found our cattle rustlers. They came into the ER today. She recognized one of them had the same cut in the heel of his boot that they'd found at the scene of the crime, and called Chief Pittman. Both men confessed and they're in jail."

"Oh my gosh! No! I hadn't heard. It's good to know who they are and get them locked up so it doesn't happen again, but it doesn't bring your cattle back."

"No, they're gone."

"Did you know the men who did it?" she asked.

"Well, everybody knows everybody around here, so yes, we knew them, but the rub was they were our neighbors. Jack even went to school with one of them."

"What a shame," Cathy said. "I'm assuming there was no violence or danger to Hope?"

"No danger at all. Once she called Lon, she was out of the picture." There was a brief moment of silence between them, and then Duke asked, "What's on your agenda for tomorrow?"

"I'm going to Savannah. I need clothes and shoes. All I own is what I was packing on my back. And I'm going to look at cars, too, if I have time. If I do decide to buy one in the next few days, I'll need a ride to Savannah to pick it up. I can always get an Uber out of Savannah to come get me, but you told me to ask, so—"

"You absolutely do not hire someone to come get you and take you to Savannah. I'll take you, gladly."

Cathy smiled to herself. "Okay. Just checking," she said, and then put the phone on speaker and began taking the cookies off the baking sheet and putting them on a plate.

"I'm coming to the bank day after tomorrow. If you're not going to be busy, I'd love to take you out for dinner at noon."

"I accept," Cathy said.

"Granny's okay?"

"Granny's is perfect," Cathy said. "I'll be here. Come by when you've finished with your business. You don't need to call first."

"I'll see you then. Save me some of those cookies," he added.

"I will," Cathy said, and then sighed as the connection was broken. She could listen to that deep, raspy voice all day, but for now she'd settle for phone calls and lunch.

———————————

Cathy left for Savannah just before 9:00 a.m. the next morning. It was a beautiful fall day and the Thanksgiving dinner she'd been invited to was now only four days away. A perfect time to be out and about, and she made the drive to Savannah in a little over an hour.

She'd done a little research last night on her phone, checking out mall locations and car dealerships, and had decided to do the shopping first and a quick reconnoiter of the dealerships last—just to get an idea of the models that appealed to her.

Her timing was perfect as she arrived at the Savannah Mall on Abercorn Street. It was just after 10:00 a.m. and the mall had just opened, so parking was not an issue. She picked a spot closest to one of the entrances and got out, locked the Jeep, then dropped her keys in a small fanny pack she was wearing—which was a good reminder to add buying a purse to the list of things to purchase—and headed inside.

She found one of the mall maps just inside the entrance to check out locations of different stores. She'd been quite the shopper in Vegas, but her lifestyle had demanded it.

Today was different. Cathy bypassed all of the high-end shops and headed to a Dillard's to buy pants and tops. Once she tried on a brand and a size, she began choosing outfits from the selections. She bought some that came as a set, and some that were all mix and match. Her arms were already full of purchases, and she hadn't even begun to look at a few dressier outfits or lingerie, so she made a quick trip out to her car, noticing that the parking lot was filling up fast.

She dumped her bags in the back, locked the car, and headed back inside. This time she went to jeans, long-sleeved knit tops, and a couple of sweatpant outfits before moving to the socks and underwear area.

Once again, her arms were full, and she was on her way out to unload when a woman came hurrying out of a side aisle and almost knocked her down.

"Oh, I'm so sorry!" the woman cried. "I wasn't looking where I was... Oh my God, Cathy Wagner!"

Cathy stared in disbelief. Pamela St. James! Her husband did business with Blaine. She'd been to their parties in Vegas. What the hell was she doing in Savannah? And why had fate seen fit that they must meet like this when Cathy had gone to all this trouble to disappear?

"I'm not Cathy Wagner," she said.

Pamela grabbed her by the arm. "Yes, you are! You disappeared from Vegas. We all wondered what happened to you."

"Let go of my arm."

Pamela was so shocked by the hard edge and aggressive tone in Cathy's voice that she not only turned her loose, but stepped back.

"I am not Cathy Wagner anymore. I'm Cathy Terry, and I didn't disappear. I left. And what was it to you? You conveniently forgot to be a friend when I was no longer the key to your invitations to the famous Wagner parties."

Pamela's face turned a bright shade of pink. Truth hurt, and without the circle of friends she ran with to back her up, she wasn't as willing to challenge this woman as she'd been back in Vegas.

"It wasn't like that," she muttered.

"Yes, it was like that," Cathy said.

Pamela quickly shifted the conversation. "Do you live here now?"

"You think I'm going to tell you my business? I came to the other side of the country to get away from all of you."

Pamela persisted in spite of Cathy's very blatant rejection.

"I'm here because my grandmother died. Her services are tomorrow. I thought I'd pick up a little something to wear to—"

"My sympathies to your family," Cathy said, and went out the door. She left her packages in the car and went back in another entrance to get shoes.

She didn't know or care if Pamela was watching or following her, but she wasn't going to panic and run. Not anymore.

Pamela had been watching, and when Cathy went back inside the mall, she ran outside to Cathy's car and took a picture of the car and the license tag, and then headed for her mama's Lincoln that she'd borrowed to go shopping. Once inside, she pulled up the Houseparty app on her phone, and as her friends began joining her, she happily spread the news.

Before long, all of Cathy's old inner circle of friends knew where she'd gone, and as Pamela put it, "how shabbily she'd been dressed." Since all of them were well aware of the huge settlement Cathy had gotten in the divorce, they knew how she dressed had nothing to do with a lack of money.

"Maybe she just went back to her roots," Pamela said in a catty little tone, which made all of the girls shriek with laughter.

"Her mother worked in a casino, remember?" one of them said.

"Well, so did she!" Pamela said. "That's where Blaine

met her. It's no wonder their marriage didn't last. He married beneath himself."

"She is really pretty," one of the girls said.

"Pretty girls in Vegas are as plentiful as the sand on which the city was built," Pamela snapped. "Anyway, I solved the mystery. Now we know where she went."

"I wonder if Blaine knows?" another woman asked.

"Why would he care?" Pamela asked.

And then one small voice in the crowd said, "I don't know, but I heard he had someone watching her the whole time she was still in town. That would freak me out. I don't blame her for leaving."

It was like throwing ice water on a pair of fighting tomcats. The hush that followed was obvious, and then one by one, they each began to sign off until Pamela was alone. She saw a text from her mother and sighed. Time to get back to family duties. The sooner they buried Mamaw, the quicker she could get home to Vegas.

It took exactly two hours from the time Pamela initiated the Houseparty chat with her friends to Blaine's phone ringing as he was on his way to lunch. It was one of his golfing buddies, and he smiled as he answered.

"Hello, Donny, are you ready for me to whip your ass on the back nine again?"

Donny Burton laughed. "No, and I was just having a bad day...but I have a little news I thought you might find interesting."

"What's that?" Blaine asked.

"I know where your ex went."

The skin crawled on the back of Blaine's neck, and then he smiled. He'd been thinking about letting all this go, but this was a sign.

"And you know this, how?" he asked.

"Pamela St. James's grandmother passed, and she went back to Savannah for the services. She ran into Cathy at a local mall. Pamela doesn't know where she lives exactly, but she was buying lots of clothes and driving a rental car. I think my wife said Pamela even took pictures of the rental and the tag. I guess she thought she was really playing detective, right?"

"Savannah, Georgia. Interesting," Blaine said. "Give me a call when you're ready for another game of golf, my friend."

"Will do," Danny said, and disconnected.

The moment he was off the phone, Blaine called Rand Lawrence.

Rand answered on the second ring.

"Hello. This is Rand."

"It's me," Blaine said. "I have a big lead on Cathy. Pamela St. James saw her in Savannah, Georgia, in a mall. She has to be using credit cards. And contact Pamela. I was told she took pictures of the tag and the car Cathy is driving. I want a firm location. Even if you have to go there to find her, do it."

Blaine hung up in his ear without giving Rand time to respond.

"Dammit," Rand muttered.

Kellie was making them sandwiches for lunch when the call came in, and when she saw the look on Rand's face as he listened, she stopped, waiting for him to hang up.

"What's wrong?" she asked.

"That was Wagner again. He has a big lead on his ex's whereabouts and wants me to chase her down...even go to Georgia to do it."

Kellie stopped, her eyes narrowing angrily.

"I've just about had enough of this. I don't care how much money he's paying you to hound this poor woman. She's no longer his business, and what he's doing is stalking her. There are laws against this, and you're going to wind up in jail doing his dirty work. I'd like to think you have enough honor and decency to tell him no, but I'm about to give you some incentive. If you continue on this case for Wagner, I'm feeling the need to reconsider what kind of man I thought you were. You may not be the right man for me after all. It's one thing to go on stakeouts to get information, but this is way beyond good sense, Rand."

Then she put his sandwich down in front of him and walked out of the room.

Rand was speechless. He'd never seen this coming and at first was upset. But the more he thought about it, the more he realized she was right. He got up and followed her into the bedroom.

"I'm taking the file I've accumulated on her to his office and telling him I quit. No amount of money is worth losing you, and you're right. Cathy Terry deserves to be left alone."

"Thank God," Kellie said, and hugged him.

Rand sent Blaine a text.

I need to speak to you in person. Name a time and place.

Then Rand and Kellie sat down and ate lunch together without mentioning another word about Wagner or his ex.

Blaine received the text during lunch and frowned. He did not like the tone of it, and ignored it. Saving it for later.

It wasn't until midafternoon when he was on his way back to the office that he responded.

> On the way back to the office. I have an hour before my next appointment. The time is yours.

Kellie was out with a friend, and Rand was working in his office when he finally got the response from Wagner. He had the file ready to go, so he grabbed his car keys on the way out of the apartment and took back streets to get to Wagner's office.

He parked and hurried into the building, then up the elevator, thinking he was actually glad to be rid of Wagner and his continuing demands for revenge.

"Mr. Wagner is expecting me," he said, as he entered.

The woman behind the desk buzzed her boss. "Mr. Lawrence is here."

"Send him in," Blaine said, and rather than giving Rand the courtesy of standing to greet him, he remained seated behind the desk.

Rand entered, nodded briefly, and then sat down without an invitation and slid the file across the desk.

"This is everything I've accumulated regarding your ex-wife. I respectfully decline to continue working on this."

Blaine's mouth opened, but he was so surprised that it took him a few moments to react. When he did, it was with anger.

"What the hell are you talking about? You don't quit me! I demand to know what's going on."

Rand sighed. He hadn't expected this to be easy, and he'd been right.

"I'm just not comfortable doing this anymore. It comes too close to stalking for me."

Now Blaine was up and leaning across his desk, his face contorted in rage.

"Nobody quits me. I'm the one who says when you can go."

Rand shuddered. All of a sudden he was realizing how truly unhinged Wagner was, and how desperate Cathy Terry must have been to feel the need to disappear to get her life back.

"I can't do this anymore. I'm sorry," Rand said.

Blaine glared. "I can ruin you, you know. I can make sure you never get another job here as long as you live."

Rand stood, staring back. "You aren't the only one with cachet in this world. Private investigators have their own brotherhood. We don't infringe on each other's cases, and when the need arises, we have each other's backs. Big time. You threaten me, and you threaten all of them. Do that and there won't be another PI in Nevada who will work for you. It might be time for you to go have it out once and for all with your ex and get on with your life. And don't call me again. Ever. I don't work for people I can't trust."

Then he turned and walked out of the office without looking back.

Blaine was furious, but the warning was real and he knew it. He couldn't make enemies of men he depended on for information, so he called another PI and put him on the case, asking only for a specific location where she could be found.

———————————

After buying the shoes she needed, Cathy was out of the mood to car shop and headed for home, far less happy than when she'd left Blessings. Seeing Pamela had just burst the bubble in which she'd been living. She didn't know what the consequences of that chance meeting might be, but she knew that world. Someone would tell Blaine. And all of this was for nothing. Now she had to hope he would just let it go.

When she got back into Blessings, she thought about stopping at the Curl Up and Dye to make an appointment for tomorrow to get her hair layered and trimmed. She had new clothes, and with Thanksgiving becoming an imminent event, she wanted to look her best for her first-ever dinner party in Blessings, but then she changed her mind and went home instead.

CHAPTER 10

DUKE HAD BEEN IN THE OFFICE ALL MORNING AND HAD just finished paying invoices and posting to their farm account. He got up to take his empty coffee cup to the kitchen, and as he did, suddenly thought of the trail cameras he'd put up. Since the rustlers had been caught, he might as well take them down.

He went out to the barn to get their old farm truck and stopped by the shop where Jack was working on the engine of their dad's old Ford tractor.

"Hey Jack, since the Gatlins are in jail, I'm going to bring in the trail cams. I won't be gone long."

Jack nodded without looking up.

Duke loved this time of year. The leaves on the trees were as varied and colorful as the old patchwork quilts they'd slept under as children. And the sky today was a clear, cloudless blue—the same color as Cathy's eyes.

The cows saw him driving across the pasture and looked up, hoping to see he was slowing down, which meant they would get fed. But when he kept driving, some moved beneath a small stand of shade trees, while others moved to the feeders with the big, round bales.

Duke had put up the cameras within a couple of hundred yards' radius and facing the direction where the rustlers had come in before.

He walked a few yards into the trees to pick up the first cam and took it down. Out of curiosity, he stopped and rewound it to watch some of the footage and grinned at the view he'd caught of the backside of a boar raccoon waddling through the woods. He fast-forwarded through the minutes with nothing, then watched the footage of two black squirrels foraging on the ground.

There was more to be seen, but he could watch it at home if he wanted, so he packed it up, then started walking through the trees to the next location, where he retrieved the cam and put it in his backpack before moving on to the last.

As Duke approached the tree where he'd mounted it, he noticed a lot of paw prints in the area. They were from either dogs or coyotes, and if there was a pack of dogs running in the area, he wanted to play the tape back to see.

He was all the way on yesterday's footage before he saw the coyote, and then it turned to face the camera. Duke gasped, watching as the coyote started staggering toward the camera, its head down, swinging slightly from side to side and foaming at the mouth. At that point he groaned, then stopped the camera.

The hair stood up on the back of his neck as he looked around at where he was standing. He'd only seen an animal with rabies maybe twice in his life, but the coyote he caught on the trail cam exhibited all of the symptoms.

They had to find it and put it down before it spread the disease to other animals. Something like that could easily become an epidemic. He needed to get home and call the county wildlife department and then notify the neighbors.

Duke drove home as fast as he could, then ran into

the house carrying the cameras. He dumped them on the kitchen table and headed for the office. He had a friend who used to work for the county wildlife department and would know what to do and who to call.

He sat down without bothering to take off his jacket, found the number on an old business card, and made the call, then waited for someone to answer. This was the last number he'd had for Will, and he hoped it was still good.

And then the call was answered.

"Wildlife Animal Control, this is Carol."

"Yes, ma'am. I'm trying to locate a ranger by the name of Will Polson. Does he still work there?"

"Yes, who's calling please?"

"Tell him it's Duke Talbot."

Duke was put on hold, giving him time to put his cell phone on speaker. And then he heard a familiar voice and smiled.

"Well, hello, Duke Talbot! How the heck are you? Are you still out on the family farm?"

"Hi, Will. We're doing good here, and yes, I'm still here. Listen, we have a problem out here. We had some trouble with cattle rustlers on the farm, so I put up some trail cams in the area, hoping if they came back I'd catch them. But they recently got themselves arrested. Today I went to take down the cameras and had quite a shock when I saw what was on the last one. It was a very obviously rabid coyote, and the last thing we need to have happen is to let this disease spread. There are a lot of farms around here, and people with kids and pets who roam the hills and creeks, not to mention the other wildlife that could get infected."

"Oh man, this isn't good. We haven't had to deal with a

rabies case in months," Will said. "What were the date and time when you caught it on film?"

"Yesterday about this time of day," Duke said.

"There's no telling where it is by now, but I'll get a crew together and head your way. You might notify as many neighbors as you can about the problem. Tell them to keep their dogs up until we find it. You said you're still on the family farm?"

"Yes. Do you need an address?"

"Nope. I still remember how to get there. Can we drive up to the area?" he asked.

"Yes. To a point, and then the trees will be too dense. It will all be on foot from there."

Jack came in the back door, greasy and muttering beneath his breath as Duke walked into the kitchen from the hall.

"What's wrong?" Duke asked.

"Oh, that damned old engine. I need a part but it might not be so easy to find. The older stuff gets, the harder it is to find ways to repair it." Then he saw the trail cams. "So, find anything interesting on them?" he asked.

"Check this out," Duke said, and played the footage for his brother. When the coyote suddenly appeared on the screen, Jack jumped.

"Oh shit! Are you kidding me? Is that thing rabid?"

"Looks like it to me," Duke said.

"What are we going to do?" Jack asked, thinking of all the livestock.

"I've already called Wildlife Animal Control. Remember Will Polson? My old college buddy?"

Jack nodded.

"He's still a ranger there, and he's going to get a crew together and head this way."

"What if you can't find it?" Jack asked.

Duke shrugged. "We'll figure that out as we go. Right now I've got to start calling neighbors."

He took a bottle of Coke from the refrigerator, then went into the living room to start making calls, but he wanted to check on Cathy before they got too involved in this hunt.

He called her number, then counted the rings. He was guessing he was going to have to leave a voicemail when she answered, and she sounded breathless.

"Hello?"

"Hey, honey, did I disturb you?"

She laughed. "No. I just couldn't find my phone."

"Are you back from Savannah?"

"Yes."

"How did it go?" he asked, and then heard her sigh.

"Oh, the shopping went great. I just had the misfortune to run into a woman who used to be one of the 'friends' I hung out with in Vegas. I couldn't believe it when I saw her, so I guess my general location is no longer a secret."

Duke frowned. "Are you worried?"

"No. Maybe…at least a little, and mad that it happened," she said. "But enough about me. What's going on at the farm?"

"Well, that's why I called. I had trail cams up because of the rustling, but now that the men were arrested, I went to take them down and saw a rabid coyote on one of the cameras."

Cathy gasped. "Oh no! What are you going to do?"

"I called the county wildlife department, and they're on

the way to see if we can track it and put it down. I'm just hoping we get to it before rabies spreads throughout the area. I have to start calling neighbors, but I wanted to check in with you first. There's no telling how long we'll be involved with this."

"Is there anything I can do to help? I am a good shot and a better tracker."

Duke was stunned. She'd just offered to join a hunt for a dangerous animal without a hint of anxiety.

"That is probably one of the more amazing offers I've ever had in my life, but no way do I want you out there and in danger in any way."

"I tracked a rabid wolf with Daddy when I was ten. It came into our camp and killed one of Mother's milk goats. I wasn't scared. I was mad because our goat was dead."

"Just the same, I'm not taking you to the woods to chase a rabid coyote. I'll see you tomorrow at lunch."

The thought of seeing him again made her happy. "What time?"

Duke laughed. "How about I come by your house and pick you up about eleven thirty?"

"That would be awesome. I'll see you then," she said, and disconnected.

Meanwhile, Duke began making calls and then asking neighbors to call their neighbors to tell them what was happening. The men who were home immediately volunteered to join in the hunt, and within the next fifteen to thirty minutes, they began arriving at the farm.

By the time the crew from Wildlife Animal Control arrived, there were ten men, including Duke and Jack, waiting to join the hunt, all of them armed with hunting rifles of one kind or another.

The rangers and trackers got out, and Duke made the introductions.

"So, do you still want to start where I caught it on the trail cam?" Duke asked.

"Yes," Will said.

"We have to open and close two gates to get there, so load up and follow Jack and me. We'll open the gates. Whoever is in the back vehicle has to be the one to close them, okay?"

One of their neighbors raised a hand.

"We'll do it, Duke. Lead the way."

Will loaded his crew back up in their van and followed Duke, past their outbuildings, then past the barn and corrals to the gate into the first pasture.

Jack jumped out to open it, then got back in the truck with his brother.

"We've got something of a convoy," he said.

His brother glanced up in the rearview mirror and nodded, and kept driving. Jack got the next gate, and then they were headed through to the trees where the trail cams had been mounted.

Duke drove as close as he could get before he stopped, then he and Jack got out.

He got his hunting rifle from behind the seat, checked to make sure it was loaded, and then pocketed more ammo while waiting for all of the trackers to arrive.

As soon as they were all out of their vehicles, Will brought the three trackers and their hounds to where Duke was waiting.

"If you'll show us where that trail cam was, we'll see if we can pick up a trail from there."

"Will your dogs be okay doing this?" Duke asked.

One of the trackers nodded. "Yes, sir. They've all had their rabies shots."

"Okay, then, follow me," Duke said, and led the way through the trees. It took about ten minutes to reach the last location, and then he stopped a ways back so as not to disturb the site and pointed. "It was on that skinny pine. See where the ground has been disturbed in that little clearing?"

"Yes, yes, I see," Will said. "Okay, everybody. Just stop here a bit and let us see if the dogs can pick up any kind of scent. If they do, then fan out in a line and move forward. I want to make sure we don't have anyone with a loaded gun walking behind someone else."

"Got it," Jack said. "We're just here until you tell us to do different."

Will nodded, and then waved to his men. "Put them to work, boys."

The trackers led the dogs to the site, keying them onto the scents around the visible coyote tracks, and then set them to hunt.

The dogs whined and then took off through the trees, moving at a fast clip in silence. It wasn't until the first one let out a yip that they knew it had picked up a trail.

"That's it," Will said. "Let's do this."

Duke was at the far end of the line and moving forward with the men spaced out about twenty yards apart. Jack was on his right and within Duke's sight. They could hear the dogs' occasional yips, which meant they were still following a trail.

The first hour came and went before the men began to realize they were less than three miles away from Blessings, and the dogs were moving parallel to the creek that ran through the city park and behind the trailer park in town.

Duke's first thought was of all the people who could be in danger and didn't even know it. But Will was on the opposite end of their line of searchers, so Duke called him.

Will had his phone on vibrate, and when he saw caller ID, he quickly answered.

"What's up, Duke? Did you see something?" he asked.

"No. It's not that," Duke said. "But my best guess is that we're less than three miles from town, and this creek we're following goes straight through the trailer park on the outskirts of town, and through the city park as well. I'd like to think that coyote crawled off somewhere and died, but your dogs keep tracking, which tells me wherever it is, it's somewhere up ahead. I think the PD needs to be notified, Will. My brother-in-law is the chief of police. I'm going to text you the number to the PD."

"Oh hell. I didn't realize we were that close," Will said. "Yes, send the number. I'll give him a call."

Chief Pittman was on patrol when his radio squawked, and then he heard Avery requesting his presence at the PD. He radioed in and headed that way, wondering what was going on, and then parked behind the building and came in through the back and up the hall to the front desk. The fact that the place was empty except for Avery was puzzling.

"What's going on? From the tone of your voice, I thought I'd be walking into trouble."

"We just got a call from a ranger with the wildlife department. His name is Will Polson, and he has a search party on the trail of a rabid coyote. He said they're less than three miles from town and the dogs are still tracking."

"Oh no," Lon muttered. The ramifications of this were huge. "I wonder how they even learned about the coyote."

"That's the rest of the story," Avery said. "Duke had trail cams up after the rustling incident, and when he took them down earlier today, he had footage of a rabid coyote, so he called it in. Bad part is that the timeline on the footage was from yesterday so there was no way to tell where the animal is now. So they brought dogs and trackers, and they've been on the trail for more than an hour. They're still tracking it on a route that runs parallel to the creek that goes through Blessings. Given the twenty-four hour lead the coyote has on them, they're worried the animal might be holed up sick and dying somewhere in town or be still mobile."

"This is not good news," Lon said. He took off his hat and combed his fingers through his hair. "Call in the two officers who are on patrol, and then call everyone who's off duty and tell them to come to the PD. We need to figure out how we're going to deal with this."

"Yes, sir," Avery said, and reached for the phone while Lon went back to his office.

Cathy wanted to get out of the house for a bit. She didn't really want to go for a drive, because she'd already done that, but she had a nice little gazebo out in the backyard that she'd never used, and she thought about checking it out.

So she put on a lightweight jacket before going outside, and once she got beneath the roof of the gazebo, she could tell by the looks of it that it had been here for years.

The floor of it was littered with dry leaves and a healthy layer of dust. The seating within it looked rough. It needed more than a dust cloth to get back in shape, but with some repairs to the inner circle of benches built into it, it would be an awesome place to sit. All in all, it looked sound, just in need of a cleanup and some paint.

Now that she had a project to consider, Cathy wanted to begin so she went back into the house to get a garbage bag and a broom. She was coming back out of the house with her hands full when she thought she heard someone scream.

She stopped—listening.

Then she heard it again—and this time the sounds of more than one person screaming—and froze. That wasn't the sound of children playing, and it wasn't a scream of anger between two people. That was terror, and they were screaming for help.

Her first instinct was to run to their aid, but with no way of knowing what she'd be running into, she went back into the house for her handgun, checked to make sure it was loaded, then put it into the inner pocket of her jacket and took off out of the house.

The screams were coming from behind her house, and without a fence around the yard, she darted straight up an alley and kept running. Now she could hear more people screaming and shouting, and they all sounded like women and children.

Her mind was racing, trying to imagine what could

possibly be happening, as she came out of that alley, then darted across the street into the next alley, and then the next and then the next, until she came out facing the park.

That's why she was hearing so many voices. Something was happening at the park. Something bad. She thought she could hear sirens now, but they were a distance away.

Cathy dashed across the street and into the park, and within seconds saw a half-dozen women running toward her. Some were carrying children, and others were holding their children's hands as they ran. She still couldn't see what they were running from, but the terror on their faces was enough to know whatever it was, it was bad.

As she began running toward them, one of the women began waving her away, screaming something she didn't at first understand. But when Cathy got close enough, she realized what the woman was saying.

"Mad dog! Mad dog! Run!"

Cathy's pulse kicked. Could this possibly be the coyote Duke and the rangers were searching for? She paused as the women and children ran past her, and then when she saw nothing, she kept running.

A coyote appeared less than thirty yards away, staggering and trembling, with foam dripping from its mouth. Cathy had a moment of déjà vu, then pulled her gun and fired.

The coyote dropped.

Cathy moved a few steps closer to make sure it was down, the gun still in her hands. Only she needn't have worried. The time she'd spent at the shooting ranges in Vegas had kept her skill as a marksman honed. She'd put a bullet in its head.

She had left the house without her phone, so she had

no way of calling for help, but as it turned out, that didn't matter. The sirens were louder now.

She moved back from the dead animal and was putting the gun back on safety just as the first police cars arrived on the scene.

Two officers bailed out of the cars and came running across the park with their guns drawn. And then they saw the animal lying dead and the new little redhead in town standing nearby holding a gun.

Deputy Ralph was the first to reach her.

"Ma'am, are you all right?" he asked.

Cathy nodded. "I was outside. I heard screaming. Lots of screaming." Then she handed him the gun. "I have a permit. It's at my house."

"Thank you," he said as she handed it over. "Just bring the permit down to the station, and we can release it back to you."

"Yes, I understand."

At that point, another three police cars arrived, and the chief was in one of them. The women and the children met him at the curb, all talking at once and pointing. He looked off across the park and realized the woman they were talking about who'd saved them was Cathy.

He knew from hearing Mercy and Hope talking that Duke was sweet on her, and he knew Duke was in that search party. He needed to let Ranger Polson know the animal had been taken down, and he needed to let Duke know Cathy had been the one to do it.

But duty called, so he notified Polson first.

Will was focused on the underbrush through which they were walking when his phone vibrated.

"This is Will Polson."

"This is Chief Pittman. Your coyote is down. The carcass is in our city park. How far away are you now?"

"Oh, good news!" Will said. "Hang on a minute. Let me call off the search."

Will pulled his walkie-talkie. "Stand down. Search is over. Our target is down. Call in the dogs and reconnoiter here with me."

The news spread, and a cheer went up. Duke heard the news and sighed with relief. He was tired, and Jack looked exhausted. He thought about the long trek they had to get home, and then headed toward the other end of the line where Ranger Polson was waiting.

Polson got back on the phone. "Thanks. I just needed to call in the dogs and their trackers. So as you were saying... you located it in the park."

"We didn't. A local woman heard screams, got her handgun, and went to see what was happening. The coyote interrupted a children's birthday party. They were running away from it when she appeared on the scene and killed it."

"We'll need to recover the carcass and dispose of it properly," Will said.

"Yes, sir. I have a couple of men guarding it now. If you're not far from town, just keep walking. You should come out somewhere in the trailer park. Get to the entrance, and we'll have rides waiting to take you back to your vehicles."

"Thank you, Chief. That would be much appreciated," Will said. "See you soon."

He disconnected, then sat down on a dead tree and breathed a sigh of relief, waiting for the others to join him.

———————————————

Duke and Jack were talking as they went.

"I'm glad that's over, and I think it's closer to walk into Blessings and hitch a ride home with Hope than it is to walk back home," Jack said.

"Agreed. Give her a call and tell her not to leave town without us," Duke said.

Jack was calling Hope when Duke's phone began to ring. He saw caller ID and smiled as he answered.

"Hey, Lon."

"Hey. I know you're in the search party, so you're going to find this out anyway, but I thought you might like to know that your little redhead is the one who killed the coyote."

Duke almost stumbled. "What? What the hell are you talking about? Is she okay?"

"She's fine. Not sure how she got to the scene of the incident so fast, but there was a birthday party in progress at the park. Some mothers and a bunch of little girls had gathered there after school was out, and just as they were about to blow out the candles and cut the cake, the coyote came out of the bushes down by the creek. They realized it was rabid and started grabbing kids and running. One of the women told me they were screaming for help as they ran, and had been for a couple of minutes, when all of a sudden this woman appeared in the park running toward them. They said they tried to wave her away, warning her they were running from a mad dog, but she ran right past them, and when they turned around to look, they saw her shoot. She took it down with a handgun…in one shot. I don't know where she came from, but she's got country girl written all over her."

"I can't believe this just happened," Duke said. "I told her earlier about what I'd seen on the trail-cam footage, and that we were going after it. Although she's never been to the farm, she offered to help us hunt it down. I told her no way was I taking her anywhere that would put her in danger. Now what are the odds that we would wind up flushing it straight down to her? Or that she would be the one to hear the women and children's cries for help?"

"Well, she did. And she's still here at the park. Where are you?" Lon asked.

"Probably ten minutes or so from the trailer park. Maybe a little more. There's a whole bunch of us who are going to have a long walk back to the farm."

"I told Polson to get his men and dogs to the park. We'll get all of you back to your farm."

"Hope is going to pick us up," Duke said. "But there are a bunch of my neighbors needing rides as well."

"Duly noted. I already told them to wait at the entrance to the park. I'll have rides waiting. Might be some volunteers, but we'll make it work," Lon said.

Once the officers were through talking to Cathy, she started to go back home. But the mothers were still at the curb, waiting for the children's parents to come pick them up. When they saw Cathy coming back their way, they ran to meet her, exclaiming over her bravery and thanking her over and over for saving them.

One mother was in tears. "I'm Phyllis Mays. My daughter, Carrie, is the one who was having the birthday. I was so scared our babies were going to be hurt. Oh my God, I will have nightmares about this forever. I don't even know your name, but I will never forget your bravery. Thank you, thank you so much," she said, and threw her arms around Cathy's neck and hugged her.

"I'm Cathy Terry...kind of a newcomer to Blessings. It was just a fluke I happened to be outside, or I would never have heard the screams."

"Where do you live?" Phyllis asked.

"A couple of blocks off Main."

Phyllis gasped. "But that's at least five blocks from here. How did you get here so fast?"

Cathy shrugged. "I run a lot. Most mornings I run at least three or four miles."

"Well, that's just amazing," Phyllis said. "Oh, there are some more mothers coming to pick up their girls. I have to go."

Cathy watched her leave, and then realized as she was approaching the curb that one of those women was her landlord's wife, Alice. She saw Alice scoop up a little girl into her arms. They talked for a couple of moments, and then the little girl pointed at Cathy.

Cathy waved.

The look on Alice's face was pure shock, and then she put her daughter down and waited for Cathy to approach.

"Hi," Cathy said.

Alice had tears in her eyes. "Sweet lord, Cathy, you saved my baby's life. We almost lost her last year when she fell off a cliff during a school trip, and when I got the call about this incident, I couldn't believe it was happening again. This is my daughter, Patty. Patty, this kind woman who saved your life is my friend Cathy Terry."

Cathy knelt, and then held out her hand. "I am very pleased to meet you, Patty. Your sweet mama came to check on me when I hurt my ankle."

"Thank you for saving us," Patty said, and instead of shaking Cathy's hand, she kissed her cheek.

"I was just in the right place at the right time," Cathy said to Alice. "All's well. Go home and take care of your baby."

Alice hugged her again. "I am your friend for life. Just know that."

At that point, Cathy slipped across the street and disappeared up the alley. She kept thinking about that urge she'd had to get out of the house, even after she'd spent the better part of the day shopping. She should have been resting with her foot up, but she'd had an urge to be outside, and now she knew why.

When she was little, her mama used to tell her how sometimes God used real people to perform miracles for Him. Now she understood what that meant. It was no coincidence that she felt the need to be outside. That was God getting her in the right place at the right time to help.

She took a deep breath, and when she exhaled, it felt as if she'd let go of more than the incident from today. Maybe the last demons from her past were gone, too. She'd never been able to stop the devil she'd lived with, but she'd stopped that coyote, and put an end to the devil it had turned into from the disease.

And so she kept walking, crossing streets into the next

alley, and then the next, until she was walking into her backyard, right past that gazebo and all the way to where she'd dropped the broom and the garbage bag. She picked them up and went inside. Today was not the day to clean the gazebo after all.

———————————————

Hope swung by the trailer park to pick up her boys. That's how she thought of them. Her husband and his brother. She'd taken the both of them on the day she said "I do" and hadn't regretted one moment of it since. She watched them walking toward her and smiled. Duke was at least two inches taller and his hair was darker, but it was easy to see they were brothers.

They looked as tired as she felt, but with good reason. It was thirty minutes by car from the farm to Blessings, and the search team had walked the whole way down tracking that coyote.

CHAPTER 11

"THERE'S MY GIRL," JACK SAID AS HOPE PULLED INTO the park. "I am so ready to sit down," he added, and headed toward her with Duke beside him.

But as soon as Jack reached the car and opened the passenger side door, he saw the exhaustion on Hope's face.

"Oh, Hope, honey...you look exhausted. I'm driving home."

"I won't argue," she said. "It was a hectic shift in the ER."

She got out and gladly took the front passenger seat as Jack held the door. Working and pregnancy were really pulling her down.

Duke got in the back seat, then tapped his brother on the shoulder.

"Would you please drive me by Cathy's house before we leave? I want to check on her."

"Sure," Jack said, and headed toward Cherry Street, while Hope reclined the passenger seat and closed her eyes.

It only took a few minutes to get to Cathy's house, and when Jack pulled up in the drive and parked, Duke got out.

"I won't be long."

"Take your time," Hope said. "I'm off my feet, and that's all that matters."

"Same here," Jack said.

Duke's heart was pounding as he headed for the house. He'd never been scared for a woman's life before. At least not that he could remember. It was a feeling he didn't know how to process. All he knew was that seeing her made him happy, and when he left her, she was all he thought about. If that was love, he was so deep in it he was drowning.

And then he reached the door and knocked.

Cathy was washing up at the kitchen sink when she heard a knock at the door. She grabbed a towel to dry her hands and went to answer it, expecting it to be more fallout from the coyote incident. But the moment she opened the door, Duke stepped over the threshold, wrapped his arms around her, and just held her.

Cathy sighed. It appeared that he knew what had happened, and who was she to turn down a hug like this?

All the worry Duke had been feeling settled the moment she was in his arms. He went from the hug to a kiss, and when her arms slid around his neck and she leaned into the kiss, he groaned and finally pulled back.

"This isn't a stopping point," he said. "Consider this moment on pause."

Cathy's lips were tingling from the passion of the kiss, and her heart was pounding. Someday soon they were going to make love. They had to, or she was going to die from the want of it.

Duke cupped her face, then brushed one last kiss across her lips.

"Hope and Jack are in the car waiting for me, but I couldn't leave town without seeing you. I needed to make sure you were okay and to remind you about our lunch tomorrow."

"I'm not about to forget anything to do with you," she said softly.

Duke sighed, then leaned down until their foreheads were touching. "You are something special, girl. See you tomorrow around eleven thirty. I'll come by and pick you up, okay?"

"Yes, very okay," Cathy said.

Duke ran the tip of his finger down the curve of her cheek, then traced the shape of her lower lip with his thumb, and all Cathy could do was stand motionless beneath his touch.

"You make me crazy," he whispered, and then he was gone.

Cathy stood in the doorway and waved as the Talbots drove off, and then the moment she closed the door, she did a little two-step and danced her way back to the kitchen.

"Oh my lord! He says I drive him crazy?" she said, and then shivered longingly at the thought of lying in his arms.

———————————

Duke got back in the car and then said nothing as they backed up and headed home, but Hope wasn't settling for silence.

"Is Cathy okay?" she asked.

"Hmm? Oh...yes, she's fine. Didn't appear to faze her. She's pretty amazing."

"I wonder how she got so proficient with guns?" Hope said.

"Spent the first twelve years of her life living off the grid in Alaska with her parents," Duke said, and then took off his hat and set it on the seat beside him.

"Really?" Jack asked.

Duke nodded. "I suspect she has skills in survival that we haven't even thought of."

"I remember she told me at the hospital that she'd hiked and backpacked her way to Blessings. What she did was amazing, but how on earth did she know those women and the children were in danger?" Hope asked.

"She was outside. Lon said she heard them screaming. She had no way of knowing the coyote had gone in this direction, but I told her about it this morning. Maybe it was instinct that led her to do it. Who knows? The bottom line is that the animal is no longer a danger. However, if I was a pet owner, I would be making sure all my pets were vaccinated. There's never going to be a way to know if rabies has already been spread in the wild because of it," Duke said.

"I'm going to hold the intention that doesn't happen," Hope said. "And just so you know, you two get the showers. I call dibs on the tub so I can soak. I don't know which hurts more, my feet or my back."

Jack frowned. "Bless your heart. You soak as long as you want. Duke and I will handle chores and supper."

"Thank you. I always look forward to gathering eggs and putting the hens up at night when I work the day shift, but I'll gladly forego it tonight."

Duke leaned forward and gave her a gentle pat on the shoulder.

"I'm so sorry, honey."

Hope chuckled. "I suspect this is just the beginning of aches and exhaustion…and after the baby gets here, it will only get worse. I'm beginning to think your sudden desire to move out has to do with abdicating from baby duty."

Duke frowned. "That's not true. I will happily help, once it gets big enough that I think I won't break it."

The honesty in that comment made Jack and Hope laugh out loud.

"What?" Duke said.

Hope was still chuckling. "Nothing. It's just me picturing giant you holding a teeny baby."

Duke grinned. "Oh. Well, I can't change that."

"You don't need to change anything for anyone. You're pretty damn awesome as you are," Jack said.

"I'm taking Cathy to lunch tomorrow," Duke said.

"Well, that's one way to change the subject," Jack said. "Good for you."

Duke leaned back and let the conversation roll on without him. He was thinking about making love with a woman he hadn't known two weeks. But the way he looked at it, she was a gift he'd never thought about, and certainly never saw coming, but she was here, and he was falling in love with her. The rest that came with it was the blessing his life had been missing.

He'd thought of her the whole time he was looking over the old Bailey homestead, and as soon as the appraiser got back to Rhonda Bailey, she was supposed to call him. He wanted to show Cathy now. But the place wasn't his yet, and it was still too soon. He and Cathy were on the verge of everything, and yet she was still running from a past that had both scared and hurt her. And because of that, giving her that heads-up was his way of giving her back the sovereignty of her own life that she'd lost.

Cathy didn't know it, but by nightfall she had become a celebrity in Blessings. The heroine of the day. The pistol-packin' mama who took down a monster. Most people hearing the story had no idea who she was before, but they did now.

She'd even received a huge bouquet of flowers from the parents of all the little girls, which had caused no small amount of turmoil for Myra Franklin at the flower shop. She was less than an hour away from closing when she got the call, and with insistence that it must be delivered today.

Myra hadn't heard the story, but the order was a pricey one, and she wasn't turning down money like that. And since her hubby expected his supper on the table at 6:00 p.m., she called and told him to go to Granny's to get his food, and to bring some home for her, too. She had a big order to fill.

The order was for pink roses—one for each of the children and the women that she'd saved—and luckily Myra had them in stock. So she chose one of the nicer crystal vases and began arranging the roses one at a time, adding greenery as she went to fill it out. It was fifteen minutes past her close time when she finished, but she was satisfied. So she cleaned up the work station and loaded the vase in her car to deliver on her way home.

When she pulled up to the little blue house with the white trim, she knew it was one of Dan Amos's rental properties. She saw the car in the drive and recognized it as a rental from the insurance agency, because every now and then she saw a resident driving it if their car was in the shop. So this Cathy Terry didn't own a vehicle, but she owned a handgun. Interesting.

Myra pulled up in the drive and got out, then carried the arrangement to the door and knocked. Moments later, she heard footsteps, and when the door swung inward, she realized she'd seen Cathy before, running past her shop.

"Cathy Terry...I have a delivery for you," Myra said, and then waited. She lived for the smiles her arrangements received, and she wasn't disappointed.

"Oh! They're beautiful! Thank you," Cathy said, as Myra handed her the vase.

"By the way, my name is Myra Franklin. I own the flower shop on Main Street, and I see you running past my window quite often. It's nice to finally meet you."

"The pleasure is all mine," Cathy said.

Myra beamed and took herself home as Cathy closed the door and then carried the bouquet to a small table in the hall. As soon as she put it down, she pulled the card from the arrangement and read it.

Thank you from all of us for saving our babies today. Then there was a list of names beneath the message, including Alice's. It was such an unexpected gift, and so thoughtful.

After a last glance at the roses, Cathy went back to the kitchen to finish peeling a potato. She'd had a hunger for plain fried potatoes just like her mama used to make. They were going to be the side dish she was adding to a hamburger steak she was cooking, along with coleslaw she'd bought from the deli at the Crown. It wasn't one of the gourmet meals of Blaine's liking, but it was the food of her people, and the smells were wonderful. She couldn't wait to dig in.

She ate supper in the living room while watching television and, every now and then, glancing at her roses. She suspected there would be a lot of unsettled children going to bed tonight, but there was no easy way to get over a scare like that. Time would dull the worst of the memories, but they would never forget it.

She finished off her meal with one of the molasses cookies she'd baked, and after cleaning up the kitchen, she went to shower and get ready for bed. Normally, she undressed and showered without conscious thought of how she looked anymore, but tonight was different.

Stark naked, she paused in front of the mirror to assess herself. One thing about backpacking across country... nothing jiggled that wasn't supposed to. Her belly was flat. The muscles in her arms and legs were lean and toned. As for the shape of her, that was God's doing and her parents' DNA. She turned from one side to the other, and then nodded.

"So, this is me, Duke Talbot. I hope you like what you see, because I am falling for you in a very painful way. Please don't let this be a flash in the pan. I don't think I could bear one more disappointment from a man I thought I could trust."

Then she turned away, grabbed a hair band and put up her hair, and stepped into the shower.

The irony that Duke was doing the very same thing would have made the both of them laugh, but right now, he was operating on instinct. This woman called to his heart. And a second chance at love only happened once in a blue moon. Duke couldn't change who he was or how he looked, but he wanted her in his life, and this thing that was happening

between them had to work. He didn't care how long it took
her to be at ease with him, or to trust him with her whole
heart. He just needed it to happen.

———————————

Gage Brewer, the new investigator Blaine Wagner hired,
didn't waste time on the job. Once he got the pictures
Pamela St. James had taken of Cathy's car and license tag,
the trace he ran turned it up as belonging to a rental agency
in a place called Blessings, Georgia. But he couldn't tell if it
had been rented as she was passing through, or if she'd taken
up residence there. However, it was time to report what he'd
discovered, so he called Wagner first thing the next morning, catching Blaine in the limo on his way in to the office.

———————————

Blaine was checking the stock market on his iPad as Paddy
deftly wound the limo through morning traffic. Blaine
paused to top off his cup of coffee and was making mental
notes to pass on to his broker when his phone rang. Seeing
it was from his new PI pleased him.

"Mr. Brewer. This is an early call. I hope it's good news,"
he said.

"Good morning, Mr. Wagner. I do have some information for you."

"Tell me," Blaine said.

"The car in Mrs. St. James's photo is a rental from an
agency in a place called Blessings, Georgia. I can't say if
that's now your ex-wife's place of residence, or if she simply

rented the car passing through, but that's what I know for sure."

"Are you free to travel?" Blaine asked.

"Yes," Brewer said.

"Then I want you to go to Blessings, and if she's living there, I want to know where and what she's doing. I'll transfer some more money into your account for travel expenses. Get a hotel. Be discreet about your investigation."

"Yes, sir. I can do that. If I can get a flight out, I'll leave today."

"Excellent," Blaine said. "Stay in touch."

Gage disconnected. He knew Rand Lawrence had been working off and on for Wagner for some years, and the fact that Rand had quit made him a little anxious. Why turn down easy money? Then he shrugged it off. One man's loss was another man's gain.

He got online to book a flight to Savannah, with a connection through Denver, reserved a rental to be picked up when he landed, and then began looking for accommodations in Blessings. He already knew the town was small, and was pleased by the looks of the website of the Blessings Bed and Breakfast. He booked a room with a late arrival this evening and an open-end for checkout, threw some clothes in a carry-on, added a few of his favorite tracking devices and his laptop, and headed for the airport.

With less than an hour before boarding, he barely made the gate, and sank into his first-class seating with relief. Since Blaine Wagner was footing the bill for this trip, Gage saw no reason to fly coach. After a slight delay on takeoff, Gage Brewer was in the air.

Unaware trouble was coming to find her, Cathy was in a good mood and happy. She was wearing one of her new outfits to lunch today: chocolate-brown denim jeans, a long-sleeved white V-neck T-shirt, and natural suede Chelsea boots. The sky was scattered with clouds, and the wind was a little gusty, so she'd added a leopard-pattern jacket for comfort. It was a big change from the clothes she'd come to town with, and she liked the feel of being stylish again. As for the usual disarray of her copper-red curls, she used them to finish the look—like a cherry on a hot-fudge sundae.

She had her wallet and keys in a new shoulder bag and was impatiently waiting for Duke to arrive. When she finally saw his big truck pull up in her driveway, she tensed. And then she saw him getting out, and her heart skipped a beat. Blue jeans, dark-brown cowboy boots, a pale-blue shirt and a brown leather bomber jacket.

Drop-dead gorgeous.

And then he was coming up the steps. But when he knocked, she didn't quite pull off the casual approach she'd planned as she opened the door.

"Hi!" she said, and then winced. A little too exuberant.

Duke didn't seem to mind.

"You look gorgeous!" he said, then leaned down and kissed her—not enough to mess up her makeup, but enough to let her know he meant it. "Are you hungry?"

"Yes, for everything life has to offer!" she said.

He grinned. "This may be the shortest lunch I've ever had in my life."

Cathy threaded her fingers through his. "No need to hurry about anything. I'm not going anywhere."

He kissed her again, and this time she reached up and wiped her lipstick from his mouth.

"Just sprucing up the Duke," she said, and then locked the door behind her.

They were still high on life when they walked into Granny's Country Kitchen. Lovey's eyes widened when she saw Duke's arm around Cathy's shoulder.

"Hail the conquering heroine!" Lovey said. "Good job you did yesterday."

"Thanks," Cathy said. "This place always smells so good."

Lovey beamed. "And thank you. The special today is baked ham with two sides. Follow me."

Duke's hand was in the middle of Cathy's back as they followed Lovey through the busy dining room to a table near the back.

"Your waitress will be with you shortly," she said, and left their menus as Duke seated Cathy before sitting in the chair closest to her.

Cathy was instantly aware that they were a new topic of conversation. Duke nodded at a couple of people who caught his eye, but ignored the rest of them. He reached across the table and laid his hand over hers.

"Yes, they're staring, and it's not just because you're beautiful. They know what you did and are somewhat in awe."

She glanced up then, smiling at a couple of people she recognized, and began to relax. At that point their waitress showed up.

"Sorry for being so slow, y'all. We're slammed today."

She took their drink orders, brought back some hot biscuits, butter, and honey, and then their drinks.

Duke downed one biscuit before Cathy had her first one buttered.

"I always eat the first one straight," he said.

She laughed. "Good to know," she said, then took a bite and rolled her eyes in appreciation. "Mercy sure can bake."

"Agreed," Duke said. "But you're no slouch in the kitchen. That roast I had the other day was amazing."

Cathy shrugged off the compliment. "I haven't cooked in years. I'm surprised I remembered how, but I always enjoyed it. I used to make all of our meals when it was just Mama and me. Her hours at the casino were so weird that I finally took over that job."

"Do you know what you want to eat?" Duke asked.

"Yes, the ham. It sounds good."

"I know Hope is baking turkey for Thanksgiving, so I'm choosing ham, too."

They turned in their orders when the waitress brought their drinks, and then talked about everything but the next step in their relationship.

While they were waiting, Rhonda Bailey and her brother, Robert, came in and were seated before they knew Duke was there.

Rhonda saw him first and pointed him out to her brother, who turned, then got up and went to their table.

"Hey, Duke, how's it going?" Robert asked.

"Good to see you, Robert. Have you met Cathy Terry yet? She's our newest resident to Blessings. Cathy, this is Robert Bailey. His sister, Rhonda, is the nurse who was with you in the ER."

"Oh. Your sister was so sweet to me. It's nice to meet you."

"She's that kind of person," he said. "Welcome to Blessings."

"Thank you," Cathy said, and then turned and waved at Rhonda.

"I won't bother you at your meal," Robert said. "But Rhonda said you asked about Dad's place. We got the appraisal back today, and we're meeting with our brothers later to set a price. She said she promised you first dibs, and that's just fine with us. We would all love to see the place back the way it was when we were growing up."

Duke nodded. "I'll be waiting to hear from her."

Robert nodded at Cathy again, and then went back to where his sister was sitting.

Duke glanced at Cathy. He could tell she was curious about the conversation, but she wasn't asking. He wanted to talk about it and feel her out at the same time.

"Their homeplace adjoins ours," Duke said. "It was the access the rustlers used to get to our cattle because the house is unoccupied now. Their father had to go to a nursing home almost a year ago, and the place is a little run-down now because it's been vacant so long."

"So they've decided to sell?" Cathy asked.

"Yes, and I expressed an interest in buying it if the price was right."

"Makes sense," Cathy said. "But what are you going to do with the house?"

"If I buy the place, I'm going to fix it up and live in it."

Cathy's eyes widened. "But you live with Hope and Jack."

"I do, which is exactly the point. With the baby coming, their whole lives are going to change, and it's past time they had a home to themselves. I thought about building on the property, but then I saw that old house and discarded that idea. I like a home with a little character to it."

"How exciting," Cathy said. "I hope you get it, then."

Before he could answer, their food came and the conversation shifted to other things.

As they were eating, Cathy was telling him a story about her daddy falling through the ice one winter while he was running traps.

"Oh wow... How on earth did you two get him out?"

"Mama didn't have time to panic. It was only seconds before he would be too cold to help himself. So she grabbed a rope off the dog sled and went belly down on the ice until she was close enough to throw the lasso end of it across the ice. But he was too cold to hold on, and she began yelling and screaming at him, 'Don't you dare quit on me,' and he managed to get it over his head, then beneath one arm. At that point, Mama backed up off the ice, grabbed the team, and mushed the dogs forward. It pulled him out like a cork out of a bottle...all the way to shore. He couldn't move, but he was still breathing."

"My God. How far were you from home?" Duke asked.

"Two miles. Mama shouted and cried, and cursed at him to move because she couldn't lift him, and finally we got him into the sled. She set me between his legs, wrapped the both of us up in the furs, and told Daddy to hang onto me for warmth, then mushed that sled like a pro and got us home. It was quite a ride. Mama stripped him in front of the fireplace, while I put water on the propane cookstove to heat for a bath. It was a scary time."

"That's like something out of a movie," Duke said.

Cathy shrugged. "I guess. But life off the grid anywhere is hard. In Alaska, it can be deadly."

Duke had no comprehension of that kind of hardship, and was in awe of the matter-of-fact way she thought about it.

"How old were you then?" he asked.

Cathy paused, frowning a moment, and then looked at him. "Probably close to eleven."

At that point, the waitress appeared again to refill their glasses. They finished their meal and waved at the Baileys as they went back to the front lobby to pay, then left the building. But once they were in the truck, instead of starting it up, Duke sat for a few moments in silence.

"Is everything okay?" Cathy asked.

"Do you have plans for this afternoon?" Duke asked.

"Today is all yours, why?"

"I want to show you our farm. And I want to show you the house on the Bailey place."

"Oh my gosh, yes, yes."

He eyed her new clothes. "Want to go change first, so you don't get dirt on your pretty clothes?"

She grinned. "You read my mind."

CHAPTER 12

"Come in while I change," Cathy said. "There are still molasses cookies if you want dessert."

"I never say no to cookies," Duke said, and followed her into the house.

"You know the way to the kitchen. They're in that little plastic container on the counter. I won't be long."

Duke went one way while she went the other. She had never changed clothes so fast in her life, then headed for the kitchen.

Duke was working on his second cookie when she came in.

"I'm ready. This is turning into the best day ever." She took a cookie for herself and a couple of bottles of water. "For us," she said.

He followed her out the door, eyeing the sway of her hips and the bounce in her curls and smiled.

Us. She said us. I like the sound of that.

Cathy buckled herself into the seat of the truck and then set the bottles of water in the console between them as Duke headed out of town.

She glanced at his profile. There was such strength in the cut of his jaw and the breadth of his shoulders, but it was the kindness and the joy in him that filled her heart. Happy to be with him in this moment, she broke her cookie in half.

"Here you go," she said. "I don't like to eat alone."

"I already had two," Duke said.

"I'm not counting," she said, and handed it to him.

He grinned and popped it in his mouth.

Cathy settled back against the seat to enjoy the scenery. Every now and then they'd drive past a house, and when they did, Duke would tell her who lived there.

"Oh, that's a pretty house," Cathy said, as they passed a big white farmhouse with navy-blue shutters.

"That's where Jake and Laurel Lorde live. Jake works online for some big-city advertising agency, and Laurel has her own cleaning service. It's grown from just her being a single mother trying to make ends meet to at least two full cleaning crews. The Lordes are good people," Duke said.

"I'm beginning to realize that is the norm rather than the exception in Blessings," Cathy said.

"What do you mean?" Duke asked.

"Good people. The town is full of them," she said.

Duke's eyes narrowed thoughtfully. "Growing up here, I guess we take all that for granted. Sometimes it's good to see the world through new eyes."

"You have no idea how unique and special this place is," Cathy said.

"Special enough to stay?" Duke asked.

Cathy glanced at him. "Yes, special enough to stay," she said.

Duke reached for her hand and gave it a quick squeeze, then began slowing down enough to take the turn off the highway onto a blacktop road.

"Our place is about fifteen minutes farther. The road actually ends at the farm. Our grandparents homesteaded the place and built the original house, but our parents added to it."

"So what's going on at the farm today?" Cathy asked.

"Nothing out of the ordinary. Jack texted while you were changing clothes and said he was on the way to Savannah to pick up a part for Dad's old truck he's been working on, and Hope is at work. So it will be me giving you the grand tour."

"I'm really looking forward to it. It's been forever since I was on a working farm. We homesteaded, but farming wasn't a thing. It was more about growing sustainable food, raising chickens, goats for milk and cheese, things like that."

Duke glanced at her, then back at the road, but the animation in her voice matched the expression on her face. She wasn't just being polite about seeing their place. She was really excited. This just kept getting better and better.

He didn't realize he was holding his breath as they came around a corner in the road and the white two-story farmhouse appeared, but when Cathy gasped, he exhaled slowly.

She liked it, he could tell.

The house was nestled against a backdrop of neatly painted outbuildings, a big red two-story barn, and fenced pastures with silver-gray gates. Several head of cattle in the nearest pasture were eating from a round bale of hay, while others had grouped beneath a stand of oaks.

"Oh Duke! It's beautiful! Picture-postcard perfect, right down to the grazing cattle."

He pulled around to the back of the house and then parked.

"I know you'll be here day after tomorrow for Thanksgiving, but I wanted to show you the house first, as it normally is."

Cathy jumped out of the truck without waiting for him to help her, then went in the back door with his hand at the small of her back. Her first impression was of all the modern conveniences in the kitchen, and how perfectly they'd blended them into the character of the house. From a long oak table and chairs in the kitchen to the antique sideboard and an old cuckoo clock hanging above it, ticking away the time.

"It's perfect," Cathy said, running her fingertips along the surface of the old table.

"Nobody has ever lived in this house but Talbots. I was born in a room down the hall."

Cathy stopped, and then put a hand on Duke's arm. "Are you going to be sad to leave?" she asked.

Duke shook his head. "Not like you mean. I've never lived life for me before."

Cathy slid her arms around his neck. "I wouldn't mind if you saved a little spot in your life for me while you were at it."

Duke pulled her close. "Fair warning...I'm saving more than a little spot."

"Is that a promise?" she asked.

"No. It is a fact," Duke said, and then kissed her— softly at first, and then longer...harder—until they were lost in the feel of being in each other's arms.

Pillow-soft breasts pressed against a hard, muscle-toned chest—both of them forgetting to breathe—then the sensation of floating in the passion building between them.

A gasp of wonder. The undertone of a moan from the want for more. The ache of unfulfilled urges.

All it would have taken was one word, and Duke would have taken her to bed right there and then. But she didn't ask, and he wouldn't push it, so he ended it with a deep, heartfelt sigh of longing.

"You destroy every ounce of good sense I ever had," he said softly, and brushed one last kiss across her lips. "So if you want to see the rest of the farm, I suggest we get as far away from my bedroom as possible."

Cathy laughed out loud.

"What?" Duke asked.

"That was the most perfect invitation not to make love that I've ever heard. And I'll go along with it…for the time being."

Duke grinned. "What do you want to see first? The chickens or the—"

"The chickens! We had chickens when I was a kid. They were my pets."

Duke sighed. "Doesn't do much for a guy's ego to know the woman he's falling for chooses chickens over making love."

"Don't be ridiculous," Cathy said. "I've been practicing being naked for you in front of my mirror. I'm not choosing chickens over you, but I am chicken about the big reveal."

Her honesty was a suckerpunch to the gut.

"I'm pretty sure anything I say right now is gonna be wrong, but I can relieve your worries about that. I dream about you…about making love to you. I've already seen you in my dreams, and you're too beautiful for words, so no more talking about being naked unless you're ready to get that way."

Cathy slipped her hand in his. "Show me your chickens, please."

He led the way out and pointed to the chicken house and the chicken-wire fence around it.

"The henhouse awaits," he said.

Their arrival set a few hens to clucking, thinking it was time to eat, but Cathy was enchanted with the fat red hens.

"What kind of chickens are these?"

"Rhode Island Reds. Hope started them because she wanted brown eggs," he said. "She likes tending to them and gathering eggs when she can, but her work schedule doesn't always permit it."

Cathy squatted down beside a chicken feeder, eyeing one big fat hen pecking at the scratch scattered about.

"Just look at you," she said softly. "You're a beauty and you know it, don't you?" Cathy stroked the chicken's head and down the back of its neck with her fingertip, cooing and talking in a singsong voice until the hen was clucking back at her.

"I think she likes you," Duke said.

Cathy gave the hen one last stroke on her back and then stood and looked up at him.

"You are so lucky to have grown up in this place," she said.

"Come walk with me," he said. "There's far more to see."

And so she did…from the barn to the machine shed, and then the corrals and the stanchions where they used to milk, to the farm pond just below the house.

"Are there fish in it?" Cathy asked.

"Oh sure," Duke said. "Dad stocked it years ago with large-mouth bass and catfish. We fish out of it and usually have a big fish fry for our neighbors at least once a year."

"I've never been to a fish fry, but I've cooked fish over an open fire."

"The fish at a fish fry are cut-up chunks that have been dipped in batter or breading and deep-fried. You'd like it, I think," Duke said.

"I love this place!" Cathy said. She threw her arms up in the air and turned in a full circle. "I love everything about it. It's beautiful."

"You're beautiful," Duke said. "And before I forget the rest of why I invited you up, I want to show you the old Bailey place."

"And I want to see it…I want to see it through your eyes…your vision of what you want it to be."

Within minutes they were headed back to the house to wash up before leaving the farm. Cathy went down the hall to the guest bath, and when she got back to the kitchen, Duke was waiting for her with cold bottles of Coke.

"Do you want something to snack on?" he asked, as he handed her the pop.

"I don't. This is perfect," she said, and took a quick sip. "How far is it to the Bailey property from here?"

"About fifteen minutes by road. But the land abuts to the back of ours, so if I do buy it, it will just be a drive through the pastures to get from one house to the other. Are you ready?"

"Always," she said.

Duke leaned down and kissed her. "Couldn't resist," he said, and ushered her back to the truck.

Cathy watched in the side-view mirror until the farm was out of sight, then leaned against the seat and sighed.

"I know there's a lot of hard work to keeping a farm running and looking that good, but it's amazing. You and Jack are obviously very good businessmen, too, or it wouldn't be that successful."

"We have our down years. So much of farming and ranching depends on enough rain, but not too much rain…

on good cattle prices…on drought-free years…keeping animals free of disease. It's a full-time job, for sure, and doesn't appeal to a lot of women."

"It's my idea of heaven on earth," Cathy said.

Duke smiled. "Yet another thing we agree about," he said, and then took a right turn at the next section line and pointed. "The Bailey place is just up ahead. You'll see the old house as we top the hill. When we do, I want you to give me your first impression. What does it look like, and how does it make you feel?"

"Okay," Cathy said, then sat up straighter and leaned forward, watching intently as they reached the top, revealing the two-story redbrick edifice sitting about a hundred yards off the road. It had two single-story wings, one on either side, that had once been painted white and a deep porch that ran the length of the two-story structure.

Breath caught in the back of Cathy's throat. "Oh, oh, oh… she looks lonesome…like she's waiting to belong again. And those two white wings are like open arms, waiting to welcome you up onto that porch. I cannot wait to see inside."

Duke was speechless. What she'd just said was how it made him feel, but he'd never been able to put it into words.

"It's pretty overgrown," he said, as he pulled up to the front of the house.

"Nothing that a good mowing wouldn't cure," Cathy said. "Is it okay that we go inside?"

"Yes. Rhonda already told me once where they hid the key. The place is old. It needs to be remodeled…updated… but the structure is sound. I think Mr. Bailey kept it up pretty good until his last year here. That's when his health began to fail. Alzheimer's made the final decision for him."

"So, let's get out," Cathy said.

"Wait. You'll be walking in grass and weeds up to your knees," he said, and jumped out and circled the truck.

Cathy opened the door, but before she could jump out, Duke scooped her up in his arms and carried her through the yard and up the steps.

Cathy was holding onto him with both arms and laughing as he set her down on the porch. Then he retrieved the key and let them in the house.

"It's stuffy...and dusty...and kind of weird. All the furniture is here, like he left to go to the store or something and never made it home."

"Family heirlooms here," Cathy said. "They'll be wanting to reclaim those before the house sells."

Duke nodded. "So, what do you think?"

"The possibilities are endless. How high are these ceilings? Twelve...maybe fourteen feet? And look at the crown molding, and I love the arched doorways."

"Come look at the kitchen," Duke said. "It's really big, but of course it would need to be gutted. And I'd like to widen the opening between the eat-in kitchen and the formal dining room."

As they began going from room to room, their ideas for what needed to be done began to mesh. By the time they reached the second floor, Cathy was already seeing the finished product in her mind as she listened to his plans.

"There are five bedrooms up here, but they're small. I'd pick the first two, knock down a wall and make a big master bedroom with a master bath and a big walk-in closet, and then move some walls around to make a couple more decent-size bedrooms for guests."

"Yes, and downstairs, make the east wing into a butler's pantry, laundry, and mud room, and the west wing into an office."

Duke turned to her then and put his hands on her shoulders.

"I'm going to ask you something, and if it makes you uncomfortable, or I've asked this too soon, will you be honest with me and tell me?"

And just like that, all the fantasy of playing house was gone, and the reality of what was growing between them was back again.

"Yes...I'll always tell you the truth of how I feel," she said.

"Will you do this with me? For us?"

Cathy's heart skipped. "For real?"

"Yes, ma'am."

Her eyes welled. "Oh, Duke..."

He groaned. "Too soon. I'm sorry, I didn't—"

"No, no, no, it's not that. I just never thought I'd be happy again...until you. Yes, I'll do this with you...for us."

Duke sighed. "Thank you, Jesus," he whispered, then wrapped his arms around her and kissed her.

Cathy was lost in his touch, matching him kiss for kiss and wanting more. But the rumble of thunder shifted the moment from wanting to weather.

"It sounds like we have rain coming. I'd better get you home before it hits," Duke said.

They hurried back downstairs, then out the door, pausing long enough to lock it back and return the key to its hiding place.

Then he went down two steps and stopped. "Hop on, and I'll take you piggyback," he said.

Cathy climbed onto his back, wrapping her arms around his neck and her legs around his waist.

"Hang on," he said, and made a run for the truck through the knee-high grass as the wind began to pick up.

She was safely inside and buckled up, and he was turning around when the first raindrops splattered on the windshield.

"We're good," he said. "It's either gravel or blacktop all the way back to the highway."

"I wouldn't fuss about being stuck in the mud with you," Cathy said.

Duke grinned. "Well, I would be fussing about getting stuck, so there's that."

His phone rang while they were on the way back to town.

"It's Jack," he said, and answered. "Hey, what's up?"

"I'm home and checking on you."

"I have the phone on speaker. I'm taking Cathy back to town. Be home soon. I gave her a tour of the farm and of the Bailey place this afternoon."

"Awesome. Hi, kiddo… The turkey is thawing in the refrigerator as we speak. See you soon."

"I'm looking forward to it," Cathy said.

Duke disconnected, and then dropped the phone in the console between them.

The rain was coming down heavily now, and they were almost to the blacktop when Duke suddenly slammed on the brakes and shoved the truck into Park.

"What's wrong?" Cathy asked.

"I think I see the taillights of a car down in those trees. Stay here."

"Take your phone!" Cathy said.

"Right," Duke muttered. He dropped it into the inside pocket of his leather jacket, tossed his hat in the back seat, and glanced at her. "Promise me you'll stay here."

"I promise," Cathy said. "Just be careful."

Moments later, Duke was out of the truck and running. Cathy could see the red taillights now—like glowing red eyes looking up from between the trees—as Duke slipped and slid his way down the slope.

"Whoever it is, please God let them be okay," she said, and pressed her face as close to the window as she could get, trying to see through the downpour.

Big Tom Rankin had spent the night with his girlfriend, Ethel, and stayed over this morning to help her repair a hole in the fence around her chicken house. They had discussed the notion of getting married more than once, but neither one of them wanted to give up their own homes, so overnight visits to Ethel's had become a twice-a-week thing.

His son, Albert, didn't seem to mind. Ever since they'd lost Junior, Albert's older brother, in the aftermath of the hurricane, Albert had become something of a recluse and was perfectly capable of tending to their livestock on his own when the need arose.

Big Tom had dozed off in the recliner after their noon meal, and Ethel let him sleep until she saw the thunderstorm brewing and hurried into the living room to wake him.

"Tom, honey...there's a big storm approaching. If you want to get home before it hits, you'd best be leaving."

"Hmmm, what? A storm, you say?"

"Yes, and you said earlier you were going to help Albert get that cow with the lame calf up to the barn."

"Right…okay, thanks for waking me, Ethel."

He got out of the chair, kissed her goodbye, and grabbed his car keys on the way out the door. He was surprised by how dark the clouds were and made a quick call to Albert as he was turning around.

Albert answered on the second ring, and sounded a little anxious.

"Hello?"

"Son, it's me. I'm on the way home," Tom said.

"I saw the storm brewing and already got the cow and calf up."

"I'm sorry I didn't get there to help. I fell asleep in the recliner after dinner. Ethel just woke me up," he said.

"It's okay, Daddy. No need to hurry."

"Well, hell, I'm not gonna beat that rain," Tom said as the first raindrops splattered across his windshield.

"Drive safe," Albert said.

"I will," Tom said, and disconnected.

The rain was coming down in sheets, making it difficult to see any distance ahead, and Tom was really having to pay attention to make sure he didn't veer off the road.

Just as he came over a hill, something darted out of the trees to his left and ran right in front of his car.

Startled, Tom swerved to keep from hitting it, and when he did, he lost control and went flying off the road, then down the slope. He saw the trees coming up fast and braced himself for impact, and then everything went black.

The next thing he knew, there was rain on his face and someone was shouting his name.

"Tom! Tom! Can you hear me?"

Tom groaned, and managed to open his eyes. "Duke? Is that you?"

"Yes. Can you move?"

Tom winced, then cried out from a sharp pain below his knee.

"I don't think so."

"I already called an ambulance, buddy. Hang in there. I'll stay with you until it's here."

"Albert…" Tom muttered.

"Yes, I'll call him later. Right now, let's just focus on you. Both doors are jammed, or I'd be inside with you," Duke said. "What happened?"

"Something jumped in front of the car. Maybe a deer. I swerved to miss it…I think. I just remember the trees coming up in my face." Then he reached toward his forehead. "Hurts," he said.

"You cut it… It's bleeding."

Tom groaned, and then passed out again.

Duke felt Tom's pulse. It was steady enough, so he turned and ran back up the slope to let Cathy know what was happening.

When she saw him scrambling back up the slope, she breathed a quick sigh of relief and rolled down the window as he reached the truck.

"It's Tom Rankin, a neighbor. He swerved to miss some animal and went off the road. He came to once, but he's passed out again and I can't get to him. The car is wedged between two trees. I already called for an ambulance. I'm going back down to wait with him."

"Is there anything I can do?" Cathy asked.

"No, and there's not anything I can really do, either, except stay with him."

He leaned in the window, kissed her quick and hard, and then took off back down the slope.

Cathy rolled the window back up and then felt her lips. They were cold and wet from his kiss, and he'd already disappeared again. She shivered, both from the chill of the storm and the anxiety of what was happening, and prayed for help to arrive.

As it happened, a deputy from the sheriff's department got there first.

Cathy saw him pull up behind her, and then he got out on the run and knocked on her window.

"Ma'am, we got a call about a wreck out here."

"Down there," Cathy said. "Duke Talbot is with the man. He said the car is wedged between two trees and he can't get to the driver. He said he already called an ambulance, too."

The deputy gave her a thumbs-up and ran back to his cruiser to call for a tow truck just as the ambulance arrived on the scene.

After that, it was collective chaos. Duke came back up the hill and jumped in his truck, chilled and shaking as he started it up.

"I've done all I can, and the best thing I can do is get out of the way. The tow truck will be here shortly, and the driver is going to need some wiggle room to get that car pulled up out of the trees before they can get Big Tom out."

"Find a place to turn around and go back to your farm," Cathy said.

"But I need to—"

"What you need is to get warm and into dry clothes, and don't argue," Cathy said. "Are you too cold to drive?"

"No. I'm okay," Duke said, and then quickly found a place to turn and headed back home, out of the way of the tow truck and the rescue vehicles that were now lining the side of the road. "I promised Big Tom I'd call his son. Would you please scroll through my contacts until you find the name Albert, hit Call, and then put it on speaker for me while I drive."

Cathy's hands were shaking, but she did as he asked, and as soon as the phone began ringing, she held it up so Duke could talk without taking his hands off the wheel.

Albert answered on the fourth ring.

"Hello, this is Albert."

"Albert, this is Duke."

"Hey, Duke. What's up?"

"First off…don't panic, but your dad's had an accident. He ran off the road and is pinned in his car for the time being. I've been with him the whole time, and now help has arrived. He's got the car wedged between some trees, and we couldn't get the doors open to get to him."

"Oh my God! I was beginning to worry why he wasn't home."

"He asked me to call you, so I am. They'll take him to the ER in Blessings."

"Thank you, man. Thank you."

"Sure thing. Just keep me posted, okay?"

"Absolutely," Albert said, and disconnected.

Cathy put Duke's phone back in the console, and glanced up at the road.

"We're almost there, right?"

Duke heard the concern in her voice. "Yes, honey. Just a few minutes more, and we'll be back at the farm."

She glanced at him once, thinking to herself how fearlessly he'd gone down that hill without knowing what he'd find, and then stayed with his friend until help arrived.

"You do know you probably saved his life," she said.

Duke frowned. "No, I just—"

"How much traffic is on that road?" she asked.

"Not a lot," he said.

"If you hadn't seen those taillights, there's no telling how long he would have been there before someone found him."

Duke shrugged. "Some things are just meant to be. And, we're home," he added, and pulled around to the back of the house, getting as close to the back porch as he could.

Jack came out the kitchen door as they were getting out, took one look at Duke, and frowned.

"What happened to you?" he asked, as he ushered both of them inside out of the rain.

"Tom Rankin had a wreck," Duke said.

"Go," Cathy said, pointing. "Hot shower. Dry clothes. Hot coffee will be waiting."

Duke grinned. "Yes, ma'am," he said, dripping water as he went.

CHAPTER 13

"TALK TO ME," JACK SAID, AND TURNED AROUND TO MAKE a fresh pot of coffee.

So Cathy began to relate what had happened, right down to reiterating what she'd said before, about Duke saving the man's life.

"Wow," Jack said. "Listen, make yourself at home. I'm going to go check on my brother. Help yourself to coffee. Cream is in the refrigerator…sugar is on the table."

He left the room on the run as Cathy went down the hall to the guest bath to freshen up. By the time both men came back down, she was sitting at the table nearest the window, watching it rain. She looked up as they walked in.

"Have you heard anything yet? Did they get him out of the car?"

"Yes. I'm sure he's already at the ER being treated, and his car has been towed away. The road is clear now, if you're ready to try this again."

"Not unless you take hot coffee with you," she said.

Jack grinned. "Finally, someone is telling Duke what to do for a change."

Duke poured a cup of coffee into a travel mug, then popped the lid on it.

"Will this work?" he asked.

"Are you still chilled?" she asked.

"No. Seriously, I'm fine," Duke said.

"Okay then, but only because the rain is beginning to let

up. Jack, thank you for your hospitality and coffee. I will see you day after tomorrow."

"Yes, ma'am," Jack said.

"You're gonna get a little wet," Duke said.

"I haven't melted yet," Cathy said.

Duke grinned, then opened the door and stood aside as she strode out onto the porch. They stood for a few moments staring into the rain, and then looked at each other and shrugged.

"I'm game if you are," he said.

"Let's do it!" Cathy said, and leaped off the porch. In just a few steps they were both at the truck and climbing in.

"Lord," Duke said, as he slammed the door shut behind him, then glanced at Cathy. The curls around her face had turned into corkscrews brought on by the weather, and the rain had long since washed all the makeup off her face. "You look like you're about sixteen, and I feel like a dirty old man for what I'm thinking," he said.

She grinned. "Well, looks are deceiving, and your reputation is safe with me."

"Buckle up and let's try this again," he said, and drove away from the farm.

Whatever mud and tracks that had been on the road during the recovery of Big Tom and his car had long since been washed away by the rain, and this time the drive back into Blessings was uneventful.

Duke pulled up into the driveway at Cathy's house and parked behind her car.

"Do you have to hurry back?" Cathy asked.

"No," Duke said, and gave her a look that made her heart skip.

"Want to come in?" she asked.

He nodded, and opened the door, then ran around to help her out. Soon they were on the porch, and then inside the house. As soon as Cathy locked the door, he took off his jacket and hat and then pulled her into his arms.

Cathy sighed. "This is happening, isn't it?"

"It is unless you send me home," Duke said.

"I don't want you to go home."

He heard the want in her voice, and cupped her face with his hands and then kissed her.

"Are you sure you know what you're getting into with me? Work is always dirty, and nothing is for sure…especially after all those years of living in the bright lights of Vegas."

"Bright lights are just that…bright lights. The world behind the scenes is like anywhere else. People live normal lives, raising families and going to ordinary jobs there, too. It has its own level of beauty, but your world speaks to my heart. It's like the way I grew up…just less dangerous. And I want a life with someone who loves me like Daddy loved Mama. I'm tired of running, Duke. I don't want to be afraid anymore."

"Then be with me…be my love. I'll keep you safe, baby. You won't ever have to be afraid again."

Breath caught in the back of Cathy's throat.

"Then follow me," she said.

But he didn't follow. He swung her up into his arms, instead.

"Where's the bed?"

"Down the hall. First door on the left."

He carried her out of the room and then down the short hall into her bedroom and put her down beside the bed.

Cathy pulled back the covers and kicked off her shoes as Duke toed off his boots, and then they began shedding clothes.

What might have been awkward was overshadowed by desire. When Cathy tossed her last piece of clothing aside and stretched out on the bed, Duke slid in beside her, then paused, taking his time to admire the beauty before him.

"You are so beautiful," he said softly, and when he lowered his head, her arms slid around his neck.

"Make love to me," she whispered, and so he did, taking his time to map every inch of her body with his hands and with his lips until she was aching for him.

Duke took her slowly…gently…afraid he'd hurt her, but his fears were unfounded. He'd only meant to love her…not set her on fire.

It was in the moment of joining that it happened. A recognition of souls—from lives long past. And without words to explain it, and no way to understand that frantic moment of sexual greed after a lifetime of unfulfilled longing, all they could do was hang on for the ride.

The ending came between one breath and the next— without warning—without that sensation of a building climax—shocking the both of them to total silence.

One minute turned into two, and then three before Cathy was able to breathe and think at the same time.

"What just happened?"

Duke rose up on one elbow.

"You happened. I just didn't expect a resurrection to come with it."

Cathy touched his face, then ran her finger down the curve of his chin.

"Well, whatever it was, it was magic, and you are one fine magician."

Duke grinned. "Well, hocus pocus and abracadabra. I think we need to see if we can do that again."

Cathy sighed with sudden longing. "Lord, I hope so," she said.

And so they did.

Duke stayed longer than he'd meant to, but then leaving wasn't as easy as it had been before.

"I don't want to leave, but I need to get back."

She wrapped her arms around his waist and laid her cheek against his chest, listening to the steady thump of his heartbeat. She didn't want him to go, either.

"I know. Jack is going to wring both our necks if I keep you here any longer."

Duke buried his face in the thick tumble of red curls beneath his chin and sighed.

"I love you to distraction, but you already know that," he said.

Cathy's pulse kicked, and then she leaned back in his arms.

"I love you, Duke Talbot…and in a way I didn't know existed, and I'll see you again day after tomorrow."

"I'll come get you," Duke said.

"No. I'll drive myself up and back. There will be a lot going on, and they'll likely need your help."

"We'll talk about this again," he said, then cupped her face and kissed her one last time. "Love you. Be safe. Call me anytime."

And then he was gone.

Cathy stood in the doorway waving as he drove away,

then backed up and closed the door. It was still raining, and she felt a chill to the house now that he was gone. She turned up the thermostat, then looked at the little house that had welcomed her to Blessings and thought about the big house they were going to redo together.

She had never been so certain about a man in her life as she was about Duke Talbot. Whatever the connection they had between them, it was magic, and she didn't intend to lose it by worrying about propriety. They weren't even a month into knowing each other. They'd just made love for the first time, and she knew in her heart it was meant to be. If the speed of this didn't bother Duke, she sure wasn't going to let it bother her. It wasn't as if they were kids who hadn't lived enough of life to make a sensible decision. It was more of a feeling that the lives they'd led before they met had been lived for other people and never for themselves.

This was the urgency within them.

Never to waste another day apart.

It was still raining when Gage Brewer arrived in Blessings. He found the bed-and-breakfast using the GPS on his phone, and parked. The huge porch spanning the length of the front was welcome shelter from the rain as he ran up the steps, then stopped to shake the water from his jacket before going inside.

The welcome warmth and the aroma of baking sweets enveloped him as he approached the man at the front desk.

"Hi, I'm Gage Brewer. I have a reservation."

"Yes, Mr. Brewer… Welcome to Blessings. I'm Bud

Goodhope, the proprietor. We have your room all ready for you. Will you be staying with us long?"

"I'll be here until my business is finished," Gage said. "Hopefully it won't take long. A day or two at best."

Bud nodded. "Breakfast is served from 6:00 a.m. to 10:00 a.m. every morning, and there are several different places here in town to get your other meals. Granny's Country Kitchen comes highly recommended by all of us, but there's also Broyles Dairy Freeze and a good barbecue place as well."

"Good to know," Gage said. "It's almost 7:00 p.m. How late does that Granny's place stay open?"

"Until 10:00 p.m. every night. Same goes for the other two places as well. There's not a lot of night life here, but if anyone gets an itch for that, Savannah is just an hour's drive away. Now...if you'll follow me, I'll show you to your room."

"Do you lock up the front door at a certain time each night?" Gage asked.

"Midnight, unless we're expecting a late arrival," Bud said.

Gage picked up his bag and followed Bud up the stairs, then down the hall to his room.

Bud led the way inside and then began pointing out the amenities.

"As you can see, there's a Keurig and K-cups in different flavors, as well as some of my wife Rachel's homemade goodies. She is a phenomenal cook."

"Everything looks very inviting," Gage said. "I'm sure I'll be comfortable here. I've been traveling all day, so I think I'll not go back out in this weather. I'll stay in for the night and avail myself of some of these goodies for dinner."

Bud pointed to the phone. "There are cookies and cinnamon-sugar muffins in the welcome basket, cold pop in the mini-refrigerator, and as I pointed out, your Keurig. Just press 7 if you need anything, and rest well."

"Thanks," Gage said.

He'd almost asked the man if he knew Cathy Terry, and then didn't. He didn't want her to know someone was asking about her, and take a chance on her running again.

Blessings, Georgia, might be one of the smaller places he'd ever been in his life. How hard would it be to find one redheaded woman driving a rental car in a little place like this?

Duke was on his way home when he got a phone call from Rhonda Bailey. The family had finally come up with an asking price for their dad's property, and Duke accepted it without question. He knew the price was fair, and he also knew they needed every penny they were going to get for it to pay for their father's long-term care.

"I want it," he said. "Are you going through the local realty company?"

"Yes. They'll handle getting everything brought up to date. As soon as there's paperwork to sign, I'll let you know. But they said you need to put up earnest money."

"Yes, of course. Are we doing this before Thanksgiving?"

"No. As far as we're concerned, your word is gold, and we're happy to know you're the one who's going to buy it."

"Thank you, Rhonda. It's a beautiful old home. I'm looking forward to making her shine again."

"Thank you, Duke. I'll tell my brothers, and happy Thanksgiving to all of you."

"The same to all of you," Duke said, and disconnected.

He got back to the farm in time to help Jack with the evening chores, and updated him on his plans.

Jack didn't know whether to congratulate him or be sad, but Duke was so elated that Jack couldn't bring himself to burst the bubble.

Hope didn't get home until after dark. She was in the ER when the ambulance arrived with Big Tom Rankin and had spent the next three hours attending Dr. Quick as he assessed and diagnosed Tom's injuries before admitting him to the hospital for overnight observation.

Tom had a concussion, staples in his head, cracked ribs, and a fractured kneecap, and was lucky to be alive.

His son, Albert, arrived only minutes after Tom was brought in, and thanks to Albert's phone call, Ethel was right behind him. They were both horrified by what had happened and grateful Tom was alive.

But Hope's exhaustion was evident when she finally got home. She'd thought about her waning energy level for most of this week, and when she walked in the back door and found Jack waiting for her, she burst into tears and fell into his arms.

Jack was startled, and then worried. "Honey! What's wrong?"

"I'm just so tired," Hope said. "Can we talk?"

"Absolutely," he said. "You sit. I'm going to heat up your supper, and you can talk while you eat."

She nodded, and then took a big drink of the sweet tea he put in front of her before heating up the meatloaf and mashed potatoes.

"Thank you, darling," Hope said, as Jack slid the plate in front of her and then handed her a fork.

"Eat...then we talk."

She nodded, and took the first bite. As always, the comfort of home, food, and the man she loved was just what the doctor ordered.

Finally, she laid down her fork and pushed the plate aside.

"I'm not holding up like I thought I could," Hope said. "There are other nurses there who work clear up to a month before they deliver, but I don't know how they do it. I'm so tired by midafternoon that I don't feel like I'm giving my patients the care they need."

Jack reached across the table and took her hands.

"We don't need the income, honey, and you know that. We've been banking most of yours for years. Just give notice and come home. You can sleep in on the days you don't feel good, and enjoy the days that you do without added pressure. I would love it if you were home."

Hope sighed. The relief was huge. "I'll turn in my resignation when I go back. I think it's the right thing for me to do."

Jack got up and then pulled her into his arms and hugged her.

"Get in the tub and soak. You have the next three days off anyway. Before you go to bed tonight, make a list of the stuff you're going to need for the dinner, and Duke or I will go get it for you."

She wrapped her arms around his neck. "Thank you for understanding, and for always being my biggest cheerleader. I am the luckiest woman ever. I'll make the list after a while."

Jack gave her a light pat on the backside as she left, which made her laugh. He was still grinning as he cleaned up after her late meal, and then went through the pantry and started the list for her, leaving the details for her to finish.

Duke overheard enough of the conversation between Jack and Hope to know she was going to give notice at work. He supported that wholeheartedly and, at the same time, felt a greater urgency to give them personal space. At least he knew for sure now that the Bailey place was going to be his—his and Cathy's.

Later that night he went up to his room, showered, and got ready for bed, but he couldn't think of sleeping without telling Cathy goodnight, so he gave her a call.

—————————

Cathy was sitting up in bed watching television, but she kept thinking back to the afternoon. She could still smell Duke's aftershave on the pillow and was hugging it to her as she waited for the late night news to come on. And then her phone rang, and she knew before she looked that it was him.

"Hello, you," she said.

Duke smiled. "Hello, darlin'. I called to tell you goodnight, and give you a little bit of news. Rhonda Bailey finally called me this afternoon with a price on her homeplace, and I accepted it. We have all the paperwork to go through, but the place is ours."

"Oh honey…this is wonderful! I'm so excited for you… for us."

"Me too. Either Jack or I will be coming into Blessings tomorrow to do some last-minute shopping for

Thanksgiving, but we're on a tight schedule. Hope has everything all planned out, and we are her runners."

Cathy smiled. "And fine ones you are, I'm sure. Please remind her that I'd be happy to bring something. Just let me know, okay?"

"Yes, I'll tell her, but I think she's got everything covered. I just wanted to tell you good night."

"Good night. Love you," Cathy said.

"Love you, too," Duke said, and disconnected.

Cathy put her phone back on the charger and then snuggled down into the bed, pulled the pillow up closer beneath her chin, and fell asleep.

She didn't see the end of her movie or the late night news. And when she woke a few hours later, she turned off the television and her lamp, and went back to sleep, unaware that Blaine Wagner had not only found her again, but had a man on her tail.

CHAPTER 14

GAGE BREWER CAME DOWN TO A BREAKFAST BUFFET that would have put any Las Vegas buffet to shame. There were four other guests in the dining area when he arrived, and a very attractive middle-aged woman was bustling in and out of the kitchen with fresh food every few minutes. When she saw him walk in, she came to greet him with a smile.

"Good morning. You must be Mr. Brewer. I'm Rachel Goodhope. Hot drinks are all on the sideboard, and the rest is self-explanatory. Enjoy your breakfast."

"Thank you, ma'am. It looks good," Gage said, and hung his jacket on the back of a chair before going to the buffet.

He started with a plate of crispy fried bacon strips, scrambled eggs with cheese, and hot biscuits with gravy, and when he got up to refill his coffee cup, brought back a short stack of pancakes soaked with blackberry syrup.

It was the best meal he'd ever eaten in his life, and if nothing came of finding Cathy Terry here, this meal alone was worth the trip.

Rachel came by later with a carafe of hot coffee to top off her diners' cups. She paused at Gage's table to warm his up, and he took the opportunity to feel her out about Wagner's ex-wife.

"This meal was amazing," Gage said, as Rachel topped off his coffee. "You could make a fortune in Vegas cooking like this."

"Oh, are you from Las Vegas?" Rachel asked.

He nodded, and stirred more sugar into the coffee she'd just poured into his cup.

"Yes, I am. I have an acquaintance from Vegas who recently moved here. Maybe you know her? Her name is Catherine Terry. She's going to help me do some genealogy research at the cemetery here in Blessings."

Rachel started to say yes, and then something stopped her.

"The name doesn't ring a bell," Rachel said.

Gage hid his disappointment with a shrug. "I understand. She hasn't been here long."

Rachel saw his expression fall, which made no sense. Why would he care whether she knew his friend or not?

"So you're into family research. How fascinating!" Rachel said. "Then you'll be visiting our All Saints Cemetery while you're here, I guess. What's the family name you're researching?"

"Um…my father's side…the Brewers."

"Well, happy ghost-hunting," Rachel said, and then smiled again before heading back into the kitchen.

But the moment she was there, she grabbed Bud by the arm.

"That new guy who checked in last night…Gage Brewer…he asked if I knew Cathy Terry."

"So?" Bud asked.

"He said she's going to help him do family research at the cemetery here, but I don't believe him."

"Well, he hasn't broken any laws," Bud said. "So don't go causing trouble for no reason."

Rachel sniffed, but she already felt a measure of loyalty

to Cathy Terry for her recent heroism at the park. She felt the need to warn Cathy, just in case, but she didn't know how to contact her.

"I wish I had her phone number," Rachel said. "I'd at least call to confirm she knows this man."

Bud sighed. "I heard Duke Talbot is seeing her. Hope probably has the number. You could call her."

"I think I will," Rachel said. "You make another run through the dining room. I'm going to the office."

"Okay. Whatever it takes to make you happy," Bud said, and winked, but Rachel missed the wink. She was already on a mission. Unaware that inquiries in small towns piqued both curiosity and suspicion, Gage finished up his coffee, then put on his jacket and left. He wasn't quite sure how to go about looking for Cathy Terry, because cruising up and down streets would only call attention to the presence of a stranger in a small town, which was the exact opposite of what he intended.

But as it turned out, the streets were busier than usual because of Thanksgiving, and the busiest place in town was the Crown. Shopping for groceries for family feasts was happening in large numbers.

After a couple of turns up and down Main Street, Gage pulled into the parking lot at the Crown and set up a kind of stakeout…watching for a curly-haired redhead driving a black Jeep Cherokee. Once he found out where she was living, he'd call it in and still make it home for Thanksgiving with a neat little bundle of money for his trouble.

But Rachel was on a mission in direct opposition to Gage Brewer, as she made the call to Hope.

It rang a couple of times and then Hope answered.

"Hello, this is Hope."

"Hi, honey, this is Rachel. Did I catch you at a bad time?"

"No, no, I'm fine. I'm off work for the next two days. What's up?"

"I was wondering if you have Cathy Terry's phone number. I need to call her about something."

"Duke does. Hang on a second," Hope said, then went down the hall to where Duke was putting extra leaves in the dining table. "Duke...Rachel wants Cathy's phone number. Can you help her?"

"Sure," Duke said, and pulled up Cathy's number in his own phone as Hope handed hers over. "Hey, Rachel. Hope said you want Cathy's number?"

"Yes...I may be overreacting, but we had a late-arrival guest last night, and this morning during breakfast he said he was from Las Vegas. Then asked me if I knew Catherine Terry. Then gave me some dubious story about Cathy being a friend from Vegas and that she was going to help him do research at the local cemetery for family history. I never heard where Cathy was from, so I didn't volunteer anything about her."

The hair rose on the back of Duke's neck. He knew she'd run into the old friend in Savannah just a few days ago, and now some guy from Vegas had shown up asking about her. This didn't feel right.

"What was his name?" Duke asked.

"Gage Brewer. Listen, Duke...I don't know much about Cathy's story, but if this sounds fishy to you, I think she needs to know there's a stranger in town asking about her."

"I do know her story, and it's fishy," Duke said. "I'll call her right now, and if it's nothing, then thank you so much for caring enough to give her a heads-up. And if this is what I think it is, you've just done her a huge favor."

"Okay…thanks. I feel better leaving this in your hands," Rachel said, and disconnected.

"What's going on?" Hope asked as Duke handed back her phone.

"Someone from Vegas is in town looking for Cathy."

Hope gasped. "Is she in danger?"

"I don't know yet, but I'm going to call her," Duke said. He took his phone out onto the front porch and sat down in one of the white wicker chairs to make the call, dreading it even as she answered.

"Hello, my love," Cathy said.

Duke sighed. "Hi, baby. What are you doing today?"

"I slept in, and I'm just cleaning house. Does Hope want me to bring something?" she asked.

"That's not why I'm calling. Rachel Goodhope—the woman who runs Blessings Bed and Breakfast—just called me. She was a little concerned about their late check-in last night. He's from Las Vegas. And this morning he was asking if she knew you."

Cathy moaned, and dropped into the nearest chair.

"No, no, no. It was that damn Pamela St. James. She went straight back to Vegas and told everyone she saw me. I knew she would. I was just hoping Blaine would let me be. I should have known better."

"Blaine Wagner didn't check in. It was a man named Gage Brewer. Have you ever heard of him?"

"No."

"Well, he told Rachel you were going to help him in some family history search at the local cemetery."

"That's a lie," Cathy said. "Where is he now?"

"I don't know, honey. Probably somewhere in town looking for you. Just stay in the house. I'm coming to get you."

"I'm not hiding," Cathy said. "And I'm not running. Not again."

Duke's heart stopped when she hung up.

"Oh dammit, you little hothead," he muttered, and grabbed his jacket and car keys as he ran through the house. "Sorry. Gotta run into Blessings. I won't be long. If you need anything, text me and I'll bring it back," he said, and then was out the door.

He jumped in the truck and took off toward town, trying to call Cathy back as he drove. It just kept going to voicemail, so he called Lon, filled him in on what was happening, and asked him to find either Cathy or Gage Brewer before they found each other.

———————————

Jack came out of the utility room as Duke went out the back door.

"Where's he going?" he asked.

"Someone from Vegas showed up in town looking for Cathy. I think it has to do with her ex-husband," Hope said.

Jack frowned. "That's not good."

"No, it's not, and Duke's about to put himself in the middle of it."

Jack felt a moment of panic, and then let it go.

"Duke's a grown man in love with a woman who needs him. Now what do you need me to do next?"

Hope grinned. "I guess finish putting the leaves in the table. That's what Duke was doing when I interrupted him."

"You got it," Jack said. "Don't worry about my big brother. He can take care of himself."

Cathy googled Blessings Bed and Breakfast to get Rachel's number, but Bud answered.

"Hello, Blessings Bed and Breakfast. Bud Goodhope speaking."

"Bud, this is Cathy Terry. Is Rachel there?"

"She just left to go to the Crown," Bud said. "Can I help you?"

"Your guest, Gage Brewer, is looking for me, and I think my ex-husband is having me followed again. What's he driving?"

Bud blinked. Wow...Rachel's instincts were better than he'd imagined.

"Uh...a silver Cadillac Escalade. Late model."

"And what does he look like?" Cathy asked.

"Are you in trouble?" Bud asked.

"Not yet, but he might be. I need a description."

"Tall, slim, sandy-brown hair. I think he left wearing a black leather jacket."

"Thank you," Cathy said, and hung up.

Bud frowned. It sounded as if trouble was stirring in Blessings.

Cathy got her jacket and keys, then thought about the handgun she still hadn't recovered from the police station and decided it was just as well she didn't have it. But she still wasn't going empty-handed, and dug through her hiking gear for the pepper spray. She found it and then headed out the door.

Her phone was ringing like crazy, but she guessed it was Duke and just let the calls go to voicemail. He'd try to talk her out of this, but it was time to stand her ground.

She got in the car with the pepper spray in the seat beside her. Logic told her Gage Brewer was looking for her, and if he was using Pamela St. James's info, they probably knew what she was driving. So she was going to drive around the main part of Blessings and see if a silver Escalade popped up in her rearview mirror.

The first place she went was by the bed-and-breakfast to make sure he hadn't gone back there. She didn't even have to pull in to see he was gone, so she swung by All Saints Cemetery just to make sure that story wasn't true. The only vehicles there were the groundskeepers' and one little blue sedan, so she headed back toward Main.

Even though she came out on the far end of Main Street, she was surprised by the amount of traffic, and then guessed it was because of people shopping for Thanksgiving. The majority of traffic on Main was either coming from the Crown or going to it, so she decided to check out the parking lot next. It would be the perfect place to watch most everyone in town coming and going today, so she drove in behind an old red truck and a shiny black Lexus and then began cruising the parking lot on the pretense of looking for an empty parking place.

Everything was taken toward the front half of the lot, and the empty places were farther back. So she turned at the end of an aisle of cars and was headed toward the back of the lot when sunlight suddenly flashed on the windshield of a car, which caught her attention.

The strangest thing about it was that the driver was parked against the chain-link fence and had backed into a parking spot so that the car was facing the store.

On the face of it, that wasn't an unusual thing to do, but backing into that particular space put the trunk of the car up against the fence, making it impossible to load groceries into it. And as she got closer, she realized it was, in fact, a silver Escalade...and the driver was wearing a dark leather jacket.

She accelerated toward the back of the lot, then pulled up directly in front of the car, blocking him in. The look on the man's face went from shock to confusion...and then she got out, carrying the pepper spray.

She saw the recognition on his face as she started toward him, then watched him roll his eyes and slap the steering wheel with both hands. He knew he'd been made.

"Get out of the car," Cathy said.

Gage hesitated. "Look, lady, I—"

"So...now I'm a stranger? I thought I was your friend Cathy from Las Vegas who's going to help you with family research, and now you're acting as if you don't know who the hell I am? Get out of the car!"

Gage hadn't expected confrontation. He opened the door and got out to try to minimize the noise she was making, because people were beginning to stare, and to his horror, a man had pulled out his cell phone and was recording them...sound and all.

"I'm out. So now what?" he said.

"Why are you here?" she snapped.

"I'm just doing a job. Nothing more," he said.

"And the job was to find me? Then what? Are you the hitman Blaine Wagner sent to kill me?"

Gage gasped. "What? Hitman? Oh, hell no! I don't know what you're talking about. I'm just a PI working a case."

"And I'm your case. My ex-husband, Blaine Wagner, is stalking me. I ran to get away from him after he threatened my life, and he obviously hired you to find me...so now when I turn up dead you're going to be an accessory to murder."

Gage felt sick. So this was why Rand Lawrence quit.

"Oh, Jesus, lady. I didn't know. All he wanted from me was to find out where you were living."

Cathy glared. "Why would he need to know that? We've been divorced for close to a year. I'm calling the police. I'm filing charges against you for whatever they can pin on you. You can work out the details of your job versus my safety with the local police. You are a low-life, scum-sucking..."

Gage forgot about the boy with the cell phone as he lunged toward her, intent on stopping her from following through on her threat.

Cathy screamed and staggered backward, getting in one good shot of pepper spray just before a big black truck came flying out of nowhere. She heard a screech of brakes, got a brief glimpse of Duke coming out of the truck, and the next thing she knew, he'd body-slammed Brewer against the Escalade.

Gage's face and eyes were on fire, and he was in a panic. He didn't know where the hell this man had come from, but he hit him like a linebacker and knocked the breath clean out of him. He couldn't inhale. He couldn't talk. Then when the man spun him around and shoved him facedown onto the hood of his car, he thought he was going to die.

"My eyes, my eyes… Can't breathe…" he finally gasped.

Duke grabbed him by the back of the neck, yanked him upright, and then twisted both of his arms behind his back.

"Move and I'll break your neck," Duke said.

It was the calm, deadly tone in the threat that ended Gage's struggles.

Cathy was still in shock. "Where did you—"

"You didn't answer your phone," he said.

Defiant, she lifted her chin. "I was busy."

He arched an eyebrow.

Gage Brewer couldn't see, but he was getting his breath back and trying to talk his way out of this.

"My eyes… my eyes…I need help."

"You need to shut up," Duke said.

Gage groaned. "I'm a licensed private investigator on a case. You have no right to—"

Duke tightened his grip. "You lost your rights when you went after my girl."

"Oh God…please, my eyes…I need help. You have to believe me, I am innocent in—"

And that's when Chief Pittman finally rolled up on the scene. He got out of his patrol car, shaking his head at Cathy.

"You still have my gun," Cathy said, and handed him the pepper spray.

Lon glanced at Duke, who had the perp still pinned to the car. "It appears she found him first," Lon said.

Duke shrugged. "I warned you. I took him down as he was about to grab her."

"I wasn't going to hurt her! I have identification. I'm

a licensed PI," Gage said, and then moaned. "My eyes...
Someone help."

"I'm Chief Pittman. An ambulance is on the way. They'll
wash them out."

Gage felt like an idiot. He was trying to plead his case,
and he was crying like a baby from the spray.

"I didn't commit any crime. I was just parked here. I was
hired to find her, and she approached me and started all of this."

Cathy shook her head. "No, that's not the whole story,
Chief. My ex-husband threatened my life back in Vegas.
He's had people watching me and stalking me for months.
It's why I left Vegas, and I had no reason to believe this man
wasn't a hitman. I want him arrested for stalking...and
whatever else you can charge him with."

Gage groaned. "I was just sitting in my car."

"Why did you come to Blessings?" Cathy asked.

Gage repeated the same story. "To find you. But it was
just a job."

Duke twisted Gage's arms a little tighter. "Chief, he lied
to Rachel Goodhope at breakfast and told her Cathy Terry
was a friend. He told Rachel that he and Cathy had plans to
spend the day together."

Lon turned and looked at Cathy.

"Miss Terry, do you know this man?"

"No."

"So you are a stranger asking her whereabouts...and
setting up a timeline that would give you the freedom to
abduct her without anyone thinking she'd gone missing.
How is she supposed to react when she's already afraid of
her ex?" Lon asked.

"But I didn't know that," Gage said.

Lon put him in handcuffs. "What I know is that you came to Blessings to find her. And then I find you staked out at the busiest place in town, hoping she'd show up," Lon said. "Only she found out about your presence before I did. Now, you're under arrest for stalking and attempted assault. Even if they don't stick, those are the charges for now. And your boss might have some questions to answer, too, before all this is over."

The ambulance arrived, and by now, half the people shopping in the Crown were either watching from the parking lot or looking out the windows of the store.

Gage groaned as the chief led him to the ambulance. The EMTs flushed out his eyes, and then the chief took him to jail.

Duke took one look at Cathy and saw past her defiance to the muscle ticking at the side of her jaw and cupped the back of her neck.

"Can you drive yourself home?" he asked.

She nodded.

"I'm right behind you," he said.

Cathy was beginning to shake from the drop of adrenaline as she drove back to her house with Duke on her tail. She got all the way inside before she turned around, walked into his arms, and burst into tears.

"It's never going to be over," she sobbed. "I will never be free of him. Why won't he just leave me alone?"

Duke didn't talk. He just held her...pulling her closer, holding her tighter, until her tears lessened and she could breathe without choking.

He kissed her forehead. "Go pack a bag. I'm taking you home with me. We have two extra bedrooms upstairs."

Cathy sighed. "I can't hide there forever. And I'm not taking trouble into your house."

"Then at least consider yourself a house guest for the holiday," Duke said.

"Not until you clear it with Hope and Jack."

Duke pulled out his phone and made the call in front of her.

Hope answered. "Duke? Is everything okay?"

"It is now. I want to invite Cathy to stay in one of our guest rooms for a couple of days. I'll take her home after Thanksgiving."

"Absolutely," Hope said. "You don't have to ask us to invite people into your own home, honey. Is she okay?"

"She will be. We'll be there as soon as she can pack a bag."

"You can put her in the room next to yours. I'll send Jack to change out the sheets. Everything else is fine. And tell her we'll love having her with us."

"I will. See you soon," he said, and hung up. "You've been doubly invited, and they're happy to have you."

Cathy's shoulders slumped. Defeated, she went into her bedroom to pack.

Junior Cooper ran into the newspaper office, waving his phone. The *Blessings Tribune* had recently been sold, and Mavis Webb, the new owner, was still waiting to prove herself.

She'd covered all of the new births and a funeral or two, along with coverage of the local football games at the high school, but she'd told Junior to be on the lookout for spur-of-the-moment news.

She'd expected something along the lines of accidents or following the police answering calls at the Blue Ivy Bar until Junior, her photographer, came into the front office, yelling, "Boss...do I have a story for you!"

Mavis looked up from her desk.

"Well, don't keep me in suspense...talk."

"Watch this," Junior said, then hit Play and handed her his phone.

Mavis's eyes widened, and she was already envisioning a front-page spread when she heard "threatened to kill me" and "hitman."

"Holy Ghost! Who is this woman? I want to get a statement from her. And who's the hero who saved the day?"

"The woman is Cathy Terry. The lady who took down the rabid coyote in the park. She's new to Blessings. The hero is Duke Talbot. He grew up in the area. He and his brother have a farm outside of town."

"Do we have contact info?"

"No, but I can get it from Chief Pittman," Junior said.

"Then get it. I want to get a statement from her before I run the story. Meanwhile I'm going to watch this again. I didn't get the name of her ex-husband."

"Oh...Blaine Wagner from Las Vegas," Junior said. "The dude who got arrested is also from Vegas. He kept claiming he was a PI Wagner had hired to find her."

Mavis rubbed her hands together and grinned.

"Get me contact info, please."

"On it," Junior said, and ran to the office phone to call the PD.

Avery, the day dispatcher, answered. "Blessings Police Department."

"Avery, this is Junior Cooper. Is the chief in? I need to talk to him."

"Hang on a sec. I'll ring his office."

Lon was in his office writing up the arrest report, while Deputy Ralph booked Gage Brewer into jail. When Lon's phone rang, he put it on speaker and kept typing.

"Hello, Chief Pittman speaking."

"Chief, this is Junior Cooper from the *Tribune*. I videoed the confrontation between Cathy Terry and the man you just arrested on my cell phone, and my boss is going to do a story on it. She wondered if you might have Ms. Terry's contact info to get a statement from her."

"I'll call her. If she wants to give you a statement, I'll call you back with her number, okay?"

"Yes. Thank you," Junior said. "I'll be waiting to hear."

Lon disconnected, then called Cathy's cell.

Cathy was in her room packing when her cell phone rang. When she saw it was from the PD, she frowned.

"Hello?"

"Cathy, this is Chief Pittman. It appears the photographer for the *Blessings Tribune* got your altercation with Mr. Brewer on video, and his boss at the newspaper wants to get a statement from you. Are you okay with me giving her your phone number?"

Cathy groaned. "Oh my God. Really?"

Duke was walking down the hall when he heard her phone ring, and walked in just in time to hear her.

"What's wrong, baby?" he asked.

"Chief, hang on a second, please," Cathy said.

"Sure."

Cathy covered her phone. "The photographer from the newspaper videoed that mess, and now they want a statement from me."

Duke immediately saw a way to put a positive spin on Cathy's situation.

"What would happen if the news of this got back to Vegas? What would Wagner's friends think about this?"

Cathy's eyes widened. "Oh my God! This would be a complete embarrassment...and his business associates would not like the publicity of this at all."

Duke was still angry at what had happened to her, and the hard tone of his voice echoed what he was feeling.

"So, give them a statement they won't forget. Tell your whole story...from the threat he made to the onset of being followed to having to run for fear for your life. And then the fact that Wagner had you followed all the way across the country, leading you to believe the PI was a hitman."

"Really?" Cathy said.

"Yes, honey. Really."

Cathy returned to the call. "Yes, you can give them my number. I'm willing to make a statement."

"Will do," Lon said, and immediately called Junior back with her number.

"Thanks so much!" Junior said as he wrote it down, and then headed back to Mavis's desk. "Got it!" he said, and plopped it down in front of her.

"Awesome," Mavis said. "Now upload this video to my website, and while you're at it, make me some stills. Pick out scenes you know would be good front-page fodder, and then research the name Blaine Wagner and Las Vegas and see what pops up while I talk to her."

Junior hurried to his desk while Mavis called the number.

Cathy had finished packing and was sitting in the living room waiting when her cell phone rang.

"Here goes nothing," Cathy said, and answered. "Hello, this is Cathy Terry."

"Ms. Terry, this is Mavis Webb, the editor of the *Tribune*. Thank you for talking to me. We will be running a story about the altercation at the parking lot of the Crown. There were some serious allegations made on that video, and I would like to hear your side of the story."

"Yes, ma'am, and call me Cathy."

"And I'm Mavis. So…start from the beginning of your story and just talk to me. I promise not to twist your words, and I promise not to sensationalize your situation with jokes and sarcasm. I'm a truth seeker, and I don't have one ounce of empathy in my body for abusive men."

Cathy took a deep breath, and then began talking. Every now and then Mavis would interrupt her to ask a question, and then tell Cathy to proceed.

It lasted over thirty minutes, and when she was finished, it felt weird to have the scariest time of her life encapsulated like this…and Mavis was silent.

"Uh…Mavis? Are you there?" Then she heard the woman clear her throat.

"Yes, I'm here. And I'm in shock. You are one tough cookie, Mary Cathleen. I will not play down your situation."

"Thanks," Cathy said. "So…are we done?"

"Yes, and thank you," Mavis said.

Cathy disconnected. "Well, that's over."

Duke stood. "Come here," he said.

Cathy slipped her arms around his waist and laid her cheek against his chest. Being in his arms was all it took to make her world okay again.

"Are you ready to go home with me now?" he asked.

She nodded.

He picked up her bag and carried it outside while she locked the door behind them.

CHAPTER 15

"I GET A PHONE CALL," GAGE SAID AS HE WAS BOOKED into jail.

"That's at my discretion," Lon said. "But I allow one if the prisoner is not combative."

"You're making a big mistake," Gage muttered.

"No, sir. You're the one who made the mistake," Lon said, then slammed the cell door and locked it.

"My boss will just bond me out," Gage said.

"Well, you aren't in the big city, sir. And you will await the pleasure of our local judge as to when you get your day in court."

Gage groaned. "I want to make my call."

Lon walked out and came back a few minutes later with the cell phone they'd confiscated.

"One call, and you will make it in front of me."

"What about my privacy?" Gage asked.

"You lost that when you violated the privacy of Cathy Terry, didn't you? You took money to go find her from a man who has no legal rights to her whereabouts. That's harassment... That's stalking a woman who is in fear for her life."

Gage took the phone, pulled up Blaine Wagner's number from his contacts, and called him, praying that it wouldn't go to voicemail.

Blaine was in a meeting when the call came through and almost let it go to voicemail, but then something told him to take it.

"Excuse me, gentlemen, but I need to take this call," he said, and walked out of the room as he was answering. "I assume you have news."

Gage sighed. "Yes, sir. She's here, and I'm in jail."

Blaine froze. "What the hell do you mean, you're in jail?"

"She was tipped off as to my presence and confronted me. She caused a big scene and accused me of being a hitman you sent to kill her."

Blaine's gut knotted. Once again, he had underestimated his ex-wife.

"That's ridiculous," he said.

"I need a lawyer," Gage said.

"Yes, yes, I'll see to it immediately," Blaine said. "Just sit tight."

"Well, sir, I have no other options considering I'm behind bars right now because you misled me about this job. I had no idea you had threatened her life."

"I already told you, that's not true," Blaine said.

"Your word. Her word. And I'm stuck in the middle of it."

Blaine felt his control of the situation slipping. Gage Brewer was obviously angry and unaccustomed to being jailed for anything, and Blaine didn't want this getting out.

"Yes, yes, we'll get this all sorted out," Blaine said. "I'll have a lawyer there to bond you out before dark."

"That isn't going to happen today. This is small-town America. It appears judges aren't available at a moment's notice around here. I am trusting you, Mr. Wagner, to keep your word."

"And I'm trusting you to keep my confidences," Blaine countered.

"Yes, well, I'm not your doctor, and I'm not your lawyer, and what you omitted to tell me about all this before I took the job got me arrested, so fix it."

The line went dead. Blaine told himself the jailer ended the call. He didn't want to think that Brewer had hung up on him, because that would constitute something of a threat to his own well-being.

He made a quick call to his lawyer, explained the situation, demanding swift action and the end result he expected, and went back to his meeting.

Gage Brewer handed his phone back through the bars.

"Can I have some water for my eyes?" he asked. "They're still burning."

Lon pointed at the sink inside the cell.

"There's your water."

"That's harsh," Gage muttered.

"Shit happens when you get in bed with the wrong people," Lon said, and walked out.

Cathy was humiliated by the ugliness of her past coming into the lives of good people, and she stayed silent all the way back to the farm. If it wasn't for Duke, she would have packed up and started running again. But she'd fallen in love with a man worth fighting for, and didn't have it in her to give him up.

Finally, Duke reached for her hand. "Cathy…honey… talk to me."

"About what? That whole scene was ugly and embarrassing. Your life isn't like this. You don't deserve to get mixed up in this."

"None of this is your fault, and no one thinks it is. You are a victim of what I would consider a dangerous man, and I think it's time to turn the tables on him."

"What do you mean?" Cathy asked.

"What if some of the heat he's throwing burned him a little? Who do you know back in Las Vegas who would be willing to leak his complicity in a stalking complaint? Would it make any difference in his life if people knew he'd threatened your life?"

"But I can't prove any of that. No one heard him but me," Cathy said.

Duke shrugged. "He's playing dirty. I think the only way he's going to back off is to protect himself. In the world we're living in, facts don't seem to matter. All it takes is the story to be told, and that first step has already been taken by the local newspaper."

It was the first time since all this happened that Cathy even had an inkling that she might be able to fight back. She had the ammunition. She'd just never thought to use it.

"Well, it could make him madder," Cathy said.

"Or…if his threats were ever made known and publicized in social media in some way, it would put the spotlight right on him, should anything ever happen to you," Duke said.

Cathy's eyes widened. "You're right. He would be the first suspect."

"Exactly," Duke said. "So, with his name attached, the story you just gave to the local paper could wind up on the national news. Who do you know in Vegas who would be willing to use the story from the *Tribune* to publicize the fact that Blaine Wagner has been stalking you ever since your divorce? That he has threatened your life, and that the latest man he hired to stalk you has been jailed, and the pending charges against that man could include Blaine as well?"

"Even if no charges are filed?" Cathy said.

"The wording is 'could be,' which doesn't lock you into a definitive statement. He's fighting dirty, baby. I think it's time to give it back to him…and we're home," Duke said as the farmhouse came into view.

Cathy hated to admit it, but she was relieved to be here. Gage Brewer's appearance in Blessings had ruined her sense of safety.

"I'll have to think about it a bit. Nearly everyone I know would side with him against me."

"Just a suggestion," Duke said, and then pulled around back to park.

The house was warm, and good smells were emanating from the kitchen. Hope was at the stove, and smiled as she turned to greet them.

"Welcome, Cathy. We're so glad you're here. Duke will show you to your room. You get yourself comfy and then come back down and join us. We're in the middle of making stuff ahead for Thanksgiving. Another pair of hands will be welcome."

And just like that, the last bit of Cathy's hesitance to intrude into their world was gone. God willing, she was soon going to be a real part of this family.

That afternoon with the Talbots turned into one of the best times of her life. The lighthearted banter between them was funny, and they constantly included her so that she didn't feel like the odd one out. When it came time to go feed the cattle that evening, she was excited to go with Duke.

Hope shook her head. "You are setting a bad precedent."

And when both men grinned, Cathy knew there was a punch line waiting.

"What do you mean?"

"They're taking you to open and close the gates," Hope said. "Trust me."

Cathy laughed. "Okay, I have been warned. But I still want to go."

Duke hugged her. "That's my girl."

Still teasing, Hope shook her head. "The new wears off fast."

"Hush," Duke said. "Don't scare her off."

"I'm not scared...not of this...and not of anything here," Cathy said. "Let's do it."

Hope was right, but Cathy's delight at the newness of it all and the joy of being with Duke was worth it. Then, when he took her all the way to the back pasture, he pointed out the Bailey property on the other side of the fence.

"This is where we'll build a road from our place to the homeplace," Duke said.

"Another gate?" Cathy asked.

Duke laughed. "No. We'll put up a cattle guard."

"Awesome," Cathy said. "Why don't you have cattle guards instead of gates everywhere?"

"Because sometimes we have to move the cattle from

one pasture to another, and that still means having a gate somewhere to make that happen."

"Ah...that makes sense," she said. "Oh well. As long as there are gates, I'll be the gatekeeper."

"A gatekeeper...I love that," Duke said.

Cathy smiled. "And I love you." Then her smile disappeared. "I don't think I remembered to thank you for rescuing me today."

"I don't need thanks. I take care of what's mine...and that includes my best girl," Duke said.

"Thank you, anyway," she said.

"You're welcome. Even if you did scare a year off my life by not answering your phone."

"I'll answer next time," she said.

Duke frowned. "Please don't let there be a next time. As for the cattle, we're done. Time to go back to the house."

―――――――――――――

Supper happened after all the chores were done, and once again, Cathy was drawn into the heart of their home with such ease that it felt as if she'd been doing this for years.

She and Duke did dishes afterward, while Hope gave up the kitchen for a long soak in the bathtub. Tomorrow was the eve of Thanksgiving, and after that, Christmas, and Cathy's year of hell would be over.

Cathy went to bed that night with new hope. She didn't know what was going to come of the interview she'd given to Mavis Webb at the *Blessings Tribune*, but it felt good not to be hiding her truth anymore.

Duke wanted to be sleeping in the bed beside Cathy, but

she'd had the day from hell, and it felt right to give her the space just to be…to rest knowing she was safe and she was loved.

When the morning paper hit the streets of Blessings the next day, it was the immediate topic of conversation. Phones began ringing and friends were talking, and everyone who wasn't on the delivery route was looking for a copy. It was the first time in years that they sold out before noon, and no wonder. The story was both shocking and inspiring. Mavis Webb was a genuine wordsmith and true to her word.

What she had found out about Blaine Wagner's blood-line and genealogy made him newsworthy, and when she learned the story had been picked up by the AP, she wasn't surprised, nor was she worried. She'd been extra careful to couch her statements so that they were all worded as unsupported accusations. And that Mr. Wagner had been unavailable for comment, which was true, because she'd tried to call the number Cathy Terry had given her for her ex but it had gone to voicemail.

It wasn't just the story the AP had picked up that was about to curdle the cream in Blaine Wagner's morning coffee.

The sensationalism of the incident and the accusations captured on the video Junior Cooper had uploaded to social media had gone viral overnight, and the three-hour time difference between Blessings and Las Vegas had already given life to the story.

Half the country had already seen it, and some big shots

on the East Coast were already making phone calls to their business partners on the West Coast—waking them in the wee hours of the morning to give them a heads-up about one of their own.

Rudy CaLucy was a big wheeler-dealer in Vegas. It was after 3:00 a.m. before he made it home, and he was getting ready for bed when his phone rang. When he realized it was the Chairman, he knew there was a crisis somewhere, and after hearing the story, he wasn't happy about any of it.

"Is this going to fall back on us?" Rudy asked.

"It's early on, so it's hard to say," the Chairman replied.

Rudy frowned. "It's true that he's really been stalking her?"

"According to my sources, yes."

"This lends credence to the murder threat."

The Chairman agreed. "Exactly."

Rudy didn't like where this was going. "Has anyone talked to Wagner?"

"I thought we all needed to know before we confront him. I'd like for us to be of one mind about how we deal with it," the Chairman said.

"So…his option is stop it now. Back off his ex, or we clean house?" Rudy asked.

The Chairman paused for effect, then answered, "It would be a tragedy that the last living Wagner died without leaving an heir."

"Are you going to do the calling?"

"Yes…later today. He doesn't deserve a heads-up. This kind of strong-arm behavior doesn't sit well with us. If she wanted retribution, she could have gone straight to the feds from the get-go. Instead, she went into hiding, which tells me Wagner made her fear for her life. We don't need that kind of publicity with one of our board members. I'll take care of it," the Chairman promised.

Rudy was confident the boss would do what he promised.

"Then I will leave this in your most capable hands, sir, and go to bed."

Gage Brewer's lawyer bonded him out of jail the same day the story broke, and with the approval of the judge, Brewer was allowed to leave the state before his day in court.

Gage promised the court to publish a public apology to Cathy Terry, explaining her innocence in the whole matter, both in the local paper and in the Las Vegas papers as well, then flew back to Vegas in a private jet with the lawyer Wagner had sent.

With the lawyer's assistance, Brewer wrote an apology to Cathy Terry and sent it as a paid notice to the *Blessings Tribune*, then sent an ad to the Las Vegas papers explaining his unintended part in frightening Blaine Wagner's ex-wife, and that he had broken off all business dealings with Wagner. It was all he knew to do to clear up his reputation, which, up to this time, had been spotless.

Then he went home, packed a bag, and headed for Reno to spend Thanksgiving with his family. He'd have some explaining to do there as well, but he felt confident the worst was behind him.

Cathy was helping Duke make pancakes when her phone rang.

"I've got it," Duke said, and reached for the spatula to turn the pancakes on the griddle so she could get her phone.

"Thanks," she said, and ran to answer. "Hello?"

"Cathy, it's Mavis Webb. I hope I'm not calling too early," she said.

"Not at all," Cathy said.

"Okay, well, I thought it only fair to warn you that your story is all over town, and we sold out of papers. It was also picked up by the Associated Press, and it ran in the Vegas papers this morning."

"Oh my lord!" Cathy said.

"That's not all. Junior Cooper uploaded the video to social media on your behalf. It went viral last night and is something of a sensation this morning."

"Uh, wait! What? You mean the whole thing...what you wrote *and* the video?"

Mavis chuckled. "Yes. The whole shebang, honey. If there's justice in this world, your ex might just be persuaded to back the hell off now."

"Oh my gosh, Mavis! Uh, I don't know what to say except thank you."

Mavis laughed. "Well, there's no way to tell how this will play out, but we've definitely put him on the hot seat. And you're welcome."

Cathy hung up, then looked up at Duke.

"That was Mavis Webb. The story she wrote was good for business. They sold out of newspapers this morning. And the story was picked up by the AP and ran in the Vegas papers this morning."

Duke grinned. "That is awesome."

"That's not all," Cathy said. "Last night, Junior Cooper uploaded the video of our little altercation in the parking lot at the Crown. Mavis said it went viral. I'd bet good money you become the hero of the moment because of it."

The smile slid off Duke's face. "Uh, well, I'm not sure all that is necessary," he said.

Cathy burst into laughter, and was still laughing when Jack and Hope walked in.

"What's so funny?" Jack asked, and then looked at his brother and started grinning. "What did you do, Duke?"

Duke frowned. "Why does it have to be something I did?"

Hope hugged him. "Because, darling…you are so good at putting your foot in it."

Cathy shook her head. "No, no, it's nothing like that. Long story short…the video of what happened yesterday was uploaded to social media, and it went viral last night. I just told Duke there was every possibility that he was going to be the darling of the internet for some time. I think it just startled him. And I'm sorry for laughing at you, sweetheart."

Duke grinned wryly. "Hey…if I have to spread myself around a little to satisfy my fans, I guess I can pull it together enough to participate."

They were still laughing when he took the last of the pancakes off the griddle, but the conversation soon changed to the food and the day, and they all forgot about what was going on beyond their walls.

CHAPTER 16

UNFORTUNATELY, BLAINE'S DAY OF HELL WAS JUST beginning. He was at breakfast when his phone signaled a text. He glanced at it and noticed it was from one of his casino managers. Thinking there must be a problem at the casino, he pulled it up, then frowned.

The message was vague, but the manager had sent a link.

Boss. You need to see this ASAP.

So Blaine clicked on the link, then quickly realized it was the confrontation between Cathy and Gage Brewer. But the shocker came when he plainly heard her say his name, and that he had threatened to kill her. His heart stopped. When she asked Brewer if he was the hitman her husband sent to take her out, he groaned.

And then his maid brought in the morning newspapers and the first one he opened had a story on the front page with a still picture of the confrontation, and his name and his ex-wife's name front and center.

"What the fresh hell is this?" he shrieked, and grabbed his phone and called his lawyer. The call went straight to voicemail, which infuriated him, so he called him again, and again, and again, until the call was finally answered.

"Hello."

Blaine frowned. The terse tone of his lawyer's voice did not sit well with him.

"Why the hell didn't you pick up? I need you."

"I was making love to my wife, and she takes precedence over everything, including you. Now what do you want?"

Blaine wanted to argue, but something told him this was not the time to denigrate a woman, especially when one had just thrown him into his own personal pit of hell.

"I'm sorry. But I have a thing happening that needs to be stopped."

"I already sent a lawyer to get your PI bonded out today," he said.

"It's not that. The whole thing is all over the morning papers, and the video is on social media. Her words, saying I threatened her life. Her words, saying I sent a hitman to kill her. I need a gag order immediately."

"Why? The words have already been said. The world has heard them. Your smartest move is to keep your mouth shut and leave her the hell alone. And that's advice coming from your lawyer."

"But she can't prove I said them," Blaine argued.

"And you can't prove you didn't," he said. "You caused this by stalking her…which, may I say, makes you look guilty as hell. How long did you have her watched and tailed before she left Vegas?"

Blaine didn't answer.

"Once she was gone, why did you care where she went? She wasn't bothering you. She wasn't interfering in your business."

Again, Blaine was quiet.

"Think about it, Mr. Wagner. Think very carefully. You need to hire a public relations firm to clean up your image and quit worrying about a woman who divorced you. If she files charges against you, you are going to have a hard time explaining why you felt the need to stalk her for all these months...and why you sent someone all the way across the country to find where she went. You, sir, are teetering on the brink of a personal disaster. And that's speaking as your lawyer, of course. If you have need of my services, you know how to reach me."

Blaine hung up. His heart was hammering against his chest in panicked irregularity. If anything happened to her now, he would be the first one the authorities would blame.

He got up from the table and walked out onto the terrace beyond the breakfast room to get some air. He needed to think. Maybe a long trip abroad would be the answer. Just let everything die down, and by the time he came back, this would all be old news.

Just as he was feeling like he'd settled on a plan that would work, his phone rang again, and when he saw who was calling, it occurred to him that he might not be able to run far enough or fast enough to get away from what was coming down on him now.

So he took a deep breath and shifted the tone of his voice into one of authority.

"Hello. This is Blaine."

"Mr. Wagner. We need to talk."

Blaine sat down on a bench out on the terrace, gripping his phone in white-knuckled fear, listening to the displeasure and the thinly veiled threat in the Chairman's voice.

"You made a very dangerous mistake, and we are not pleased," the Chairman said. "Any shadow of indiscretion on you comes back on us as well. You see that, don't you?"

"Yes, sir, I understand, but let me assure you that none of this is true," Blaine said.

"Don't lie. You aren't good at it. What you need to understand is that we expect all of this to go away ASAP. If you persist in your pursuit of this woman, then I advise you to get your affairs in order."

Oh Jesus. "I have no intention of engaging her further. I will be traveling abroad for the next few months, giving all of this time to fade away," Blaine said.

"Consider yourself warned," the Chairman said, and hung up.

Blaine's stomach roiled. He stood, then lurched to the side of the terrace, leaned over the railing, and threw up until there was nothing left in his belly but the fear of God the Chairman had just delivered.

It was just after 9:00 a.m. Thanksgiving morning when Jack saw a white delivery van coming up the drive.

"Hey, isn't that the delivery van from Franklin's Flower Shop?" he said.

Hope looked out the window as the van stopped in the front yard, and then Mr. Franklin got out and went to the back of the van. When he appeared again, he was carrying a very ornate arrangement of flowers, all in autumn colors.

Jack opened the door as Harold came up the steps.

"Wow, that's some bouquet!" Jack said.

"I was told Cathy Terry was here," Harold said. "These are for her."

"Yes, she's here. Hey, Cathy!" Jack yelled.

Cathy was in the kitchen peeling potatoes, and stopped to wipe her hands before hurrying toward the living room as Duke came down the stairs to join them.

"What's going on?" she asked, and then saw the flowers. "Good grief!"

"Delivery for Cathy Terry," Harold said. "Myra got the call late yesterday evening, and the orders were specific... that they be delivered to you today. Happy Thanksgiving, everyone," he said.

Duke took the vase.

"Where should I put this?" he asked. "It can't go on the dining room table because we won't be able to see over it."

"We'll make a place for it on the sideboard next to Mercy's pies," Hope said.

Duke did as she asked, and then plucked the card from within the bouquet and handed it to Cathy.

"Here you go, honey."

"I can't begin to imagine who these would be from," she said as she opened the little envelope and then pulled out the card. She scanned it, then gasped.

"Oh, my lord!"

"What?" Duke asked.

"Listen to this," she said, and read it aloud.

Cathy, we have only good memories of your kindness during our business dinners, and wish to express our sincere apologies for your suffering. You have our word that you will not be bothered again. Happy Thanksgiving.

"But who's it from?" Duke asked.

Cathy looked up, her eyes wide with shock. "This would

be Blaine's business partners. I'm thinking they delivered an ultimatum he will not be able to ignore."

Duke whooped with delight, then swung her off her feet and turned her in a little circle.

"This is fantastic! Your instincts to confront the PI were on target, and look what came of it," he said. "Your running days are over."

Cathy was in tears, but they were happy tears.

"I didn't think this day would ever come," she said.

Hope clapped her hands. "Best news ever!" she cried. "Now let's go have breakfast! We have lots to celebrate."

The turkey had been in the oven since 5:00 a.m., but breakfast was simple bowls of cold cereal. It had been Duke and Jack's tradition that all of the cooking on holidays was devoted to the dinner being served, and Hope had gone along with it years ago when she first joined the family. Now Cathy was part of the tradition, eating cornflakes with the rest of them, while the wonderful aroma of roasting turkey filled the room.

Lon and Mercy arrived just after eleven. Mercy came in wearing black pants and a loose turquoise shirt that accentuated her height and beauty. As always, she was the epitome of elegance. She was laughing as she entered, carrying a pie in each hand and teasing Lon about putting his thumb in the pecan pie on purpose.

The pies went on the sideboard next to the ornate bouquet. Once they heard the story about why it had come and who it was from, Lon was secretly relieved.

It had occurred to him that more trouble might follow

Cathy, and he was ready to protect her and Blessings in any way necessary, but this seemed to signify she would not be bothered by her ex again.

"Hey! There are still more to bring in," Mercy said, and sent the men back for the second load.

Two more pies were added to the sideboard, along with a big container of homemade rolls.

Mercy gave her sister a hug, then patted Hope's little tummy.

"Baby's first Thanksgiving, and he doesn't even know it," she said.

Hope grinned. "We don't know whether it's a boy or a girl," she said.

"If it's a Talbot, it's bound to be a boy," Mercy said, and then smiled at Cathy. "I'm so glad you're here to have dinner with us today."

"So am I," Cathy said. "I keep pinching myself to see if I'm dreaming. This is the nicest town, with the nicest people I have ever known in my life."

"And I am the nicest of all," Duke said, and kissed her on the cheek as he walked past with a stack of dessert plates for the sideboard.

Cathy blushed but she was grinning, while everyone else laughed, mostly at Duke for just being himself.

———————————

People all over Blessings were gathering around their tables with their family and guests.

Big Tom Rankin got to go home the day before Thanksgiving. He had a lot of healing ahead of him, and

Ethel had rescinded her vow not to move in with them and was in their spare bedroom next to Tom, to nurse him back to health.

Albert was so grateful his daddy was still alive that he didn't mind the fact that Ethel was in the house. He went into Blessings and got Thanksgiving dinner from Granny's and brought it home for them to eat.

Dan and Alice Amos had their little family, plus their neighbor, Elliot Graham. After they'd weathered the hurricane together, Elliot had become a fixture in their family.

As always, Lovey Cooper was serving Thanksgiving dinner at Granny's, and for the first time, she had family of her own to share it with. Her son, Sully Raines, and his wife, Melissa, were setting up the small banquet room for Lovey and her family and friends.

Ruby and Peanut were joining them as always, and Vera and Vesta from the hair salon were eating there, too. Mabel Jean had gone home to her family.

Jack and Dori Pine's house was nothing short of mayhem with Jack's two little brothers, Brooks and Beep, and Dori's son, Luther, who was now walking and talking and following the "big boys," rolling all over the living room floor while watching the annual Macy's Thanksgiving Day Parade on TV.

Jake, Laurel, and Bonnie Lorde were having ham for Thanksgiving because Bonnie was afraid her pet chicken, Lavonne, would get her feelings hurt if they cooked turkey.

Bowie and Rowan James arrived in a red Mustang the night before Thanksgiving to spend it with his granny Pearl and his aunt Ella. It was an interesting twist to be the first overnight guests in the house Bowie rebuilt for them after the hurricane. Pearl cried when they drove up, so happy to have her grandson, Bowie, and his new wife back in Blessings, even if it was only for a couple of days.

The Wilson family was celebrating big this year. After Melvin Lee's meltdown and his daddy's return to the family, his daddy's new job with a local plumber put him home every evening.

Melvin Lee was anxiously waiting for his mama to call them to come eat. He'd been smelling that turkey cooking all morning and was certain he might actually starve before everything was done. It was his best day ever, because his grandma was riding herd on his siblings while Mama and Daddy cooked dinner together. He couldn't remember a better Thanksgiving in his life.

And so it went all over Blessings. People were gathering together, or making the trip to Granny's Country Kitchen to have their holiday meal in the company of friends.

The Bailey family had gone to the nursing home to have dinner with their father, Mylo. It would likely be their last Thanksgiving with him. Even though the old man didn't know who they were anymore, they remembered him, and such was the circle of life.

They were down to dessert at the Talbot farm, and telling stories about holidays past, when Duke asked Cathy what her Thanksgivings were like when she was still living in Alaska.

Cathy laughed. "Nothing like this, I can assure you, and there were only the three of us. Once we didn't even celebrate it at all because we forgot about it, and one Christmas we celebrated on the wrong day. Time didn't mean the same thing there that it does now. It was sunup and sundown, and staying focused on surviving in between."

"You didn't even have a calendar?" Jack asked.

"Usually," Cathy said. "But think about it a minute. If the days aren't marked off as they pass, you lose track. And if you need something dry to start a fire and it's been raining for days, or snow is up past the windows and the fire went out because of a downdraft, you use the driest thing you have for tinder because getting warm is more important than what day it is. At that time, the driest thing in the cabin was a page from the calendar. So if we burned up October or November, Halloween and Thanksgiving went begging. And then you don't know how many days have come and gone, so you still have December on the calendar, but you don't really know when it is. That's when Mama would just pick a day and call it Christmas."

"I am in awe," Duke said.

Cathy pointed her fork at him. "That was then, and this is now. I will expect a Christmas present and a birthday present," she said.

Duke's eyes darkened. "I will give you presents every day of your life, just for the pleasure of seeing you smile."

And just like that, Cathy was looking at him through tears.

"Awww, honey, don't cry," he said.

Hope patted Cathy's arm. "Women cry good tears and bad tears. Those are good tears."

"Nothing is forever," Lon said. "Just be grateful for each day you have together. And on a happier note, Cathy, have you read the piece the *Tribune* did on you yesterday?"

She shook her head. "No. It was embarrassing enough just being in a public brawl."

Mercy arched an eyebrow and then shook her head. "Oh sugar…that was not a public brawl. I used to work in a bar in Savannah that catered to bikers and truckers. *Those* were brawls."

Cathy sighed. "Well, it's still hard to let the world see your dirty laundry."

"You need to read it," Mercy said. "You'll feel better about yourself once you do. The new owner did a fabulous job of telling your story. You came across as very brave while dealing with a scary situation. I predict you will have even more fans than you did after you took out the rabid coyote…which by the way was *so* badass."

"Truth," Lon said. "And Duke, my friend…you need to check out the video on YouTube because you're gathering yourself quite a fan club. Most of them are women, but there are plenty of men giving you a thumbs-up, too, for taking care of business."

"Lord," Duke said.

Cathy laughed. "I told you."

Jack rolled his eyes…pretending dismay. "I will never live up to my big bro's reputation."

"Oh…I think you're doing okay," Hope said. "You're the one who's gonna be a daddy."

Jack grinned. "You're right! And I'll take that any day. I'll also take a piece of pumpkin pie with whipped cream, please."

"You want more? After all we've eaten?" Hope asked.

"The first piece was pecan. We don't want the pumpkin pie to feel left out."

"I second that," Duke said, then got up from the table to bring the coffeepot back to the table.

When he got to Cathy, he not only added a little coffee to her cup, but the lingering touch on the back of her neck as he paused at her seat gave her shivers. She would not be sleeping alone tonight.

———————

It was the witching hour.

The energy in the old farmhouse was magnetic. Love was happening, moving air through the rooms like breath in and out of lungs.

A floorboard creaked—even though no man trod the planks. The grandfather clock in the living room downstairs was striking midnight as the couple in the bed upstairs continued to chase their own kind of magic.

The house had come alive within the joy of the people in it, as if sensing the burgeoning love of Duke and Cathy, and the impending arrival of a new life with Hope and Jack. Another Talbot was to be added to the generations who'd lived and died beneath this roof.

The toll of the clock had struck ten previous times... and then eleven...and then the last.

Midnight.

Another creak...a small pop...and then silence, like the long exhale of a breath—the sign a new day was just beginning, even though the occupants within were still at rest.

———————

Hope left the farm before daybreak to begin her shift and turn in her notice.

Jack went to feed the animals on his own, leaving Duke to get Cathy home.

"I don't want you to go," Duke said, as they drove away from the farm.

"I don't want to leave you, either, but our lives together will begin when we move into the new place. Not moving in with Hope and Jack."

"I know," Duke said. "And I agree, which is even more of an impetus to get a crew into the house to start renovation. The only drawback is that legally it doesn't belong to me yet."

"What all will they have to do?" Cathy asked.

"The Realtor is drawing up the papers. Hopefully, they'll be ready for me to sign soon, and once I hand over earnest money, that seals my intent to purchase. Then we'll get an inspector in so everything is in writing. We'll close as soon as we can."

"Is there anything we can do in the meantime?" she asked.

"We can't do anything to the house…but I'm going to take the tractor and brush hog over and knock down all the grass and weeds around the place. It hasn't been tended in months."

"This is where I miss having a purpose," Cathy said. "I used to volunteer a lot in Vegas, but there's not a lot of call for volunteering around here."

"Well, there is the upscale side of Blessings. There's a small country club, a golf course, and the high-end lifestyle that goes with it. I understand there's a group of women who—"

Cathy shook her head. "No thanks. I've been there, done that, and I want no part of that anymore. I'll figure something out. And when we can finally start tearing into the house, I can help."

"You should get online and start looking for design and decor. I'm no good at stuff like that. All I know is I don't want it to look sleek and modern, but I do want the modern touches that make living life easier. We won't have the house done by Christmas, but we can have Easter there. How's that?"

"Yes…Easter. That's something to look forward to, and I can start on the decor. But the first thing on my agenda is buying a car. It's time to turn in the rental."

"Then there's your purpose. As soon as you pick out the model you want, I'll take you to Savannah to pick it up," he said. Then he looked thoughtful for a moment. "I didn't know love felt like this. I have assumed a lot between us, and it occurred to me this morning that I haven't officially said the words."

"What words?" Cathy asked.

He pulled over onto the side of the road and then took her by the hands.

"Mary Cathleen Terry, I cannot imagine the rest of my life without you in it. Will you marry me?"

Cathy grinned, and then threw her arms around his neck and kissed him soundly on the lips.

"I'm taking that as a yes," Duke said.

"Yes, that is a yes," Cathy said. "In the romance books, doesn't the heroine always marry the man who saves her from the bad guys?"

"I don't know about that. All I know is you are what was

missing in my life." Then he groaned. "Crap. I never do anything in the proper order. I love you like crazy, and a ring will be forthcoming."

Cathy cupped the side of his cheek. "There is no order to love. Only a chaos of emotions and the feeling that you will die without each other."

"Then I'm there," he said, and this time their kiss was longer and sweeter before he finally got back onto the road and took her home.

There was an accumulation of newspapers on Cathy's front porch, including the one with the story about her interview. She sat down and read it after Duke left, and then cried from relief and a release of the fear that had sent her running in the first place.

This was happening. This really was happening. She had her life back, and without the worry of ever being bothered by Blaine Wagner again.

Blaine was still reeling from the throes of his own revelation. Then seeing the ad that Gage Brewer had taken out in the Las Vegas papers admitting his unintentional part in frightening Blaine Wagner's ex-wife, and the public acknowledgment that he was no longer associated in any way with Blaine Wagner and his enterprises, added to Blaine's humiliation.

The ultimatum from the Chairman had been scary as

hell, and now it felt like all eyes were on him in negative judgment wherever he went. He was getting a dose of what he'd done to his ex-wife, and it didn't feel good.

It occurred to him as he was contemplating his demise that there wasn't another Wagner in the wings. He was the last of the line. He'd refused Cathy's desire for children, and now it dawned on him what that meant.

He'd already booked a flight to Rome and, at the invitation of a college friend, was going to spend a month with him and his family in their villa. Italy was as good a place as any to look for a new wife—one who was ready to give him babies.

His father used to tell him all the time to "straighten up and fly right." He'd thought that was just an old-fogey saying from his dad's childhood, but now it was making all kinds of sense. The threat of becoming coyote food and ant bait in the Mojave Desert had a way of doing that.

But Wagner wasn't the only one in Vegas who was feeling the guilt. When Pamela St. James first read the story, then saw the video, she was horrified. She kept thinking back to that phone call she'd made to her friends the day she'd seen Cathy in Savannah. Not only had she given away where Cathy was hiding, but Pamela and her friends had made fun of her. If Cathy had been murdered, Pamela would have shared in the guilt of making it happen.

She hadn't been to church in years, but on the day Gage Brewer's public apology showed up in the local papers, she took herself down to the Catholic church where she'd been married and asked to confess her sins. It didn't change what she'd done, but in her mind, at least God wouldn't be mad at her anymore.

To celebrate the cleansing of her soul, she went shopping and slid right back into the shallow existence of her life.

Two days later, Cathy was dressed and waiting for Duke to take her to Savannah to pick up her new car. She liked driving the Jeep Cherokee she'd rented, so she had opted for a newer version of it, only in red and with four-wheel drive. If she was going to be a country girl, she wanted a car that could navigate bad roads and slick roads to get to and from town.

When she heard Duke drive up, she patted her hair just to make sure there were no flyaway curls. And moments later, he was knocking at her door.

Duke heard her footsteps and smiled. She was running. That's how he felt trying to get to her. Like he couldn't get there fast enough. And then the door swung open and she was standing there smiling—a vision in blue. He entered with a chill wind behind him and swept her up into his arms. Her lips were warm upon his cheeks, and then on his mouth, yielding to the pressure of his kiss.

"Good morning, my love."

"You are in a fine mood today," she said. "What's happened?"

He took a little black box from his pocket and handed it to her.

"Had to get it out of the safety deposit box. One engagement ring, somewhat late, but nevertheless important," he said, and then opened it.

Cathy immediately gasped at the yellow rose-cut diamond in an antique setting. "Oh Duke! Oh my God, this is beautiful."

"It belonged to my grandmother...the first Talbot woman to live in our house. If it doesn't fit, we can have it sized, but she had long slender fingers like yours."

He took it out of the box and then slid it on her finger.

"Look! It's meant to be! It's a perfect fit, and it's stunning," Cathy said. "I am so honored to be wearing it."

"If you'd rather have something new, we'll go—"

"No, no! Never!" Cathy said, and clutched her hand to her heart. "This makes me feel like I already belong."

"And you do...to me," Duke said. "Now let's go get that new car. We'll drop off the rental first."

She put on her gray hip-length peacoat and grabbed her bag, and then out the door they went.

CHAPTER 17

THE CITY WORKERS WERE HANGING CHRISTMAS decorations on the streetlights down Main as Cathy and Duke drove to the insurance agency. All of the businesses were in the act of decorating their storefronts and putting up signs in the windows advertising sales for Christmas shoppers.

Cathy went inside and turned in her Jeep, then ran out and got into the truck with Duke.

"Ready, set, go!" she said, which made him grin. Her happy spirit was contagious.

He made a U-turn and headed out of town. As they were going down Main, Duke pointed to a little girl with her face pressed to a window, looking in at the Christmas village being set up in a shop window.

"Look. She's already in the holiday spirit," he said.

Cathy nodded, but she was thinking back to her own childhood. The only holiday that was ever celebrated with great enthusiasm was her birthday. She was born on July Fourth. Her parents called her their little firecracker, even though she didn't really know what that meant until she began homeschooling and learned about Independence Day and the American Revolution.

"I'm getting in the holiday spirit, too," Cathy said, thinking about all of the good things ahead of them.

They drove out of town with the radio off, talking about the future.

"Do you want a big wedding?" Duke asked.

"I had a big wedding. It was a nightmare of planning and being careful to do and say the right things. I want what you want," Cathy said. "You grew up here. If you want it, I'm on board. If you don't, it won't be a disappointment to me. All I care about is being with you for the rest of my life."

"Then let's play it by ear when the time comes," he said.

Cathy hesitated, and then just blurted out what she'd been thinking about. "I want to remind you of something. You're taking me into your family as your wife, but I come with a big-ass dowry. You bought the place that's going to be our forever home, so I want to furnish the money to renovate it. We'll just set up a renovation account, and every expense will come out of that and won't impact the farming operation."

Duke's eyes widened. He'd actually forgotten her telling him about the money she got in the divorce settlement.

"Seriously?" he asked.

She frowned. "Of course, seriously. If we're partners in life, we're going to share stuff, mister. No mine and yours business."

He grinned. "Yes, ma'am. And for the record, that's probably going to be the unseen blessing in all of this. Not having to cut corners to meet a budget."

"Our budget will be what it takes to make the place the way we want it," she said. "The money came from the profits of gambling, but it's going to be spent on us…and there's no risk in that. I know in my heart we are a sure thing, Duke Talbot."

Duke sighed. "I have a confession to make. Duke is a nickname I've had since I was two. My legal name is Jason Lee Talbot."

Cathy's mouth opened…and then she rolled her eyes in pretend dismay. "Thank you for letting me know before we got to the altar."

He grinned. "Well, Grandpa grew up in the sixties. And there was this song he liked called 'Duke of Earl,' by a singer named Gene Chandler. He was always playing it on Grandma's old record player, and they said the first word I learned to say was Duke. Not Mama. Not Daddy. Duke. And it stuck."

Cathy laughed, trying to picture this man as a tiny little boy, and wished she'd known him a long time ago.

They kept talking about the house renovation and colors and designs until they were finally at the outskirts of Savannah. Christmas had already hit that city as well, and everything seemed to be in full holiday flow.

"Do you know where the Jeep dealership is?" Cathy asked.

Duke nodded. "I make it my business to know where I'm going at all times…except when I'm with you. In those times, I am just going crazy."

"You are impossible," she said, then felt that silly smile creeping back on her face. He had a way of doing that to her—feeding her ego and flashing her those sexy looks at the same time.

They reached the dealership and got out. Her car was ready and waiting, and the only thing she had left to do was sign papers and pay for it. They sat in the sales office for almost thirty minutes, and Cathy kept thinking of all the things Duke probably had waiting for him back at the farm.

"Duke, honey, I know you need to go home. I needed a ride, and you provided it. Why don't you go ahead and leave?"

"I don't want to leave you on your own like this," he said.

She shook her head, unsettling a few curls. "I'll be fine. I do not need a keeper. Backpacked…slept under the stars… fed myself…kept myself alive…remember?"

He sighed. "I will never not want to take care of you."

"And I will love every moment of it, too. But right now, I'm about to sign my name on a check and on a bill of sale, and then swing by the mall before I leave town."

"Okay. But will you promise to call or text before you leave the city, just so I'll know you're on the way back to Blessings?"

"Yes. I promise."

He leaned over and kissed her, brushed the tip of his finger across one of her curls, and then left.

She watched him leave, thinking to herself as he walked out the door that he looked just as sexy going out a door as he did coming in one. And then she leaned back and sighed…still waiting for the papers she needed to sign.

It took another twenty minutes of patience before the salesman came back with the papers and apologies. But her brand-new keyless-entry, push-button-start Jeep Cherokee was fueled up and ready to go, and when she left, she headed straight to the mall. She was going to the men's Big and Tall shop to look for a Christmas present for Duke.

She'd already checked out his sizes while she was at the farm for Thanksgiving, and now she wanted to find him something special.

She parked farther back in the lot just so she wouldn't have to worry about getting a door ding on her new car and was walking toward the front entrance when she saw two men getting out of a white van.

The first thing that alerted her something was off was how they were acting when they got out. The weather was cool, and the wind was brisk, so their long trench coats weren't out of place, but they were both clutching at the front of their coats, as if they were holding onto something beneath.

And even as she kept walking, there was a sense of warning washing over her. She was only feet behind them when they paused at the entrance. When they pulled masks up over the bottom half of their faces, Cathy gasped.

They heard her and spun around.

Cathy turned and ran, zigzagging across the lot toward the cars.

The rapid fire of one weapon kicked up concrete beneath her heel, and another shot went through the purse swinging on her shoulder.

She was running and screaming when she tripped and fell, sending the last of the burst of bullets over her head into the car in front of her. She was crawling on her hands and knees to get out of the shooters' line of sight when they quit her and ran inside.

Cathy was still shaking as she grabbed her phone to call 911. And even as the dispatcher was answering, she began hearing the rattle of automatic weapon fire and the screams of unsuspecting victims.

"911. What is your emergency?"

"I'm in the parking lot at the Savannah Mall. I saw two white men in long gray trench coats and masks get out of a white van. They shot at me and then entered the mall. I can hear screams and gunfire of automatic weapons."

"Are you injured, ma'am?" the dispatcher asked.

"No, all of the shots missed me," Cathy said.

The dispatcher was taking down the information as fast as Cathy was giving it, and at the same time, more calls were coming in to 911 from people inside the mall.

"Ma'am, you said you saw them and what they were driving… Did you see the tag?" the dispatcher asked.

"Yes, yes," Cathy said. She saw the van a short distance away and gave her the tag number. "I don't know anything more to tell you, and I'm getting out of here," Cathy added, and then got up and started running toward her car.

The moment she was inside, she called Duke because she knew if he heard about this shooting, he was immediately going to think she was inside the mall.

When he answered, she could hear the delight in his voice.

"Hi, honey! Missed me already?"

She couldn't tell him over the phone that she'd been shot at. She couldn't even say it aloud without screaming.

"I just need to tell you I'm fine, I'm leaving the mall, and I never made it inside."

There was a moment of silence, and then his voice changed.

"What the hell are you talking about?"

She was still rattled and breathless and didn't realize she was skipping details.

"I saw them get out of the van. They were wearing trench coats and holding onto them like there was something beneath…and then I saw them pull up the masks just before they went in the mall. I turned around and ran. I called 911 just as they started shooting. I'm in my car in the back of the lot, and I'm going home."

"Oh my God, baby… Are you telling me there is an active shooting happening in the mall?"

"Yes! I can see people running out of the mall from all over. And the first police cars are coming. I am leaving the parking lot as we speak. I'll let you know when I get home."

"If I call you again, you'll answer your phone, right?"

Cathy swallowed past the lump in her throat. That fear came from the fact that she hadn't answered before when she was chasing down Gage Brewer.

"I promise. I'll never let a call from you go to voicemail again. I'm safe. I'm already a block away from the mall and heading home."

"Do you want to stay on the phone with me for a bit?" he asked.

Cathy was shaking as she put the phone on speaker. "Yes, please." And then she started crying. "Oh, Duke. People were Christmas shopping. Some will die today. They always do. Why is this happening?"

"I don't know, baby. But I'm selfish enough to be grateful to God you aren't one of them. Take a deep breath and just drive. I'll talk to you."

And so he did, starting with his and Jack's childhood on the farm. Telling her about the time eating a whole quart of dill pickles got them out of a day of school. How they'd snuck down into the cellar and ate the whole quart between them, then didn't tell their mom why they were sick and throwing up. She thought they were coming down with something and kept them home from school the next day.

And the stories went on. By the time Cathy reached the outskirts of Blessings, she had calmed down enough to breathe without wanting to scream.

"I'm driving into Blessings right now," she said. "I feel sick. I don't know whether it's shock or the fact that I didn't eat anything yet today. I think I'm going to go on to Granny's and get a little food in me and see if it helps. Don't mention anything about me being in any way involved in that shooting. It was a fluke that I was there, and let this just be between me and you, okay?"

"Yes, sweetheart. Very okay. And just so you know...the police have taken down both shooters and rescue is on the scene. I'm sure your early report helped. Just think about that. I love you," Duke said.

"Love you, too," Cathy said. "And thank you."

"Always," Duke said, and hung up.

She noticed the Christmas wreaths were all up now, hanging in place on the streetlights, and kept driving to Granny's. She needed to displace the horrible emptiness she was feeling—to settle the ache of what she'd seen and heard, and maybe a little comfort food would do it.

But when she went to get out and saw the bullet hole in her purse, her composure slipped. She almost got back in the car to go home, but she was feeling too light-headed and sick to drive. Hopefully, a little food would help this.

The tables in Granny's were filling up fast as Sully led the way to her table, but Ruby and Peanut were sitting at a table together, and when they saw her about to sit down alone, they waved.

"Is Duke with you?" Ruby asked.

"No, just me," Cathy said.

"Then come join us," she said.

"Yes...please do, and save me from talking about perms and hair tints," Peanut said.

"Sounds like a mercy mission to me," Sully said, which made Cathy smile.

The idea of not sitting alone was appealing.

"Then yes, I'll sit with them," Cathy said.

Sully seated her and left her menu.

"We haven't ordered yet," Ruby said. "Today's special is a pork chop, mashed potatoes and gravy, one side, and dessert."

"I think I'm going to go for breakfast food," she said.

Ruby kept eyeing Cathy's hair, and finally reached out and touched it.

"Forgive me, but you have the most beautiful head of hair I think I've ever seen. And it's all you, isn't it?"

"Yes. Born with this…curls and all."

"It's gorgeous," Ruby said. "My hair has been every shade on the spectrum at one time or another, but I consider it advertising my wares."

"My hair is sadly out of shape," Cathy said. "I kept thinking I'd get down to your salon before Thanksgiving and never made it."

"I have two whole hours open this afternoon, or I wouldn't be here eating lunch with my husband. If you have time when lunch is over, come back to the shop with me and I'll fix you up."

"Really?" Cathy said. "I keep it all one length so I can at least keep it out of my face, but I am badly in need of a trim."

"Yes, really…and it will be a 'Welcome to Blessings' hairdo on me."

"Oh no, I'd want to pay," Cathy said.

Ruby leaned over and patted her hand. "Sugar, I think you've paid enough in your life for a while. Let me treat you.

I do it for all the newcomers to Blessings, so don't take it as charity."

"Then okay," Cathy said. "I'll be grateful."

About that time, two women came in and were seated next to them. To Cathy's horror, their entire topic of conversation was the shooting at the mall.

"Hey, Ruby. Did y'all hear about the shooting at the Savannah Mall this morning?"

Ruby gasped. "No! You're not serious?"

"Yes, as a heart attack. It's awful, just awful. People were shopping the leftover sales from Black Friday, and two men came in with automatic rifles and started shooting up the place. They say there's dead people everywhere."

Cathy swallowed past the lump in her throat as their waitress finally appeared with their drinks and a basket of hot biscuits. She smiled at Cathy.

"I saw you had joined them. Sully said to bring you some sweet tea."

"Thank you," Cathy said, and took a quick sip, hoping to settle her stomach and her emotions.

"We're having the special," Peanut said.

"I just want biscuits and gravy," Cathy said, and then reached for a biscuit and buttered it before taking a bite.

By the time she'd eaten half of it, she was already feeling better and had zoned out of the conversation, just nodding now and then and pretending to follow it.

When their food came, it gave her even more reason not to talk, and she ate without really tasting it, just concentrating on getting enough food in her belly to take away that empty feeling.

The waitress swung back by with Ruby and Peanut's

dessert—little bowls of peach cobbler—and brought one for Cathy on the house.

"Enjoy," she said, and topped off their drinks.

Cathy managed to eat just enough of it to be polite, and then excused herself to go to the ladies' room while they were still eating.

She made it inside before she came undone and cried until her eyes were almost as red as her hair. She knew they would notice. Hopefully, they would not remark about it.

When she came out of the ladies' room, Peanut and Ruby were waiting for her in the lobby.

"Sully said your meal was on the house," Ruby said. "Want to follow me to the shop?"

Cathy nodded, then paused at the register on their way out.

"Thank you for my meal," she said.

"You're welcome," Sully said. "Glad to have you."

Cathy got in her car and headed for the Curl Up and Dye.

Peanut dropped Ruby off at the back of the salon.

"Something's wrong," he said. "She seemed okay until they started talking about the shooting."

"I noticed," Ruby said. "I'll find out. Don't worry. The hair salon is a better confessional than the one at the Catholic church."

Peanut smiled. "I know that's the truth. I'll see you at home tonight."

Ruby waved, then jumped out and went in the back just as Cathy walked in the front.

"I've got her," she said as Vera put down her sandwich and started to go greet Cathy. Ruby sailed past them, then led Cathy back. "Girls, this is Cathy Terry. Cathy, my stylists, Vesta and Vera Conklin, and manicurist, Mabel Jean Doolittle."

"It's so nice to meet you," Vesta said.

"Ditto," Vera said.

"Welcome to Blessings," Mabel Jean said.

"It's a pleasure to meet all of you," Cathy said.

"Okay…introductions are over. Sit, child," Ruby said.

Cathy plopped down in the stylist chair at Ruby's station, while the women finished eating their lunch.

Ruby whipped out a cape and fastened it around Cathy's neck, then turned her toward the mirror. When Cathy saw herself in the mirror, she kept thinking, *But for the grace of God, I would be lying dead in a parking lot, not sitting here in this chair*, and broke into tears again.

Ruby put her arms around her.

"What's wrong, sugar? You're among friends here, and whatever we hear in this place goes no further."

Cathy kept shaking her head and then wiping her eyes with the tissue Ruby gave her.

"I'm sorry I'm making such a scene," she said.

"Are you sick?" Ruby asked. "Can I call someone for you?"

"I was at the mall," she said. "The shooters walked in just ahead of me. When I saw them pull up their masks and pull out their guns, I ran. They shot at me three times." Then she pointed at her shoulder bag with the bullet hole hanging on a hook at Ruby's station. "The only thing they hit was my purse. They turned around and ran inside, and I called 911."

"Oh my God!" Ruby said. "And all those two biddies did during lunch was drag out the gossip they'd heard about it. I'm so sorry."

"I just keep thinking about the gunshots I heard. I knew people were Christmas shopping, and I knew there were people dying. I can't stop thinking about it."

Ruby just kept hugging her, then finally patted her on the shoulder.

"Come with me to the shampoo station. A good scalp massage is relaxing. And you can tell me how you like to wear your hair after we get back in the chair."

Cathy got up and followed. When the warm water began flowing through her hair and onto her scalp, she closed her eyes.

"It's gonna be okay," Ruby said.

And by the time Ruby had her hair trimmed and styled, Cathy was feeling better.

"Thank you for everything," she said. "And thank you for not telling anyone. I've had enough drama in my life the last few weeks to last the rest of my life. I just don't want to be attached to anything else…however random."

"We understand," Ruby said. "Your story is safe with us. Go home and call that handsome boyfriend of yours. We all saw the video. We saw him come to your rescue in a most heroic way. I'm thinking he would be good for what ails you."

"Well, yes, there's that," Cathy said, and was smiling when she got in the car and went home.

But once she got there, she showered, got into pajamas, and curled up on the sofa under a blanket. She wanted to watch TV, but every local station was covering the shooting, so she scanned her guide until she found a Disney movie and settled in to watch.

She fell asleep in the middle of it, and when she woke

up, there were tears on her cheeks. She wiped them away, then threw back her blanket and went into the kitchen to make coffee. Once it was done, she took a cup of it back into the living room and pulled the blanket back over her and changed the channel.

It was almost dark when she heard a car pull up in her drive, and then she heard footsteps on her porch. She knew that stride, and was on her feet in seconds. She opened the door before Duke had time to knock.

Even though the room was dark, he saw enough by the light of the television to know she'd been crying, and shut the door behind him as he walked in.

"I don't know why you're here, but I'm glad," she said.

"I didn't want you spending the night alone."

"You're staying?" Cathy asked.

"Yes, ma'am. In your bed, with you held tight in my arms."

"Oh, honey…thank you," Cathy said.

Duke took off his hat and coat. "I had to. You're hurting, and I can't think about you going through this alone."

"I have something to tell you, and you need to sit down," Cathy said.

Duke sat. Then listened to the tremor in her voice as she told him the rest of the story and tried not to react to the horror he was feeling. But he was shocked and shaken as he pulled her onto his lap. "I feel like I should never let you out of my sight again."

The weight of his arms around her was the safest feeling in the world.

"I know things happened to me, but I realized something this evening as I was sitting here in the dark. I keep surviving them, because I'm still supposed to be here, with you."

"Thank you, God," Duke whispered, then laid his cheek against the top of her head and just held her.

They sat within the silence of the darkened house, staring through the curtains at the streetlights that had come on, and at the flashing Christmas lights on the house across the street.

"You are the best Christmas present I'll ever have," Duke said.

"It isn't Christmas yet," Cathy said. "In fact, it's not quite December."

"Today was my Christmas. Just getting you home alive is all that matters. Have you eaten anything at all today?" he asked.

"Biscuits and gravy at noon."

"Do you have ice cream?" he asked.

She nodded.

"Then we are having ice cream for supper. Get some socks on so your feet don't get cold, and meet me in the kitchen."

And just like that, her world began to settle back into orbit. She ran down the hall to her bedroom as Duke got up and pulled shades and turned on lights, and then went into the kitchen.

He took the ice cream from the freezer, then began digging through her refrigerator. By the time she got into the kitchen, he was in the act of building two sundaes. A three-scoop for him and a two-scoop for her.

"In lieu of chocolate syrup, we have chocolate chips. And in lieu of nuts, we have granola. You also have honey, which is actually a good ice cream sauce, so pick your poison."

"I'll have some of all of it," Cathy said. "Light on the granola."

He spooned and he poured, and he sprinkled and he dipped until both sundaes were finished. Then he poked a spoon in each of them and carried them to the table where she was waiting...watching.

Cathy took her first bite and then rolled her eyes. "My compliments to the chef, and I love the honey on ice cream. It's turning into a kind of taffy from the cold."

Duke reached across the table and ran his finger down the side of her face.

"Love you."

Cathy leaned into his touch. "Love you, too."

CHAPTER 18

WHILE LIFE FOR SOME HAD ENDED THAT DAY, AND families were still reeling in shock and in grief, Mary Cathleen Terry had survived. She didn't know why, and it no longer mattered. She didn't need a reason to be grateful she was alive. And Duke's presence in her life gave her the joy that had been missing.

Making love to him this night was as life affirming as rolling over in the night and feeling his arm tighten ever so slightly to secure her again, even as he still slept.

They woke to a slice of sunlight that had slipped through the bedroom curtains and made love again to celebrate the beginning of a brand-new day.

In the aftermath, Duke still held her.

"I don't want to leave you," he said.

Cathy sighed. "But you have to. You have work to do, and I will find my own way through this day. Don't make me afraid to be alone."

He hugged her. "You're right, and I acknowledge I am overprotective."

"But it always comes from love, and that's never bad," Cathy said. "Do you want me to make breakfast?"

"If I stay for that, then I will delay even more."

She smiled. "Understood, and I'm going to go to the Crown sometime today and get some chocolate syrup."

He laughed, then threw back the covers and got dressed while Cathy watched from beneath the covers, admiring the view...and then he was gone.

She was too warm and comfortable to get dressed and go out for a morning run, so she settled for sweats and a cup of coffee to jump-start the day. It wasn't until later that she went to the Crown and noticed the houses in town were being turned into winter wonderlands even though they were missing the snow.

There were a few blow-up Santas that weaved and bobbed with the slightest breeze, and down the block, a sleigh and three little plastic reindeer in the act of taking flight perched precariously on a roof, while the Santa that went with them had been unceremoniously tied to the chimney. It looked more like he'd been taken hostage than that he was getting ready to climb down the chimney, but it was the thought that counted.

She was enchanted with the displays and felt obligated to stop at the hardware store and get a few strands of Christmas lights to string along the edge of her porch. Then she added a big green wreath with a red bow, and a hook to hang it on her front door. She thought about getting a small artificial tree for inside her house and then decided not to, since she would be spending the day with the Talbots again, so she paid for her things and then headed to the Crown.

Her entrance into the store did not go unnoticed. Almost everyone she approached stopped to comment something to her about her bravery, and the people who didn't take time to come up to speak to her waved at her in passing.

Between the story Mavis Webb had published and the ad the private investigator took out in the paper apologizing for his part in what had been a fearful time for her, she had become the best-known face in town.

That was part of why she hadn't wanted anyone to know

about her presence at the Savannah Mall. She didn't want to be associated with conflict and peril. She just wanted to be Cathy who loved Duke…and the newest resident of Blessings.

She was outside putting her bags into the car when she saw a young woman come out of the store with a toddler on one hip and a little girl that might be school age trailing her. She was carrying two bags of groceries and hunched against the weight of the baby and the sacks in her hands.

The little girl at her heels was wearing flip-flops instead of shoes and only had a little sweater over her clothes instead of a coat. The baby was in lightweight pajamas, and the woman was thin as a rail.

Cathy pushed her cart back to the outside rack, curious as to which car the woman was heading toward, and then realized the woman was afoot. Without thinking she ran to catch up.

"Hi, honey. I noticed you have your hands full here and thought you might like a ride home. My name is Cathy. I live over on Cherry Street. What's your name?"

The young woman stared, almost as if she couldn't believe what she'd just heard.

"My name is Barrie. I live down in the Bottoms."

"Where's that?" Cathy asked.

"The other side of the tracks."

That's when Cathy remembered. She'd been down there before. "Okay. If you'll wait right here, I'll go get my car and load you all up and get you out of this cold wind."

Barrie Lemons had been teased about her name for years and had given up trying to make lemonade out of the lemons life had given her. So when the woman turned around and ran back to a shiny red car, she was almost certain this was a joke and the woman would drive past her laughing for falling for it.

But she was wrong.

Cathy pulled up, then jumped out and took the sacks Barrie was holding. But when the little girl cried about being buckled up and having to sit in the back on her own, Cathy quickly solved the dilemma.

"What's your name, sweetie?"

The little girl sniffed. "Lucy. My little brother is Freddie."

"Okay, Lucy, I have an idea!" she said. "How about you and Mama and Freddie all sit in the back, like you were in a fancy limousine, and I'll be your driver. You can tell me where to turn and how to get to your house."

Lucy sniffed again, and then looked at her mother.

Barrie nodded. "That would be fine."

Cathy got them settled in the back, and then got back in the car.

"Okay…we're leaving the parking lot. When I get to Main Street, which direction do I turn?" she asked.

"Turn left," Barrie said, and the little girl sitting beside her piped up, "Left!"

Cathy hid a giggle. "Yes, ma'am."

She drove all the way down Main and was almost at the gas station at that end of town when she got her next set of directions.

"Take the next street left. Cross the tracks and take the second street right," Barrie said.

"Street right!" the little girl echoed.

Cathy smiled. "Yes, ma'am. Turning now," and when she crossed the long-abandoned tracks and started downhill, she suddenly understood the meaning of the Bottoms. The cluster of houses below reminded her of dirty toadstools all clumped together...but not in a fairy ring. More like seeds in a garden that didn't all germinate...and the ones that did were stunted and sterile.

This place gave off a lonesome feeling, and Cathy didn't understand why, when Blessings was so welcoming, this was still like this. As she turned right on the second street, the little girl cried, "Dat's home!"

"The one with the leaning porch," Barrie added. Freddie had fallen asleep in her lap, so she shifted him to her shoulder so she could carry her things inside. "I sure do appreciate this."

"Oh, you're very welcome. I won't intrude on your privacy, but I will carry your things up to the porch," Cathy said. "You get your babies inside out of the cold, and then you can come back for your things, okay?"

Barrie Lemons was so struck by the continuing kindness that she could only nod for fear if she spoke again, she'd burst into tears.

Cathy parked and got out, then ran around to open the door, and when the woman and baby got out, Cathy leaned in and unbuckled the little girl.

"You did such a good job telling me how to bring you home. Thank you very much," she said.

Lucy beamed. "Welcome," she said, and ran into the house behind her mother.

Cathy grabbed the two sacks and carried them up to the door. The woman had left it ajar. The lights were on, so Cathy knew the family had electricity, but she could see inside just enough to know they were destitute. Even worse, she couldn't feel any heat coming out the door although there was obviously an electric wall heater in sight.

When Barrie came back, Cathy handed her the sacks.

"I thank you," Barrie said.

Cathy nodded, then pointed to the wall heater. "That isn't putting out much heat, is it?"

"It hasn't worked in two years," Barrie said. "Landlord won't fix it."

"Oh my God...how do you stay warm in the winter?"

"We got a space heater from Salvation Army about three years ago. We use it when it gets bad, but it won't heat more than one room." Then she turned her back on Cathy and went inside, shutting the door behind her as she went.

Cathy went back to her car and headed home, but she couldn't get that family out of her mind. She kept thinking of how some people have too much, and some will never have enough, and then she thought of Blaine Wagner's millions sitting in three banks...and an idea was born.

As soon as she got home and her things put away, she googled Peanut's office to get a phone number and then called it.

Betty Purejoy, Peanut's secretary, answered.

"Butterman Law Office. This is Betty."

"Betty, this is Cathy Terry. Might Mr. Butterman be available to speak to me?"

"Yes, ma'am. Just a moment, please."

A few seconds later, Peanut was on the line.

"Hello, Cathy! How can I help you?"

"First I just need a question answered. Who is responsible for the Bottoms? It's a disgrace."

Peanut sighed. "Yes, ma'am, it is. Except for the few

houses that were deeded over to the renters recently by their landlord at his passing, all of the others are owned by a different absentee landlord. And before you ask, I will tell you that we have tried to contact him for years without success about the deterioration of his property and the hardship it's caused for the people living there."

"So, nobody helps them just because they don't own their places?" Cathy asked.

Peanut was silent a moment. "I never looked at it like that, but it appears to be the case, doesn't it?"

Cathy let that comment lie on his conscience and asked another question. "Do you have contact information for the absentee landlord?"

"I know his name and how to contact him, but I can't guarantee he'll ever respond to your letter."

"I don't intend to write to him. I was thinking about calling."

"Ah…not sure I have that info, but I know who might. Let me do some checking around and get back to you."

"Yes, sir, and thank you for your help."

"If I may ask…what do you have up your sleeve?" he asked.

"Not sure yet. I need more info before I make that decision."

"Okay, that's fair, and for the record, it's not sir…it's Peanut. As aggravating as it is, that's my name."

Cathy grinned. "Peanut it is, and I'll be waiting for your call."

She busied herself making a sandwich, and then answered a text from Duke that made her laugh.

Just checking in. Are you still alive?
Really funny, Dude...uh, I mean Duke.
Yes, I'm still alive.

He sent a smiley face and a LOL, which made her smile.

A short while later, she got a text from Peanut with a name, address, and phone number.

"Hmmm, R.L. Meiner with a Brooklyn address. How in the world did someone from New York wind up owning land in Blessings? But there's a phone number. So, here goes nothing," she said.

She sat down and made the call, listened to a multitude of rings and then a robotic voicemail.

"Well...good grief if this is all I have to work with," Cathy muttered, and left a brief message. "Mr. Meiner, I'm Cathy Terry from Blessings, Georgia, and I want to discuss the deterioration of the property you own here. The tenants are suffering from your lack of attention. I know slum lords are a thing where you live, but not here. I would like to discuss the possibility of buying the properties from you. Please call me at your earliest convenience. Winter is coming, and some of your tenants do not have heat. Not because they're too poor but because nothing has been repaired in so long that the appliances they have don't work." Then she left her address and the phone number she was calling from, and hung up.

She didn't know what might come from this, but she also knew someone who might be willing to wave another flag on behalf of those suffering such hardship. She scrolled through her small list of contacts until she got to Mavis Webb at the *Tribune*.

Mavis answered on the second ring, and Cathy started talking.

"Hi, Mavis. It's me, Cathy. I might have the next big story for you if you're interested."

"Then get your butt down here to the *Tribune* and we'll talk," Mavis said.

Cathy giggled. "I'll be there in ten," she said, then grabbed her jacket and her purse with the bullet hole and took off out the door.

Mavis was waiting for her when she walked in. "Want a cup of coffee?" she asked.

"No, I'm good," Cathy said.

Mavis led the way to her office, then closed the door behind them.

"Sit, and tell me what's going on."

"Have you ever been to the Bottoms?" Cathy asked.

Mavis frowned. "Isn't that what they call those little houses on the other side of those old railroad tracks?"

"Yes. But did you know they're owned by an absentee landlord who has ignored requests for years to address the situation there? I took a woman and her two babies home from the Crown today, and there wasn't any heat in the house. She had electricity, but no heat, and I saw an electric heater on the wall. She said it hadn't worked in two years and the landlord refused to fix it. She said she's been using a donated space heater from Salvation Army that she was given three years ago...and she said it barely heats one room. The child was wearing flip-flops. She did not have a coat. The baby was in pajamas and no blanket, and the mother looked like she was starving. Those houses are pitiful, and I'd warrant the families are all living the same lives."

"And what do you think I can do?" Mavis asked.

"I've called the landlord, asking to buy the property, but if I can't get a response, then maybe we can shame him into either fixing the places or selling them to me."

Mavis's eyes widened. "All of them?"

"Yes."

"Can you do that?"

"I can't think of a better way to spend some of Blaine Wagner's money," Cathy said.

Mavis nodded. "Do you think they might cooperate with us…let me take pictures of everything that's broken inside their houses…and take pictures of them?"

"We can only ask," Cathy said. "We have an absentee slumlord situation in Blessings that is appalling. I can't believe it's been let go this long, and I said so to Peanut Butterman."

"Then I'm willing to run the story, but I need to get background on the landlord and contact information for him, too."

"I can furnish that," Cathy said. "Call it Operation Christmas Rescue, and talk to Barrie Lemons. She's the young woman I took home. Tell her I'm trying to contact their landlord to force him to either fix the properties or sell them to me so I can."

Mavis nodded. "We'll work on this together and see how it goes. I'll go down there later and look around for myself."

"Awesome," Cathy said, and took out her phone and gave Mavis all the information Peanut had given her. "Let me know if there's anything else I can do to help."

Mavis grinned. She liked Cathy Terry, but now she was getting a glimpse of a whole other layer to her personality.

Cathy went home, happier than she'd been in years. She had a purpose and the means with which to achieve a difference in people's lives. Now she just needed R.L. Meiner to respond.

A whole week passed without a response from the landlord, but Mavis Webb had gone into full documentary mode, made friends with Barrie Lemons and a half-dozen other residents of the Bottoms, and was on a mission to get their stories and pictures of them and their living conditions, while Cathy was torn between two different passions— Duke, and her new project at the Bottoms.

The Bailey property was officially Talbot land now. The Bailey family had cleared the house of all the furniture, leaving it a shell of its former self.

The renovation budget was in place, and the first thing Duke did was hire a crew of painters to give the two white wings of the house a fresh coat of paint and roofers to repair the broken shingles that had been damaged during the hurricane.

He had a friend in Savannah who hooked him up with a reputable contractor named George, and now George and his reno team were gutting the kitchen and widening the opening between it and the formal dining room.

The house was being transformed, and so was Cathy. She was fast becoming a fixture down in the Bottoms. Even though the landlord was still silent, that didn't mean she couldn't help them, and she began with the house Barrie Lemons was renting.

She started by replacing the heater, repairing floors and replacing windows, then a new roof and insulation blown into the attic.

Little by little, she was refurbishing the house, replacing appliances that didn't work, and putting decent furniture inside the house.

After Barrie's house was done, Cathy upped her game and hired four separate crews working full time in the Bottoms, with two paint crews, plumbers, and two crews that did flooring and tile.

The residents were ecstatic. Having decent living conditions, appliances that worked, and creature comforts was giving all of them a new sense of pride in themselves.

When Cathy found out about the large number of the men living there who had lost their jobs when their vehicles needed repairs they couldn't afford, she hired them to work on the project.

In the midst of all that, she was picking out colors and tiles and flooring for her and Duke's own house, running her selections by Duke during the evenings, and shopping and ordering local, or ordering online for delivery on the jobs.

She hadn't mentioned it to anyone, but she was afraid to go back to Savannah. One day she'd have to face that fear, or accept that those killers had done what wild animals, the Alaskan wilderness, and a cheating husband hadn't been able to do—and that was beat her.

But right now, getting those homes fixed before

Christmas was her goal, and she was pushing hard for it to happen.

Cathy called R.L Meiner every other day, asking for a decision but with no response. And then Mavis Webb finally ran her story about the absentee landlord in New York, and Cathy Terry, the Christmas Angel of Blessings. She ran pictures of the families and of the living conditions with the story, calling R.L. Meiner a hard-hearted slumlord, and again the AP picked up on another scandal and ran with it.

Cathy's philanthropy had not gone unnoticed by the people in Blessings. When they first found out what she was doing, they reacted with a sense of guilt, acknowledging this should have been done years ago, and then with a sense of purpose that it was never too late to right a wrong.

Ruby Butterman started an angel tree in her salon and picked five families from the Bottoms for her customers to buy Christmas presents for, and when she did, Lovey Cooper put up an angel tree in Granny's and added the names of five more family members, and so it went until every business on Main Street had every family member in the Bottoms on the trees.

One Sunday, Granny's Country Kitchen donated the entire day's proceeds to the families—to be divided up so that they could have their own Christmas dinners and buy presents for their own children, too. And when Broyles Dairy Freeze and the barbecue place all found out Granny's was doing that, they did it, too. Even the owner of the Blue

Ivy Bar donated the entire take from one Saturday night to the project.

And in the midst of this, Cathy Terry finally got her call from R.L Meiner.

The morning dawned raw and blustery. Cathy had paint samples and tile samples spread out all over her kitchen table when her cell phone rang. Duke was coming into town, and thinking it was likely from him, she didn't even look at caller ID.

"Hello."

"May I speak to Cathy Terry?"

It wasn't Duke.

"This is Cathy."

"Miss Terry, this is Michael Meiner. I understand you have been trying to reach my father, R.L. Meiner."

"Yes, about purchasing some property he owns in Blessings, Georgia."

"We read the story. I must say it gave our whole family a bad name," he said.

"Well, your father has given his tenants many years of a living hell."

"My father has been in a nursing home for the past seven years. He has Alzheimer's."

"I'm sorry to hear this, but surely someone has been taking care of his business?"

"My brother and I, but we were unaware of any of this. We don't know how he even came to own property in Georgia, and the messages you've been leaving weren't taken seriously. We thought it was some kind of scam, because we were unaware that the property was even in the family. It wasn't until the story ran that we realized the calls were valid."

"Okay, so now you know," Cathy said. "What are you going to do about it?"

"We have no interest in being long-distance landlords like this. And we had our lawyer check the property taxes and assess the value of the land, because it's obvious from the story that the houses are of no value."

"They are to the people living in them," Cathy snapped.

"Yes, yes, I'm sorry. That didn't come out right. What I meant was that there was no way to put a fair price on their value that would increase our asking price, and the rent doesn't even cover the property taxes that have been coming out of our father's accounts."

"Well, in the eyes of God, sir…your family owes the tenants a refund for paying rent all these years for something they didn't have, which was livable housing. So there's that."

Cathy heard a sigh, and then a slight chuckle.

"You are a sharp businesswoman."

"I just want to right a terrible wrong. That's all," Cathy said. "So before you throw out an asking price, remember this is all going to be part of a follow-up story regarding your family. So if you want to clear that good name you are worried about, don't try to pad your pockets on the backs of poor people and my good intentions."

Obviously, the knowledge that a second story would be forthcoming horrified him.

"Of course, we intend to do the right thing. Our lawyer advised us to ask a million five."

Cathy laughed. "The land is on the downslope of an old railroad crossing. I've been told they can't even grow gardens there because the soil is littered with the remnants of gravel and coal…and yes, Blessings is that old, and if this property hadn't been neglected for so many years, it might be worth about two-thirds of what you asked. But you let it go to ruin. So you reap what you sow, Mr. Meiner. I will give you half of your asking price and not a penny more. Seven hundred and fifty thousand dollars."

"And we'll get our family name and all of the misunderstandings cleared in the follow-up story?"

"Yes."

"Done. We'll have our lawyer contact you."

"No. Have your lawyer contact my lawyer. His name is P. Nutt Butterman. He practices here in Blessings."

Meiner laughed. "You're kidding, right?"

"Do you hear me laughing?"

"No, ma'am."

"I will expect the paperwork to begin this process within the week. And you will be responsible for all closing costs. You have lax business practices, sir," Cathy said.

"But we didn't know," Meiner said.

"You do now. Have your lawyer contact my lawyer, and no dawdling. Christmas is upon us, and I'd like for these people to have a blessed one this year."

"Yes, ma'am. We'll be in touch."

Cathy hung up, and then called the *Tribune*.

Mavis Webb answered, and then heard Cathy's squealing.

"Oh my God, Mavis…we did it. We did it! And wait until you hear the end of this story about the Bottoms."

"Then come on over," Mavis said.

"Can't but I'll give you the lowdown while I'm waiting on my sweetie to take me to lunch."

And so Cathy told the story once again, right down to them agreeing to sell her the land and the houses on it.

Mavis crowed. "Holy crap. I hope your sweetie is ready for you, because you are one hell of a woman."

Cathy grinned. "Oh…he's fine. He has my number and the line it comes in on."

Mavis sighed. She'd seen Duke Talbot. He *was* fine, in so many ways.

"Okay, and congrats. Once the deal goes through, I will run a follow-up."

"Thank you," Cathy said.

CHAPTER 19

SHE MET DUKE AT THE DOOR WITH A SMILE AND A KISS that took away his appetite for anything other than making love to her.

"I don't know what that's for, but I'll take seconds," he said, and did.

"I finally heard back from Meiner. It's quite the revelation. The owner has Alzheimer's. That's why no response. And his sons, who are taking care of his business properties, had no idea he owned anything in Georgia. It was Mavis's story about New York slumlords in the South that got their attention."

Duke laughed and hugged her. "Way to go. So what did they say?"

"They're selling it to me for a steal in the hopes that the follow-up story paints a better image of the Meiner family."

Duke shook his head. Like Mavis, he was realizing what a shrewd businesswoman she was turning out to be.

"Where are you with the renos?"

"About a half dozen more to go…most of it roofing and paint and replacing appliances and furniture, although a couple have floors that are in horrible shape. But it doesn't matter right now who owns it. I just want it done."

"I am in awe," Duke said. "Let's get some food, and then I'd love a tour…and to meet some of the people you've made friends with down there."

"Deal," Cathy said. "Let's get something from the Dairy

Freeze and then drive to the park. We can sit in the truck to eat if it's too cold, but I like to look at all the Christmas decorations."

"Sounds good to me," Duke said, and after a sweep through the drive-through, they headed to the park with burgers, onion rings, and drinks.

"Want ketchup?" Cathy asked, as she dug a ketchup packet out of the sack.

"No, thanks. I'm good with it just like this."

Cathy took a bite of an onion ring, and then used it for a pointer.

"Do they decorate the park like this every Christmas?"

Duke nodded. "You should see it during the Peachy Keen Festival."

Cathy grinned. "What's that?"

"Well…Georgia is famous for peaches, right? And lots of places in the state have their own celebrations of them during harvest. Every year, some young high school girl is chosen Miss Peachy Keen, and it's the biggest freaking deal in town. You'd think they were vying for Miss America. LilyAnn who works at Phillips Pharmacy was the Peachy Keen queen once."

"That sounds like a lot of fun and a lot of tears. Competition against each other is brutal, and when it's an all-female event based on looks and personality, and it takes place in a small town, there's nowhere to get away from being the losers," Cathy said.

Duke nodded. "They used to have to bring a peach pie that they'd baked as part of their events, but when it became clear that most of the mamas were doing the baking, and two of them got into a squabble about one being a better baker than the other in front of the judges, it was phased out."

Cathy grinned. "Oh, my lord! Are you serious?"

He nodded, and took another bite of his burger.

"Is there ever a Peachy Keen king?" she asked.

"Nope. It's all about the queen." They ate in silence for a few moments, and then he added, "There have been quite a few people who got married in that gazebo…Ruby and Peanut were the latest, I think."

Cathy looked at it with new interest.

"I'm assuming it was warm weather when that happened?"

"Yes. The only thing threatening was rain, but it stayed clear for them. And…they invited the whole town. With both of them being in business in Blessings, they didn't know where to start and where to stop on an invitation list, so they just told everyone they were invited, and to bring blankets and their own picnics and eat on the ground with them after the ceremony…and they furnished cake for everyone."

Cathy's eyes widened, imagining how that would have looked.

"That was such a unique and special way to include all of their friends," she said.

"Yeah…but that's a little over the top for me."

"Ditto," Cathy said. "And I don't want to wait for warm weather to become your wife."

"Agreed," Duke said, then took the last bite of his burger. "Are you finished?" he asked.

She nodded, and sacked up all of their refuse. Duke got out, dumped it in a nearby trash bin, and then got back in the truck.

"I'm ready to tour the Bottoms," he said.

"You know the way," Cathy said.

The closer they got, the more excited she became. It had already undergone a huge transformation from what it had been, and they weren't finished. But coming over that rise of the old tracks and looking downhill at new roofs and houses bright and clean with fresh paint was uplifting, not to mention seeing the windows that had been replaced and the porches and steps that had been rebuilt.

"It's been a long time since I've had occasion to drive this way, but I remember it as being what my mother would have called tragic. This is amazing, and I am so proud of what you're doing," he said.

Cathy sighed. "Thank you, honey. Sometimes I think I'm not paying enough attention to our renovation for all that's going on here, but it matters so much that this wrong be righted."

"No, no! Never think that," Duke said. "We're not destitute. We're blessed. This is where your attention is most needed now. We'll have our house, and I'll have you for the rest of our lives. This matters."

"Thanks for backing me. It means everything," she said. "Drive down that way and turn right at the second street. Barrie's house was the first one we worked on, and she's really helped us get the rest of the people living here involved in the process. I want you to meet her."

"Will do," Duke said. When he pulled up to the house Cathy pointed out and he saw the pale-yellow paint and white trim on the house, and a new porch, he smiled. "This is sunny, just like you."

She beamed. "Come on. Barrie's here."

"How do you know?" he asked.

She pointed. "I see her peeking out the window," she said, and jumped out.

The moment Barrie recognized it was Cathy, she came out to meet her.

"Barrie, you've heard me talk nonstop about Duke. I wanted you to meet him," Cathy said. "Duke, this is Barrie Lemons. Barrie, my fiancé, Duke Talbot."

Barrie smiled shyly. "It's a pleasure, sir. Would you like to come inside and see what magic your lady has created?"

"I would love it," Duke said, and walked into a little house filled with warmth, and color, and a little baby crawling on a large magenta-and-blue area rug beneath the furniture.

"I keep these here to remind me of the gift she's given," Barrie said and handed over the still photos Mavis Webb had taken of the interior of her home before the renovations began.

Shock left Duke momentarily speechless. He looked up at Cathy, then at Barrie, and shook his head.

"I am looking at two of the strongest women I think I've ever known. If you don't mind me asking…how did you come to be living here?"

"My man brought me to the Bottoms," Barrie said. "We were gonna get married, but we just kept putting it off. His old truck quit on him, and we didn't have the money to fix it. He got down on himself, got mixed up with meth, and died in a motel in Savannah. I had just found out I was pregnant with Freddie, my baby, and had nowhere else to go."

"I'm sorry," Duke said. "I hope your life takes a happy turn one day soon."

"Oh, it already has," Barrie said. "She did it. She cared about us. That's more than we've ever had."

The baby had already crawled over to where Cathy was standing and pulled himself up by holding onto her leg.

Cathy laughed. "Well, hello, little man," she said, then swooped him up in her arms.

When he laughed and patted her cheeks, Duke could tell she'd done this before. And seeing her with a baby in her arms made him aware of how much life he'd been missing.

"Freddie likes you," Duke said.

"Down here, everyone loves Cathy," Barrie said.

"Well, I have good news," Cathy said. "I finally heard back from your landlord. To his credit, the old fellow has been in a nursing home with Alzheimer's for years. His sons didn't know he owned property here and, I think, chose to ignore the messages he was getting. But they finally called, and we made a deal. I'm buying all of the property here, and I can promise you as long as I live, this will never happen to any of you again."

"Oh my God! That is wonderful news!" Barrie said. "Can I tell the others?"

"Yes, ma'am, you sure can," Cathy said; and then looked around for the little girl. "Is Lucy in school?"

Barrie nodded. "Yes, now that she has clothes warm enough to go."

"I'll bring cookies next time I come," Cathy said. "I know snickerdoodles are her favorite."

"And mine," Duke said.

Cathy grinned. "Every cookie is your favorite."

"Guilty," he said, which made Barrie smile. She couldn't remember the last time she'd been happy with a man.

Cathy kissed Freddie's little cheek, and then put him back down on the floor and handed him his toy.

"We need to go. Thank you for letting us intrude, but

I so wanted Duke to meet you and see what's happening down here."

"Miracles are happening in the Bottoms because of our Christmas angel," Barrie said.

"Christmas angel?"

"That's what we all call her," Barrie said.

Duke slid his hand across her shoulder. "And I consider her my Christmas gift. Happy holidays to you and your family."

"Thank you," Barrie said, then waved goodbye from the window as they drove away.

They drove through the rest of the area, seeing the houses in different states of repair and stopping once to talk to some of the residents who were outside replacing chain-link fences.

When they finally left the Bottoms, Duke was beyond impressed with what was being done and praised Cathy, but she shrugged it off.

"You can do many good things if you have the money to do it," she said.

"Yes, but not everyone with money does good things. You chose to make a difference in other people's lives. You have a loving heart, and I am most grateful that you're spending part of that love on me."

Cathy sighed. "Oh honey…I'm spending all of my love on you. The other stuff is purpose with a passion. I need purpose to feel like I'm making a difference, and I need to make a difference. After all the wasted years I spent in Vegas—and all the wasted money spent on useless, frivolous things—this feels awesome…like I hit the jackpot."

Duke nodded. He understood purpose.

The day was brisk but the sun was shining, which was a good thing because Santa Claus was due to arrive at the park. The crowd was growing, and Santa's elves were all waiting in their red and green suits.

Junior Cooper was the official photographer for the day and all set up to take pictures of kids sitting in Santa's lap.

Santa's big overstuffed armchair was in the gazebo, in front of a potted pine with branches heavily laden in fake snow. The candy-filled stockings were stacked nearby in boxes, and the line was beginning to grow when two buses pulled up at the park. Everyone turned to watch as parents and children from the Bottoms began coming out of the buses. They were hesitant to join in until other people there waved them over, and soon they were standing in line with the rest of the crowd, waiting for Santa to arrive. For some of these kids it would be a first, while others were old pros at talking to Santa.

And then all of a sudden they began hearing sleigh bells, and then a jolly *Ho, ho, ho* from a loudspeaker. They turned and looked again, and then everyone began to smile as the children went silent...staring in awe at Santa and Mrs. Claus's arrival in an old farm wagon being pulled by a team of mules.

It was a less-than-classic arrival, but no one seemed to care as a very tall Santa and a tiny Mrs. Claus stepped down from the wagon.

There wasn't enough padding in Blessings to make Peanut Butterman fat enough to have a belly that shook like a bowl full of jelly, but he was jolly enough as he swept through the crowd in his red and white suit, holding Mrs. Claus's hand.

Santa took his place in the chair, and Mrs. Claus stood at his side, ready to hand each child a candy-filled stocking as soon as they told Santa their wish.

"Ho, ho, ho!" Santa said. "Welcome to all of the children. Let's get this party started."

Mrs. Claus sighed and then whispered in Santa's ear.

"Santa doesn't say 'get this party started.'"

Santa grinned beneath his beard. "This one does. Hang in there with me, honey. This is gonna be a long three hours, I can tell."

The first child up was a little boy of about three. His mother plopped him down on Santa's lap. The toddler took one look at the bearded man and let out a shriek.

Santa winced, and then glanced at the name tag on the little boy's shirt.

"Hello there, Raymond. What do you want for Christmas?" Santa asked.

"Mama!" the little boy shrieked.

The mother looked at Junior. "Did you get the picture?"

"Yes, ma'am," Junior said.

The mother yanked the kid off Santa's lap, took the candy, and walked out of the gazebo and disappeared into the crowd as the procession continued.

Cathy had been waiting for Santa's arrival as anxiously as everyone else, and when the bus arrived with the residents from the Bottoms, she relaxed. Another project checked off her list.

She recognized Peanut and Ruby as Santa and Mrs. Claus almost instantly and took pictures of them and the

wagon and mules and sent them to Duke, who was overseeing the appliances being installed at their house.

They were already working on the master bedroom and
bath upstairs. Electricians and plumbers were overseeing
the installation of central heating and air, light fixtures, and
the big black-and-gold six-burner range being hooked up in
the kitchen.

Cathy's claw-foot, cast-iron bathtub that she'd found at
a salvage yard had been refinished and refurbished. But it
was so heavy, it had taken six burly men to carry it upstairs
to the master bath.

"This is one big tub," one of the men remarked as they
settled it into place.

Duke eyed it, picturing the curly-haired redhead he
knew in it and up to her chin in bubbles. It was a damn fine
image to have.

"Let's get it hooked up," he said, and then got the text
from Cathy and paused to look. When he saw the pictures
of Santa arriving in a wagon pulled by a team of mules, he
laughed out loud, and then showed his workers. "Looks like
we missed the boat with Santa this year. He's at the park in
Blessings, and here we are hooking up a bathtub."

The last house in the Bottoms was finished five days
before Christmas, and the furniture to go in it arrived that
afternoon.

Cathy stood beside the truck as it was being unloaded,
watching the family's excitement as all their new furnishings were being put into place.

She walked to the front door as the delivery truck drove away, but they were all so excited about moving furniture around to fit their space that she just pulled the door shut and went back to her car.

The adrenaline that had carried her through the mad rush to get this done was crashing. By the time she got home, she was stumbling. She dropped her purse and coat on the sofa, kicked off her shoes in the hall, and fell onto her bed fully dressed. The last thing she remembered hearing was the central heat kicking on.

Duke had intended to be there with her, but ended up helping Jack get an injured steer into the barn so it would be sheltered while it healed. They didn't know what it had gotten into that put such a gash in its hip but the vet had been out, and now all they could do was wait for the animal to heal before turning it back in with the herd.

Later he sent Cathy a text, but when she didn't answer he called, and when she didn't answer the call either, he got in his truck and drove into town. She'd promised never to ignore a phone call or a text from him again, and now he was worried.

The relief of seeing her car in the drive at her house was huge, but when he got to the front door and knocked, it swung open.

His heart skipped. He walked in, saw her purse and coat on the sofa. When he realized her phone had fallen out of her purse onto the floor, it was apparent why she hadn't heard it ring.

Then he saw her shoes in the hall and headed for her bedroom. The door was ajar, and when he walked in and found her sprawled belly down on the bed, he had to get closer to make sure she was breathing.

And she was.

"My poor tired sweetheart," he said softly, then got a blanket from the foot of the bed, covered her up, and walked out of the room, closing the door behind him.

He went into her kitchen to check and see if she had food she wouldn't have to cook, and then wrote her a note.

> *You didn't answer your phone. Your door was unlocked. I covered you up and am locking you in. Sleep well, my love. Call me when you wake.*
>
> *P.S. We're gonna have to get married, and soon. I'm wearing out the rubber on my tires. I need you in my life. I need you in my arms every night. I need you.*

And then he was gone.

Hours later, Cathy woke up. She didn't remember getting the blanket she was covered with, and she didn't remember closing her bedroom door.

She got up and went into the living room, then into the kitchen and found Duke's note.

"Oh, honey," she said as she read it to herself, then went to get her phone to call him.

It was dark outside, and she pictured them all in the kitchen together making supper. He answered on the third ring.

"Hey, Rip Van Winkle. You woke up!"

"I need you, too," Cathy said. "I'm sorry I didn't hear the

phone, but the renovations are done, and after the last load of furniture arrived, I came home and passed out. I can't believe I didn't even lock the door."

"You not only didn't lock it, but when I knocked it just swung inward, so the latch didn't fully catch, either."

"Lord," Cathy said. "I need a keeper."

"You have one. Me. I will keep you in my heart. I will keep you safe. Set a date before I lose my mind."

"How big a wedding do you want?" she asked.

"I want to get married at the farmhouse. I just want family and our closest friends, and as soon as you can find a dress, I'm there."

"We need to get that marriage license," she said.

"Then I'll pick you up in the morning and we'll go to the courthouse."

Duke heard her take a quick breath, but then she said nothing.

"Cathy, honey…what's wrong?" he asked.

"I need a wedding dress, but I'm afraid to go back to Savannah."

The tremor in her voice broke his heart.

"Sweetheart, I'll take you to a bridal shop…to all the bridal shops in the city. I will sit in the truck at every stop until you find what you want. I will be with you every step of the way, but I won't go inside."

"Really?"

"Yes."

"Can you get away before Christmas to do that?" she asked.

"The perk of being my own boss is that I can do any damn thing I want to make you happy," Duke said.

"You know the stores will be crazy with last-minute shoppers," she said.

"I don't know how many last-minute shoppers there will be looking for wedding dresses, but I don't care," he said.

"If I can find a dress and get it fitted..."

"We'll find it," he said.

"Then let's aim for getting married on New Year's Eve and see what happens. I know they aren't finished with our house, but I don't care."

"The downstairs is mostly done. The kitchen is finished and wearing a layer of dust. The master bedroom and bath will be done before New Year's Day. We can move into our own home. We'll have to live with some dust and noise until they finish the rest of the upstairs, but the downstairs and our bedroom will be done."

"I cannot believe you're that close. I got so wrapped up in the Bottoms project that I left all ours up to you."

"You couldn't help with what we were doing. You did exactly what we needed, which was to pick out the appliances and the colors and tiles and flooring. And the design of it."

"I had no idea it was this close to being done. Oh, Duke. It's really happening, isn't it?"

"Count on it," he said. "See you in the morning. I'll pick you up at nine. I checked on the requirements days ago. We need two forms of ID for the license. We'll go to the courthouse to get the license and then head to Savannah... if you're free."

"I'm free," she said. "Let's do this."

"I love you, baby. It's all going to be okay," Duke said. Then as soon as they disconnected, he went to find Jack. "Where's Hope?" he asked.

"She's on her way home from grocery shopping now. Why?"

"Cathy and I are getting a marriage license tomorrow, then I'm taking her to Savannah to find a wedding dress. She's afraid to go back by herself."

"Why? Because of that shooting?" Jack said.

"Something like that," Duke said.

"But the groom isn't supposed to see the dress beforehand," Jack said.

"That's why I'm staying in the truck at every stop."

Jack grinned. "You are the ultimate case of arrested development, brother, but I am seriously proud of you. You stayed single so long I didn't think this day would ever happen, but boy, when you fell, you fell hard, didn't you?"

Duke shrugged. "A shoe either fits or it doesn't. The same way with women you meet. They either fit or they don't. We fit. Just like you and Hope fit. Just like Lon and Mercy fit. You just know when you know."

"Hope will be excited," Jack said.

Duke grinned. "I hope so. I want to get married here on New Year's Eve. Just our family and a few close friends. No big deal. No big dinner. Just me, my girl, and a cake."

———————

As it turned out, getting the marriage license at the court-house was a breeze. The giggles, the smiles, and the con-gratulations were what slowed the process down.

The clerk who helped them was full of questions.

"This is so exciting. I'm so happy for the both of you. Are you having a big wedding?"

"No," Cathy said. "We're getting married at the family home. Just family and a few close friends."

"That sounds special," the clerk said. "Less turmoil, easier to make wonderful memories when you're not under stress about the details. It's the bride and groom and their day, after all."

"As long as she says 'I do,' it'll work for me," Duke said as he gave Cathy a hug, and then they were gone.

By the time they left town, word was already spreading. Duke Talbot and Cathy Terry were getting married.

Driving back into Savannah made Cathy's stomach hurt. She was tense and pale, and Duke knew it. So when he suddenly pulled off into a Starbucks drive-through, her focus shifted from panic to curiosity.

"Plain coffee or something fancy?" he asked.

"Dark chocolate mocha," Cathy said.

"Cookie or muffin?" he asked.

She grinned. "Chocolate chip cookie."

Duke nodded, then ordered the same thing and pulled forward to the window to pay. When their orders arrived, Duke could tell by the gleam in her eyes that this had been a good move. He'd given her something else to focus upon besides the bad memories.

"Umm," Cathy said, as she took her first sip of the flavored coffee. "This is perfect."

He took a sip of his own as they drove away.

"You're right. This is good. Really good."

"So is the cookie," Cathy said, and broke off a piece and popped it in her mouth.

"Now this is how you shop for wedding dresses on a cold day," Duke said.

"You have the best ideas," she said, and by the time they reached the first bridal boutique, her cookie was gone, she was warm inside from the mocha coffee, crumb-free, and ready to shop. She leaned across the console and gave Duke a quick kiss on the lips.

"I know what I'm looking for, and if they don't have anything like it, this won't take long."

"Take your time," Duke said. "I'm just gonna sit here and contemplate the wedding night."

She blinked, and then burst into laughter.

He grinned.

She was still smiling as she went inside.

———————————

Two hours, one pit stop, and three bridal shops later, they pulled up and parked at Le Trousseau on Broughton Street.

"Here's hoping," Cathy said.

She was thinking of her mother as she walked in.

Oh, Mama...you were with me when I shopped for my wedding to Blaine. I wish you were here now. You didn't like Blaine, and now I know why. But you would love, love, love Duke Talbot. I just know it. Is this the one, Mama? Is my dress here? You know what I want, and you know why.

A consultant approached her, smiling.

"Welcome to Le Trousseau. I'm William."

She eyed the middle-aged man in his dapper pin-striped suit and liked him on sight.

"Hello, William. I'm Cathy Terry. I know what I want, so

let me describe it, and if you don't have anything remotely like it, we'll save both of us time and trouble."

William's eyebrows arched, and then he nodded.

"This is a breath of fresh air. Talk to me," he said, and so she did, and the more she talked, the wider his smile became. "Follow me, Miss Terry. Let me show you something." And then he eyed her more closely. "What size are you...about an eight?"

"Good eye," Cathy said, and followed William back to the dressing room.

"Have a seat. I'll be right back," he said.

Cathy sat, looked up, and saw herself reflected back in the three-way mirror. She looked happy because she was. She leaned back, waiting...and when William came back a few minutes later with three white dresses over his arm, she stood.

"Oh my gosh! You did it!"

"Now let's try these on. There are subtle differences in all three, but I see where you're going here. You are going to look amazing."

Two young clerks appeared to help her into the dresses as William stepped out. It wasn't until she tried on the last one and walked out onto the showroom floor to look at herself in the big mirrors that she knew.

This is it, Mama. This is it.

"It fits you like a glove," William said. "Unless you're unhappy with the length, I wouldn't touch any part of the bodice."

"It needs to be hemmed up a bit," Cathy said.

"I agree. Let me get the seamstress in here," he said, and left, coming back minutes later with an all-business woman in boho chic with a tape measure around her neck and a pincushion in her hand.

She measured, she fussed about, and then she waved her hand.

"All done. Take it off. I'll fix it."

Back to the dressing room they went, and when Cathy came out again, she was beaming.

"When is the wedding?" William asked.

"New Year's Eve."

"*This* New Year's Eve?" he said.

She nodded.

He flew back into the sewing room, and then returned nodding his head.

"Yes, Sunny likes you. She likes your red curls. She will put a rush on it just for you."

"When can I pick it up?" Cathy asked.

"She said the day after Christmas."

"Perfect," Cathy said, then paid the deposit, picked up her paperwork, and hugged him. "Thank you. Thank you for being so wonderful about this."

William beamed. "There's nothing that makes me happier than a happy bride," he said. "We'll see you the day after Christmas."

Cathy bounced out of the store with a smile on her face, and Duke could tell she'd found the dress. Before he could get out to help her into the truck, she was already climbing up.

"I found it," she said. "They're altering the length. I'll pick it up the day after Christmas. This is the best day ever. Thank you for putting up with me."

Duke leaned across the seat and kissed her. "I'll collect

later. Right now I'm going to take you to eat at the best shrimp shack in the city."

Her lips were still tingling from his kiss as she buckled herself in.

"I am suddenly starving and shrimp sounds perfect."

It was midafternoon when they got back to Blessings, and after a heartfelt goodbye, Duke left her safe and sound inside her little house.

"It won't be long now before this business of going our separate ways at the end of a day is over," he said. "I'll call you tonight. Love you."

"Love you, more," Cathy said, and then stood at the window and watched him drive away.

But the moment he was gone, she jumped in her car and headed to the florist to order her wedding bouquet and what she wanted to wear in her hair in lieu of a veil. Then she dug through her closet to make sure the heels she planned to wear with her dress weren't any higher than the ones on her boots.

"Ta-da!" she crowed when she lined them up side by side and saw they were the same.

She didn't bother to make a list of who to invite, because she'd been here for such a short time. The only people she really cared about being there were Dan and Alice Amos, because Dan had trusted her enough to rent her a house on her word, and Ruby and Peanut Butterman. Peanut, because of his help in getting the Bottoms, and Ruby for keeping her secret about the shooting. And Mavis Webb, for being the single reason that Cathy was free of Blaine Wagner forever. Duke was the one who'd grown up here. He needed to invite the people who meant the most to him.

Christmas Day arrived in sunshine. Cathy drove herself up to the farm with a sweet potato casserole topped with a brown sugar and walnut crumble and a sack of gifts.

Duke met her at the car, and when she handed him the hot dish wrapped in a tea towel, he smiled.

"Lord, but something sure smells good," he said.

"It was my mother's recipe. Just me including her in our life."

"Can't wait to try it," he said, and then walked her inside.

She left her presents under the tree and went into the kitchen. It felt so normal to be with the Talbots now. She was only days away from becoming one herself, and so integrated within the family that she felt like she'd been there forever.

Hope's baby bump was showing now, and her last day of work had come and gone. Just being able to pace herself and her days now had made all the difference in her energy level, and Jack was happy she was home.

"Are you sure you're up for a wedding here so soon after Christmas?" Cathy asked.

Hope laughed. "Honey, we've been trying to marry Duke off ever since I came into this family, and for the most part, he wasn't having any of it. I'm so happy for the both of you that I'd do it twice just to see him smile. He is so in love with you, and that's the way life is supposed to be."

Cathy sighed. "Thank you, just the same. I've never

known anyone so entrenched in family and taking care of people as he is. I think he's perfect. He wanted to have it here, and all I want is for him to be happy, so that's how this happened."

"And it's all good. Mercy and Lon just drove up. Go find Jack for me and tell him I need the ham out of the oven."

———————————————

The day was like Thanksgiving with them, except for ham instead of turkey. Her mama's sweet potato casserole went perfect with the ham. They opened presents after dinner.

Bath salts for soaking for Hope and Mercy. Leather gloves for Lon and Jack, and a dark-blue pullover sweater for Duke that was just a shade or two darker than his eyes.

Cathy's presents from Hope and Jack were things they knew she liked from when she'd stayed with them. Thick warm socks and a soft throw. And then she opened her present from Duke.

"It's hard to think of what to buy for the woman who just bought half the town," Duke said, which made everyone laugh.

Cathy grinned, and then she opened the box, only to find a smaller box inside and then a smaller box inside that. She was laughing when she got down to the last one, and then she opened it to find a necklace.

The chain was white gold and the pendant hanging from it was an obelisk-shaped gemstone of greenish-lavender. It had been years since she'd seen this, but she immediately knew what it was.

"Oh, Duke, is this—"

"Alaskan jade. I know it's the state gem of Alaska, and I wanted to give you something from where you began."

She threw her arms around him in front of everyone and burst into tears.

"Oh lord, please don't cry. You'll make me cry, too."

"Put it on me, please," she said, and so he did.

After that, he caught her rubbing the jade countless times, and could only imagine what memories it evoked.

The day ended with football and leftovers, and it was getting late when Cathy finally left, with a promise to let Duke know when she got home.

She called him the moment she drove into Blessings.

"I'm here. Going to swing by the Bottoms just to see the lights inside the houses and rest easy knowing no one is cold or hungry there today."

"Blessings to you, my little Christmas angel. I'll pick you up tomorrow to go get your dress."

"No, you don't need to," Cathy said. "I'm going straight there and straight home, and I have to face that alone."

"Oh Jesus, Cathy. You know that's gonna freak me out."

"Then you have to get over being afraid for me, because I can't live thinking each day could be my last."

She heard him sigh.

"Deal," he finally said. "Same rules. Call me."

"Deal," Cathy said. "Love you."

Then she turned and drove across the old track bed, thinking what a difference the view was from here now. It felt good to know she'd helped fix this. But instead of driving through the streets as she'd planned, she turned around and went home.

Getting her wedding dress was a breeze. She was in and out of the city and driving back into Blessings before noon.

"I'm home," she said, when she called in.

"So am I," Duke said, which made her smile. "It's not long now, baby. Laurel Lorde and her crew are out here cleaning our new home, and I want to see you so bad."

"Come over tonight. We'll make love and make sundaes."

"I can't stay. We're working cattle early tomorrow."

"That's okay. We're on the downhill slide of my house/ your house life."

"Then I'll see you later."

He made good on his promise, and took her to bed within moments of walking in the door.

A couple of hours later they were in the kitchen, revisiting the sundaes-for-supper routine, and when Duke left, he tasted the butterscotch from her kiss all the way home.

At 5:00 p.m. New Year's Eve, the preacher who'd married Jack and Hope drove up in his car and hurried inside the house. The cars already parked outside the two-story farmhouse marked the guests who had already arrived.

Cathy was upstairs in the guest room getting dressed, and Duke was in the bedroom next door doing the same. He could hear the rumble of voices next door, and then every so often the soft sound of Cathy's laugh.

"Thank you, God, for this woman," he said, and then sat down on the side of the bed and waited.

He knew guests were arriving, but he didn't want to go visit. He just wanted to hear his woman say "I do."

Some of them were people Cathy had yet to meet—families who had been neighbors of the Talbots for two generations and who had shared troubles and joys together. The few who'd come from Blessings were at Cathy's request.

But it was the arrival of the preacher that signaled the beginning.

Jack flew up the stairs to get Duke, as Hope was zipping up the back of Cathy's dress.

"You're beautiful, girl," Hope said. "I'm going to leave you alone now to tell Cathy Terry goodbye. When you walk out of this house tonight, you will be a Talbot woman...and you are a perfect example of who they were. Welcome to the family, sister. I love you. When you hear the music, it will be time to come down the stairs."

She gave Cathy a quick kiss on the cheek, and then left her alone.

Cathy turned to face herself in the full-length mirror and then shivered.

The jade necklace Duke had given her rested in the valley between her breasts—a beautiful contrast to her winter-white dress. Whisper-soft cashmere clung to her curves all the way to her hips, then flared the rest of the way to the floor. The mandarin collar tucked beneath her chin was stark against the red curls on her shoulders, and the long sleeves all the way to her wrists had tiny bands of the best artificial ermine money could buy.

She'd let her curls fall free. No more binding...no more boundaries. The tiny sprig of green in her hair was from a pine bough, and her bouquet was holly bush, with the red holly berries and a single strand of long red velvet ribbon holding it together. She looked at herself one last time—the white for snow…the pine for the trees in which she'd lived…the fur they'd worn to stay warm in harsh winters…and red, the color of the blood often shed in a beautiful but unforgiving land—then closed her eyes and saw Alaska.

Full circle, Mama. I've come full circle.

Then she heard music and took a slow, deep breath.

The music from "A Thousand Years" led her out the door and all the way to the head of the stairs. "A Thousand Years," because that's how long it had felt before this man found her to love.

When she paused to look down, it reminded her of the moment she'd first looked down into the Bottoms…and the possibilities of change just waiting for her.

Then she saw Duke and started down the stairs toward him without looking away, drawn by the love in his eyes and the fact that he didn't look like he was breathing. She needed to correct that as soon as possible, and had to make herself walk when she wanted to run.

The rest of the night was pure magic.

All Duke remembered was the Christmas angel at the top of the stairs, and then finally hearing her say "I do."

Once the preacher announced that they were married, Duke felt complete. He'd waited all his life for this moment, and she'd been worth the wait.

Pictures were taken, but Duke and Cathy never knew it. They had eyes only for each other and shared the traditional bites of wedding cake.

The guests were still there when Duke and Cathy slipped out, her still in her wedding dress, and him still in his suit and boots.

The bags they'd packed were in his truck, and when he drove away from the farm that night, it felt right. The road that led around the section line to get to their new home was dark except for the headlights and a sliver of new moon.

When they pulled up to their home, all the lights inside the home were on, as well as the light on the porch—a welcome beacon.

Cathy was trembling. She'd come such a long way from the little girl from Alaska. Lost for a long time in the desert world of sand and sin...to running for her life, straight into this man's arms.

"Wait here a sec," Duke said. He got out and took their bags to the porch and set them inside the door, then ran back to the truck and opened her door.

Before she could get out, he lifted her out of the truck seat into his arms.

"This is how we met, and this is how we start again," he said, then carried her up the steps, pausing only at the threshold to brush a kiss across her mouth. "Welcome home, Mrs. Talbot."

And then he carried her inside.

Blessings was ringing in the new year when a man on a motorcycle rolled into town. He paused beneath a streetlight and looked up at the Christmas wreath above his head, and then accelerated up the street, all the way to the Blessings Bed and Breakfast.

It had been a long damn ride to get here, and he needed sleep before he could face what he'd come here to do.

Sharon Sala welcomes you back
to Blessings, Georgia, with

SOMBODY *to* LOVE

Available February 2021
From Sourcebooks Casablanca

CHAPTER 1

HUNTER KNOX HAD NEVER PLANNED ON COMING BACK
to Blessings, so the fact that he was riding up Main Street in
the middle of the night was typical of his life. Nothing had
ever gone according to plan.

It was just after midnight when he pulled his Harley up
beneath a streetlight, letting it idle as he flipped up the visor
on his helmet and glanced at the Christmas wreath hanging
from the pole.

From the sounds going off in town, a lot of people were
ringing in the New Year. He could hear fireworks and church
bells and someone off in the distance shouting "Happy New
Year."

Hunt wasn't looking forward to this visit, and he'd

332 SHARON SALA

planned to get some sleep first, but he couldn't. Too much time had passed already, and there was someone he needed to see before it was too late. So his reservation at Blessings Bed and Breakfast, and the bed with his name on it, were going to have to wait. He flipped the visor back down, put the bike into gear, and rode up Main Street, watching for the turn that would take him to the hospital.

The Knox family had just ushered in the New Year in total silence—eyeing each other from their seats in their mother's hospital room—already wondering about the disposition of the family home before their mother, Marjorie, had yet to take her last breath.

It wasn't as if she had a fortune to fight over. Just a little three-bedroom house at the far end of Peach Street that backed up to the city park. The roof was old. It didn't leak, but it wouldn't sell in that condition. The floor in the kitchen had a dip in the middle of it, and the furniture was over thirty years old, but right now, it appeared to be a bigger issue than watching their mother still struggling to breathe.

Marjorie had given birth to six children. The oldest, a girl named Shelly, died from asthma before she ever started school.

Four of her children, Junior, Emma, Ray, and Bridgette, who they called Birdie, were sitting with her in her room. Only Hunter, the second child and eldest son, was missing. No one knew where he was now, and all knew better than to mention his name.

Their father, Parnell Knox, died six years ago of emphysema. Marjorie always said he smoked himself to death, and while she'd never smoked a day in her life, now she was dying of lung cancer from someone else's addiction. The diagnosis had been a shock, then she got angry. She was dying because of second-hand smoke.

Sometimes Marjorie was vaguely aware of a nurse beside the bed, and sometimes she thought she heard her children talking, and then she would drift again. She could see daylight and a doorway just up ahead and she wanted to go there. She didn't know why, but she couldn't leave yet. She was waiting for something. She just couldn't remember what.

Ava Ridley was the nurse at Marjorie's bedside. Ava had grown up with the Knox kids, because Marjorie had been her babysitter from the time she was a toddler. Her childhood dream had been to grow up and marry Hunt. But at the time he was a senior in high school, she was a freshman in the same class with his brother, Ray.

She'd spent half her life in their house, making Ray play dolls with her when they were little, and learning how to turn somersaults and outrun the boys just to keep up with them. As they grew older, they hung out together like siblings, but she'd lived for the moments when Hunt was there. At that time, he barely acknowledged her existence, but it didn't matter. She loved enough for two.

And then something big—something horrible that no one ever talked about—happened at their house, and Hunt was gone.

After that, no one mentioned his name, so she grieved the loss of a childhood dream, grew up into a woman on a mission to take care of people, and went on to become a nurse. After a couple of years working in a hospital in Savannah, she came home to Blessings, and she'd been here ever since. Ava had cared for many people in her years of nursing, but it was bittersweet to be caring for Marjorie Knox, when she had been the one who'd cared for Ava as a child.

Ava glanced at Emma. She was Emma Lee, now. Married to a nice man named Gordon Lee. Her gaze slid to Junior, and Ray, and Birdie.

Junior was a high school dropout and divorced.

Ray worked for a roofing company, and had a girlfriend named Susie.

Bridgette, who'd been called Birdie all her life, was the baby, but she was smart and driven to succeed in life where her siblings were not. She was the bookkeeper at Truesdale's feed and seed store, and still waiting for her own Prince Charming.

Ava thought the family looked anxious, which was normal, but they also seemed unhappy with each other, which seemed strange. However, she'd seen many different reactions from families when a loved one was passing, and had learned not to judge or assume. And even though it was no business of hers, she knew the Knox family well enough to know something was going on. Her job was to monitor Marjorie's vitals and nothing else.

The door to Marjorie's room was open, and the sounds out in the hall drifted in as Ava was adjusting the drip in Marjorie's IV. So when the staccato sound of metal-tipped boots drifted inside, they all looked toward the doorway.

The stride was heavy, likely male—steady and measured, like someone who knew where he was going. The sound was growing louder, and they kept watching, curious to see who it was this time of night.

Then all of a sudden there was a man in the doorway, dressed in biker leather and carrying a helmet. He glanced at them without acknowledgment, then went straight to the bed where Marjorie was lying.

Ava's heart began to pound. Hunt Knox had just walked in, and the years since she'd seen him last had been more than kind. His face was leaner, his features sharper. He was taller, and more muscular, and his dark hair was longer, hanging over the collar of his leather jacket, but his eyes were still piercing—and unbelievably blue.

She forgot what she was doing and stared as he approached. It took her a few seconds to realize he didn't recognize her.

"Ma'am. I'm Hunt Knox, her oldest son. Is she conscious?"

"Not ma'am, Hunt. It's me, Ava Ridley. And to answer your question, she's in and out of consciousness. You can talk to her if you want."

Hunt's eyes widened. He was trying to see the young girl he remembered in this pretty woman's soft voice and dark eyes.

"Sorry. You grew up some. I wouldn't have recognized you," Hunt said. "Is she in pain?"

"Doctor is managing that for her," Ava said.

When his four siblings finally came out of their shock, Junior stood up.

"Where did you come from? How did you know?" he asked.

Hunt turned, staring until they ducked their heads and looked away, then shifted focus back to his mother. She had wasted away to nothing but skin and bones. Disease did that to a body. He put his helmet aside and reached for her hand.

"Mom...it's me, Hunt. I came home, just like you asked." He waited, and just when he thought she was too far gone to hear, he felt her squeeze his fingers. Relief swept through him. He wasn't too late after all. "I'm sorry it took so long for your message to reach me, but I'm here now."

Her eyes opened. He knew she recognized him. Her lips were moving, but she didn't have enough lung capacity to breathe and talk at the same time.

Finally, she got out one word.

"Sorry," and then, "love."

Everything within him was shattering, but it didn't show. He'd as soon shoot himself before he'd reveal weakness.

"It's okay, Mom. I love you, too. I made you a promise and I'll keep it. I'm sorry it took me so long to get here. I was out of the state for a while, and didn't get your last letter until I got back, but I'm here now and I'll take care of everything you wanted."

Marjorie's eyelids fluttered.

Hunt waited.

His siblings stood and moved around the bed, waiting. They hadn't seen her respond to anything in days, and all of a sudden, she was conscious. Then her lips parted.

They leaned closer, not wanting to miss a moment of her last words.

Then she said, "Hunt."

"I'm here, Mom. I'm right here," Hunt said, and gently squeezed her hand. "I'll do what you asked."

Her lips parted again. "Promise?"

He leaned over and spoke softly, near her ear.

"I promise. I'm here now. You're free to go."

Marjorie exhaled. The light was brighter, and there was no longer a weight on her heart. She let go of her son, and let God take her home.

Now all four siblings were staring in disbelief, wondering what the hell just happened? Their mother had been hanging onto life like this for almost a week, and the prodigal son walked in and told her it was okay to go. And she died? Just like that?

Ava was trying to find a pulse, but it was gone.

Marjorie's heartbeat had flat-lined on the monitor.

Emma's voice rose an octave. "Is she dead?"

Tears were rolling down Junior's face, and Ray was wiping his eyes.

Birdie, the youngest daughter, covered her face and started to weep.

Moments later an RN came hurrying into the room. She felt for a pulse, then looked up at the clock.

"Time of death, 1:15 a.m."

There were tears on Ava's cheeks. "I'm so sorry. My sympathies to all of you."

Emma hugged her. "Thank you for taking such good care of Mama," she said.

Hunt had yet to speak to any of his siblings, and was still

holding on to his mother's hand. He knew they were gathering up their things and walking out of the room, but he had nothing to say to any of them now. That would come later.

He felt a hand on his shoulder. It was Ava.

"I'm so sorry, Hunt, but I'm grateful you made it. At the last, you were all she talked about."

"Thank you for taking care of her," he said, then let go of his mother's hand, picked up his helmet, and walked out.

Ava heard pain in the pitch of his voice, but he did not need her concern or her care. Losing a patient was the hardest part of being a nurse, but in this instance, Ava was at peace. Marjorie Knox had suffered a long time. She was no longer sick or in pain, and that was the blessing.

Hunt was on his way back up the hall when he saw his siblings getting in the elevator. He pictured them standing in the lobby downstairs, waiting for him to come down next, and took the stairwell instead.

He was already out in the parking lot and on his Harley as they finally walked out of the building. They watched him ride away without acknowledging any of them.

"Well, dammit, there he goes," Ray said.

"Did any of you ever know where Hunt went when he left town?" Birdie asked.

"I didn't," Emma said.

"Me either," Junior said, while Ray shook his head.

"Mama must have known," Birdie said.

The others looked at each other in silence, finding it hard to believe that the mother they'd taken for granted had kept a secret like that for so long, but the four of them knew why.

"I wonder what Mama asked him to do?" Junior said.

Ray frowned. "What do you mean?"

Junior frowned. "You heard him. He told Mama he'd keep his promise, and do what she asked him to do."

"Oh, yeah," Ray said.

"I wonder where he's going?" Junior said. "Do you think he's going to stay at Mama's house?"

Emma shrugged. "I don't know. Why don't you drive by the house on your way home and see if he's there. If he thinks he's gonna just move in, he has another think coming. I want to—"

"What you want, and what's going to happen are two different things," Junior said. "There are four of us standing here."

"But there are five heirs," Birdie said. "Whatever money comes from selling Mama's house will be divided five ways, not four. The house is old. It's not going to bring anything worth fighting over."

"Nothing is worth fighting over," Ray said.

Emma glared at all of them. "We've already talked about Mama's funeral and stuff, and there's just enough money in Mama's bank account to bury her, and nothing more. Let's go home and get some rest."

"Did Mama leave a will?" Birdie asked.

They all stopped.

"I don't know," Emma said.

Junior shrugged. "I don't either."

"How do we find out?" Ray asked.

"Maybe Hunt knows. He already knows something about Mama that we don't," Birdie said.

"I'm going home. If you want to know where Hunt is at, go look for him yourself," Junior muttered.

Ray got in his car and left, and Junior did the same.

Emma ignored him. "I'm sad Mama is gone, but I'm glad she's not suffering." Then she glanced at Birdie. "I wonder where Hunt's been all these years."

"I don't know, but he sure turned into a good-looking man," Birdie said.

Hunt rolled up to the Bed and Breakfast as quietly as he could manage on a Harley, cognizant of the other guests who were likely asleep. He locked up his bike, grabbed his bag and helmet, then headed to the door and rang the bell.

Bud Goodhope was still up and waiting for their last guest to arrive, and when he heard the doorbell, he hurried through the hall to answer the door.

"Welcome to Blessings Bed and Breakfast," Bud said.

Hunt nodded. "I'm Hunt Knox. I have a reservation."

"Yes, come in, Mr. Knox. I'll get you registered and show you to your room. You must be exhausted."

A short while later, Hunt was taken upstairs and given a room at the end of the hall.

"It's quieter back here," Bud said. "Breakfast will be served from 6:00 a.m. to 10:00 a.m. If you need anything, just press seven on the house phone, and either my wife, Rachel, or I will answer."

"Thanks," Hunt said. "Right now, all I want is a shower and a bed."

"Then rest well," Bud said, as he put Hunt's bag on the bed. "We'll see you in the morning for breakfast."

Hunt locked the door, put his jacket and helmet on a chair, then sat down and took off his boots. The room was well-appointed and had a warm, homey feel. It had been a long time since he'd been in a place like this.

He poked around and found a basket of individually bagged, homemade chocolate chip cookies, as well as a mini-fridge of cold drinks. He hadn't eaten since noon, and it was already tomorrow, so he chose a cookie, and a cold Coke, and ate to dull the empty feeling in his belly.

When he was finished, he stripped and walked into the bathroom. The full-length mirror reflected the milestones life had left on his body. The scars of war weren't just within him. Some, like the thin silver ropes left from wounds that had healed, were visible, too.

He turned the water as hot as he could stand it to loosen tired muscles, and then washed his hair before he washed himself. By the time he got out, all he could think about was crawling between clean sheets and sleeping for a week. But there'd be no sleeping in. He'd come a long way to keep a promise, and it wasn't going to be accomplished by staying in bed.

Ava's shift ended at 7:00 a.m.

Normally, she was looking forward to a little breakfast and then sleep, but Hunt Knox was on her mind as she headed home. She wondered if he was married, if he had children, where he lived, what he did? But it appeared she wasn't the only one in the dark. From the little she'd over-heard, his brothers and sisters didn't know, either. Again, she wondered what had happened to drive such a rift within their family, and what was the promise he'd made to his mother before she died?

She was still thinking about him as she pulled up beneath the carport. The morning was cold and the sky appeared overcast. But weather wasn't going to affect her day. She let herself in, and then went through the house, leaving her coat in the front closet, and her purse on the hall table.

Getting out of her uniform was always paramount. It went straight to the laundry, then she went to the bathroom to shower. The ritual of washing all over was both a physical and an emotional cleansing—leaving behind all of the sadness and sickness of the patients she cared for last night, to the capable hands of the day shift.

She was off for the next two days, and then she would be going back on days. She hadn't minded filling in while one of the nurses had been out of town for a family funeral, but she was ready to go back on her regular shift in ER.

As soon as she was out and dry, she put on her PJs, switched her laundry to the dryer, ate a bowl of cereal while standing at the sink, then crawled into bed. She was still thinking of Hunt Knox when she fell asleep.

Rachel Goodhope met their latest guest when he came down for breakfast. She hadn't seen him in biker gear, but he cut a fine figure in the black Levis and the gray chambray shirt he was wearing. He hung a black leather coat over the back of a chair, set a biker helmet in the seat of the chair beside him, and then went to the buffet.

"Welcome to Blessings," Rachel said, and added a fresh batch of crisp bacon to a near-empty chafing dish.

"Thank you," Hunt said. "Everything looks good."

"Enjoy," she said. "If you want something to drink other than hot tea or coffee, just let me know."

"This is fine," Hunt said. "Oh…can you tell me where Butterman Law Office is located?"

"Sure. He has an office in a building directly across from the courthouse. There's a sign out front. You can't miss it."

"Thank you," Hunt said, and began filling his plate.

Rachel went back to the kitchen to take a batch of hot biscuits out of the oven. She put them on a counter beneath a heat lamp to keep them warm, and was going to bake up some more waffles when her cell phone rang. She wiped her hands, and then answered.

"Hello, this is Rachel."

"Good morning, Rachel. This is Ruby. I'm on the church calling committee, so I'm giving you a heads up about an upcoming funeral."

"Oh no! Who died?" Rachel asked.

"Marjorie Knox finally passed, bless her heart," Ruby said.

"Oh, of course! I heard they'd called in the family," Rachel said, and then gasped. "Oh! Oh my! I didn't put two and two together until now. We had a guest sign in really, really early this morning. His name is Hunter Knox. I'll bet he's family."

Ruby gasped. "Oh my word! That's the oldest son! He disappeared right after high school, and never came back."

"Well, he's here now," Rachel said. "And a fine-looking man, he is, too."

"I hope he made it in time to see Marjorie," Ruby said.

"He just asked me where Peanut's office was," Rachel said.

"I don't know if Peanut will be in the office or not, since it's a holiday. I guess time will tell how this all plays out," Ruby said. "In the meantime, just giving you a heads-up about a family dinner at church in the near future."

"Noted," Rachel said. "I've got to make some more waffles. I'll talk to you later."

"And I have more people to call," Ruby said. "I'll be in touch."

Hunt ate his fill of eggs, biscuits, and gravy, then went back for waffles. He was making up for having gone so long without real food, and had no idea what the day would bring, so eating what was in front of him seemed like a good idea.

He'd reserved the room here for at least a couple of nights until he had a chance to check out his mother's house. If it was habitable enough to stay in while he repaired it, he'd stay there. Once it was fixed, it would be up to him to see to the auction, and pay outstanding bills.

When he'd received her letter, he'd been shocked to find out his mother had named him the executor of her estate. Even though they'd stayed in touch, she never mentioned his brothers and sisters, and with good reason. She knew he wouldn't care. By the time the letter caught up with him, the postmark was almost two weeks old, and the date on the letter she'd written was a month before that. When she confessed her days were numbered, he panicked and called her, but never got an answer. The thought that she would die without knowing he would do what she'd asked, sent him on a wild, sixteen-hour ride from Houston to Blessings. He knew now she'd been waiting for him to come. She'd trusted him enough to wait. Now it was up to him to do the job.

About the Author

New York Times bestselling author Sharon Sala has 125 books in print, published in six different genres—romance, young adult, Western, general fiction, women's fiction, and nonfiction. First published in 1991, and once a member of Romance Writers of America, she is an eight-time RITA finalist. Her industry awards include the Janet Dailey Award, five-time Career Achievement winner from RT Magazine, five-time winner of the National Readers' Choice Award, five-time winner of the Colorado Romance Writers' Award of Excellence, the Heart of Excellence award, the Booksellers Best Award, the Nora Roberts Lifetime Achievement Award presented by RWA, and the Centennial Award from RWA in recognition of her hundredth published novel. She lives in Oklahoma, the state where she was born. Visit her on Facebook.

Also by Sharon Sala

Blessings, Georgia